The Priest of Evil

Matti-Yrjänä Joensuu

The Priest of Evil

Translated by
David Hackston

EURO CRIME

Arcadia Books Ltd
15-16 Nassau Street
London W1W 7AB

www.arcadiabooks.co.uk

First edition published by Arcadia Books, 2006
Originally published by Otava Publishing Company, 2003
Copyright © Matti Yrjänä Joensuu, 2003

This English translation from the Finnish, *Harjunpää ja pahan pappi*
copyright © David Hackston, 2006

Matti Yrjänä Joensuu has asserted his moral right to be identified as the author of this work in
accordance with the Copyright, Designs and Patents Act, 1988.

A catalogue record for this book is available from the British Library

ISBN 1-900850-93-1

Typeset in Bembo by Basement Press
Printed in Finland by WS Bookwell

Arcadia Books Ltd gratefully acknowledges the financial support of The Arts Council of England.
Part of this translation has been funded by FILI – Finnish Literature Information Centre.

Arcadia Books supports English PEN, the fellowship of writers who work together to promote
literature and its understanding. English PEN upholds writers' freedoms in Britain and around
the world, challenging political and cultural limits on free expression.
To find out more, visit www.englishpen.org or contact
English PEN, 6-8 Amwell Street, London EC1R 1UQ

Arcadia Books distributors are as follows:

in the UK and elsewhere in Europe:
Turnaround Publishers Services
Unit 3, Olympia Trading Estate, Coburg Road
London N22 6TZ

in the US and Canada:
Independent Publishers Group
814 N. Franklin Street, Chicago, IL 60610

in Australia:
Tower Books
PO Box 213, Brookvale, NSW 2100

in New Zealand:
Addenda
PO Box 78224, Grey Lynn, Auckland

in South Africa:
Quartet Sales and Marketing
PO Box 1218, Northcliffe, Johannesburg 2115

Arcadia Books is the *Sunday Times* Small Publisher of the Year

For Virpi, Anni, Taru, Anu, Iines and Nooa

1. *Night Watch*

Someone called out his name; rapidly, over and over, as if they were thrashing him over the head with a twig. 'Mikko! Mikko!'

But he didn't answer. He didn't want to.

'Mikko!'

He didn't want to be Mikko again, clutching terrified at someone's legs or round their neck; he didn't want to keep watch at the door any longer, because it was nasty and said bad things. All he wanted to do was curl up on top of the dressing table in Anitra's nest and be her fledgling, because Anitra was nice: she never pecked at him, she didn't scratch his bottom or pull his willy, and she allowed him to stroke her feathers, and that made him happy, almost as happy as when he was allowed to eat candyfloss.

Candyfloss always made him shiver slightly – like when he'd gone to the park without permission, or when on the first of May their taxi had run over a pigeon and its eye had popped out of its head, and Kasper had poked the end of Tuija's hat into its beak. It had stared at them the way Father's cigarettes stared at them through the night-time darkness. The feathers made him feel like Anitra was his real mother, and that Mother was only a pretend mother, some unknown, naughty boy's nagging mother. And again he felt a shiver, the same kind of chill as when someone pulled his hair, and he began thinking of the legs beneath the dressing table: dark-green lion's paws, complete with claws and everything. And even though they were made of wood, nobody dared tiptoe past them, not even the fat janitor with smelly hairs growing out of his ears.

1

'Mikko!' someone shouted again, then came another yelp: 'Are they killing each other yet?'

He was the one, he, Mikko, and all at once he sat up – there was no nest, no candyfloss and no Anitra. Nothing good ever came true. It was still dark, still night, the same wicked night. He ran his fingers along the bed and his pyjama trousers – of course: he had wet himself again, though this time there was only a little bit; it would dry out by morning and he wouldn't have to fetch the belt from the kitchen. It was hanging on a towel hook by the door, so high up that he had to use a chair to get it down.

'Not yet,' someone whispered near him; and it was then that Mikko saw him and quickly drew his arms and legs back inside the safety of the blankets. It was the skeleton man, he had a white face and white hands, you couldn't see anything else of him, and presumably there was no flesh on his bones either. He even smelt like nothing but bare bones, and Mikko could feel his heavy stare through the black holes in his face. 'Mikko?' he whispered again, his voice sounded like Marja's after she had been bawling, as though he was sucking a boiled sweet. His head nodded to one side: tick-tack! It was Marja after all.

'But Dad's got three cigarettes in his mouth and another one burning in the ashtray, you know, pacing back and forth… It's your turn.'

'Let's go together.'

'It's your turn.'

'You can have my frog man.'

The alarm clock ticked and its hands moved ever so slowly. Someone flushed the toilet on the floor downstairs, even though you weren't supposed to do it at night, and a car drove past on the street outside casting a strange light on the ceiling, like a mitten without a thumb; it turned slowly on to its back and flowed down across the wall, but never quite reached the floor. Marja's nose began to run and she secretly wiped it on the sleeve of her nightgown.

'I'm so tired!' she sobbed into her hands so as not to wake Saara, she would have started to cry too. Marja knew how. So did he, they had both learnt. 'My tummy hurts and I have to go to school in the morning. You don't!'

'Marja, please!' said Mikko, startled; it always scared him when Marja started crying. She was so grown-up, already in the second year at school. He took Rum-Rum by the hand and clambered on to his feet. The floor felt terribly cold beneath his toes, like a tin sheet the dogs had weed on during the winter. He took hold of his sister and they hugged, lulling each other as if they were dancing, and for a brief moment Mikko felt happy again; perhaps no one would die after all, and come the summer he and Uncle Eikka would be able to go canoeing round the lake again.

'I can watch him by myself,' Mikko finally tried to pluck up some courage, though his lips trembled like when he said bad words and had his mouth scrubbed clean. 'You can have the frog every now and then.'

'And you can have my bouncy ball, but only for a while. Come and wake me up if they start, but if not wait until the alarm goes off. Two o'clock, mind, not half past one.'

'OK.'

'Good night,' she whispered. There came the patter of her toes across the floor, a rustling as she crawled into bed, followed shortly by a soft murmur: 'Now I lay me down to sleep; I pray Thee, Lord, my soul to keep. If I should die before I wake, I pray Thee, Lord, my soul to take; and this I ask for Jesus' sake. Amen.' The sheets rustled once more as she turned on to her side, then everything fell quiet. Nothing could be heard but the sound of Saara quietly sucking her dummy.

Mikko was alone.

He didn't want to look anywhere.

At night his home seemed strange. Even its heart was black, though he knew that only wicked people have such a thing – and they don't go to heaven. And he knew that the table had disappeared again, and that in its place there lurked a smelly bear; he knew that three zebras were standing in front of the closet, pretending to cover their eyes, but it was all a trick. They were staring out between their fingers and would start whinnying if he looked at them. The bear would fly into a fury if someone looked at him; Mikko didn't dare so much as glance at any of them.

But he did notice one thing: the waste bin was full of little balls again – and this frightened him. He pulled his lower lip between his teeth and began biting it. It frightened him because he knew that they weren't really balls at all: they were the heads of little children. God had killed them.

'Marja,' he whispered, so quietly that only his lips moved. He waited for a moment, and when the silence continued he turned around. Light shone in from the hallway, but it wasn't good light; it was bad, as though someone were holding a dirty hand in front of a lamp, and Mikko didn't want to go out there. When he tried to walk out there he felt even more of a chill, so much so that he shivered. He held Rum-Rum against his face; he was shivering too and his eyes were wet. Mikko hushed him, stroked his bare back and whispered into his ear – perhaps it was in Swedish or some other foreign language, because he couldn't understand a word of it.

A moment later he was in the doorway; almost as if he had moved without his noticing, but there he stood nonetheless. Now there was slightly more light, and although he had heard the voices all along, now he could make them out properly. The air was full of them, like angry, squawking birds. 'Answer me, God damn it! Was this in your pocket or not?'

'I've already said, I don't want to talk about this any more!'

'You'd better believe we're going to talk about it – we're going to talk about it so we'll never have to talk about it again!'

'What the hell do you go rummaging through other people's pockets for? You're such a stupid cretin that you can't even see that it's only a sample. A bloody sample that I got in the post!'

'Of course, how stupid of me. Condoms come through the post every day…'

'Oh give it a rest, for Christ's sake. How should I remember? It could just be one of the boys at work, their idea of a joke.'

'That's right. You're a joke of a man! Is it that whore Hännikäinen? Is it her again?'

'Stop it, for crying out loud! Stop it!'

Mikko was right behind the door. Light was oozing through the doorframe; it was yellow like wee. Through the doorframe came the smell of cigarette smoke and very bad words.

On the other side of the door was the kitchen – and Mother and Father. They were the ones bellowing at each other. Yet at the same time they weren't like Mother and Father at all; they seemed strange, a pair of raging hooligans. His lips pursed together as he thought about it: what if they stayed like that? All at once he could feel a swarm of little yellow ants tingling in his cheeks and his stomach began to churn, and he could feel invisible ropes dragging him down to the floor. He began to feel very tired and almost wanted the ropes to win.

'Stop fidgeting with those cigarettes, you moron! You'll burn the house down.'

'Fine, I can finally get rid of the wife and kids – everything! And I'll sure as hell...'

'You'll what? That's right, threaten to kill us all again.'

'You keep your trap shut, woman!'

'Oh it's my fault, is it? Kill me then, I'd be better off dead than stuck here while you're out with your whores.'

'Whores!'

'Kill me, go on, kill me!'

'You can be sure I will!'

Chair legs screeched across the floor, there came a sound like the roar of a beast; something clattered and smashed on the floor. Mikko imagined the kitchen to be full of spears flying through the air, sharp spears that sailed through people, shattering them to pieces. He realised that he would have to go and wake up Marja, because they had to save Mother and Father, that was their job; but just then he remembered the Cupboard Monster. He froze and couldn't take another step. Cold, sticky drops of sweat trickled down through his hair.

At night it lurked in the hall. During the day it hid inside the wall – it could even eat stone – and that's why Mikko had never seen it. But Marja had seen it, many times. One night it had almost caught her as she was on her way to the toilet. It was a bit like a dachshund, but didn't have paws or a tail. First it would spit poison into your eyes making them sting, blinding you. Then it would crawl under your skin through your bottom or the soles of your feet and start eating your flesh, and then there was nothing you could do but cry out. Finally it would eat your heart, chewing it slowly, and then you would die.

Mikko let out a short frightened gasp. He sensed that it was right behind him. He could even hear it making noises, he tilted his head – yes, at that moment he was absolutely sure of it – it sounded as though something was crawling across the floor, panting, and he couldn't think what to do. At last he shut his eyes tightly, pressed his hands against his bottom and began raising his feet off the ground, one at a time, high into the air – he was almost flying – and he wished with all his heart that Mother and Father would notice him and come to his rescue. And all the time, barely audibly, he whispered: 'Mummy, Daddy, Now I lay me down to sleep, Mummy, Daddy...'

'Mikko! Mikko!'

'What?'

'What are you dancing about for?' Marja demanded and smacked him across the shoulders so hard that it stung. She had switched on the hall lights, and now there was nothing on the floor but shoes and a rug. 'Why didn't you wake me up? Are you deaf?' Only then did Mikko notice the constant clattering coming from behind the door, the angry grunting and shouting, and for a moment he was sure that it was a bear, but then he gradually began to make out the 'fucks' and the 'bastards', when amidst it all his mother cried out: 'Help!'

Marja wrenched the door open; the air was blue, chairs lying across the floor; a row of cigarettes lay smoking in the ashtray, a thin, curly tail rising from each of them into the air. Mother was lying on the floor. Her face was red. Father was sitting flat on top of her, his hands around her throat. Marja nudged her brother and a moment later they were in the thick of it, trying to drag Father away. Mikko pulled at his shirt while Marja tried to prise his fingers loose. Buttons popped out like teeth, there were arms and legs everywhere, and all they could hear was 'Help!' and 'Bastard!' Somehow Mikko found himself at the bottom of the pile; he couldn't see a thing and couldn't move – he could hear nothing but the screaming and could smell Father's sweaty back.

Suddenly everything stopped.

Mikko didn't understand quite how it had happened, it simply stopped. This had happened before. He rubbed his face and rose to his knees. Father was already on his feet, pacing about the room gasping for breath. A glob of spit or snot hung at the side of his mouth; Mikko tried not to look at it, he was ashamed, ashamed of everything. Father was so big; his head reached almost as high as the lamp, and as he paced back and forth across the room he resembled some kind of killer robot, building in speed. When he was angry his face became terribly ugly, like a bony tortoise that could bite everything to pieces.

'My poor darlings,' Mother started to wail. Now she too was standing up, spluttering and trying to clear her throat. Mikko gave a start – he already knew what she was going to say, though she ought not to. Marja knew too and cried out somewhere behind him: 'Mother, no! Please stop, Mother!'

'My little darlings,' she moaned on and on. Perhaps she too was genuinely afraid because her shoulders were shaking. 'Your Father's going to shoot me…'

'The pistol!' Father bellowed almost straight away: the beast had roared again. Mikko pressed his arm against his forehead so that he wouldn't have to watch it. 'Where's the pistol? The pistol! God help me, I'll shoot you all!' This time Mikko didn't burst into tears. He just looked at Marja, and she looked back at him, they both knew. Marja dashed into the hall and made it to the bureau before Father had even turned round. A second later Mikko was at his legs. He clasped his arms around Father's ankles, grabbed at his trouser legs until they lay in a bundle at his shins, but still Father hobbled towards the living room, his slippers booming against the floor. The cork flooring shimmered like thicket in Mikko's eyes, the door jamb struck his knees with a sting; the hall rug became tangled beneath them; shoes fell into the corner with a clatter. Amidst all the commotion something clinked like a ship's bell.

'Marja!' Mikko whined, repeating his sister's name over and over, as he felt that he couldn't hold on much longer, that his hands were already so numb that they ached. He thought he could hear Marja shouting back that she had got there in time. At that he loosened his grip on Father's legs and lay sprawled on the crumpled rug. Through his panting he could hear Father rattling the bureau and swearing, but there was nothing he could do about it. Marja had hidden the key just in time.

Mikko lay still, he was afraid. For it didn't stop there, it never stopped there, because Father became all the more angry when he couldn't find the pistol and shoot them all. He lay perfectly still, so still that it almost felt as though he didn't exist, as though he were almost dead, and he was certain this would make Mother and Father very happy, because in some way everything was always his fault. Perhaps they had been arguing about the fact that he still hadn't learned to get up in the night and use the potty. That was why they called him Mr Piss Pants.

Very cautiously he raised his head. Father was already rushing towards the window. In a flash his hand was on the latch; he turned it and pulled it open. The outside air flooded in; it was like water. Father was lying on the window ledge, but thankfully Marja was holding him by the belt. Mikko dashed over to help and somehow he managed to clamber on to Father's back and pull him inside – or so it seemed, at least. A red neon sign flashed on the building opposite, but he couldn't make out all of its letters yet.

'Erkki!' came Mother's voice. 'Erkki, please!'

At that everything stopped again, just as it had in the kitchen, as if by magic. The radiators seemed to have stopped rattling. No one said a word. No one looked at anyone else. Only Saara cried in the bedroom, wailing at the top of her lungs. Mikko could see her in the mirror standing up in her cot, white as a rabbit, holding on to the bars with both hands. There came a rustling sound as Father dug in his pocket for a cigarette. Mother snapped: 'Look what you've done, you little brats! You've woken up your sister. You should both be ashamed! Who gave you permission to get out of bed? Marja, go and get your sister back to sleep. Mikko: toilet, then straight back to bed like you'd never got up.'

Mikko plodded back to Rum-Rum. He was lying on the hall floor, broken. He didn't have the strength to say his evening prayers, he was so tired, but he hoped that God would forgive him this once.

2. *Sinikka*

Sinikka didn't yet know she was Sinikka. Nobody else knew either, because she was still invisible, hidden away deep inside the darkness. But this wasn't a malevolent darkness like the darkness underground; it was warm and good, it gave her strength and life, gradually preparing her for what was to come. No one could have known what the future held in store. Only one person knew, and even He didn't breathe a word about it.

But if there had been light – and if someone had been there watching – they would have seen straight away how wonderful Sinikka was. She had everything: a delicately rounded head and the tip of a little nose, like porcelain; eyes still closed but unbelievably big, and tiny wrinkled ears like ferns unravelling. And of course she had arms and legs and fingers and toes too, the kind that only fairies have, though she didn't have any wings.

Sinikka could already taste sweet things. And she could hear too, though she didn't yet know that the strange murmuring sound was speech, words that people exchange with one another.

And of course Sinikka had a mind too, though nobody could see it any more than they could see Sinikka; nobody would ever see it. Nonetheless, it must surely have been very much like Sinikka herself: delicate and fragile, almost transparent – you might even be able to see red and blue veins running through it like a network of roads and rivers.

Above all what her mind needed was for someone to take care of Sinikka, feed her, touch her softly and hold her tenderly in their arms. To love her.

3. The Brocken

If someone were to claim that right in the middle of Helsinki there stood a bare mountain, and that you could walk straight through it without possessing the slightest supernatural powers – not to mention the fact that that mountain's name was The Brocken and that inside the mountain there lived an earth spirit – he would undoubtedly be considered rather odd.

But without due cause, however, for this was almost true. No one knew about it, or rather, no one knew it to be a mountain, despite – like tens of thousands of commuters – seeing it every day, morning and night.

Perhaps the name 'mountain' was a bit too flattering, though a mountain was what it most resembled. Its sides were particularly mountain-like: steep, almost sheer, uneven and rocky. Dotted about the rock face were the marks left by drilling and quarrying. The mountain's height varied between fifteen and twenty metres depending on the precise spot; it was almost three hundred metres long and about a hundred or so metres wide. It narrowed to a point at both ends, making the whole structure resemble a diamond-shaped boiled sweet.

On a map of the city it could be found on page fifty-two, in square DJ/78. Yet on the map it was only a patch of green grass, barely the size of a fingernail. Neither had it been given a name, but then again surveyors and cartographers did not know it existed either.

The page in question showed Pasila. And Pasila was indeed where the mountain was to be found, between East and West Pasila, perhaps slightly more to the east, where the two central train lines finally divided. There it rose majestically, a lone rock castle, surrounded by trains speeding in all directions, a place nobody ever had recourse to visit.

The claim that you could walk right through the mountain was also true. From behind the Hartwall Arena ran a bridge that, after it had crossed the tracks, began to slope downwards until it eventually formed a tunnel through the mountain. This tunnel came out at Ratapihantie right in front of the city exhibition centre.

If someone were to reach the top of the mountain, they would notice that the view was much the same as from the islands in the archipelago: rolling rock faces and promontories, muddy hollows sprouting with yellowed hay and moss, brittle birches, alders and ancient, resilient dwarf spruces.

At the southern face of the mountain there was evidence that the site had once been very significant indeed. A trench about twenty metres long, now partly filled with soil, had been hewn into the side of the rock. At one end the trench led to a concrete bunker inside the quarry – perhaps this had been planned as a bomb shelter for a handful of people – while the other end of the trench wound its way round beneath a concrete platform propped up on pillars several metres high. A set of concrete steps led up to the platform and if you climbed them you could see that a rail of piping ran round the edge of the slab, with rusted mounting bolts set into the floor forming two circles next to one another. One could only guess at what this had once been – something to do with anti-aircraft defence during the war; perhaps a spotlight or two.

Almost halfway up the mountain, hidden among the thicket, was a more recently erected shack made of corrugated iron, like a flat-roofed cabin with no windows and no door. At first you could not really tell what the purpose of this was either. But if you peered inside through the eaves you could see that the surface of the walls had been replaced with heavy steel mesh, and if you listened carefully, you could make out a faint, distant murmur, as if the mountain itself were breathing. This construction must have had something to do with the bunker underneath the mountain; if you were able to gain access to the railway yard and have a look around, you would soon notice two hefty steel doors at the foot of the mountain.

Standing at this corrugated iron shack, you would finally realise that, despite everything, there were visitors to the mountain every now and then: its walls were so covered in graffiti that not even by scratching it could you reveal its original colour. And if you were to examine the area more closely you would just be able to make out a path winding away from the shack down towards the northern end of the mountain. At that point the rock face was at its lowest and the incline at its gentlest, the easiest place to climb up. Still, in order to get there these daring graffiti artists would have had to negotiate their way across the central train line, moving dangerously close to the power cables at the transformer station, and climb over sturdy mesh fences.

The ground was covered in junk, the same rubbish that was to be found in the forests around any city: broken glass, empty spray paint cans, pieces of cardboard and plywood. Somehow even a child's red slipper had ended up here. However, this rubbish did not seem particularly fresh: it was faded and rusted, having doubtless lain there as the snows of many a winter had fallen and melted.

There was a strange atmosphere on the mountain. So that no matter how badly you had wanted to go there, and even if you'd managed to arrive in one piece, you'd just want to turn around and leave. Fast.

And if you happened to look closely at the mountain from the platforms at Pasila station, as night began to engulf the blue dusk and the streetlights came on, with a bit of luck you might have been able to make out some faint movement. Just like now: it seemed as though someone had climbed up the steps and was now standing on the concrete platform above, motionless.

4. *Earth Spirit*

Killing a person was not difficult, no more difficult than killing a pigeon. All it required was a soft push – at the right time, of course, and in the right place. He of all people could sense when the time came, or rather in a mysterious way the time and place were revealed to him, and that was it: flesh was torn from the bones, guts smattered across the gravel floor, vertebrae and joints were cast about like beans, and the soul departed from the degenerate body that turns people into a devil of greed. Of course, he knew this well. He had seen it, and his nostrils had been filled with the shuddering, salty smell of raw human flesh.

Particularly beautiful was the moment when the soul was liberated from the body; it spurted up into the air in a shower of little particles, no larger than salt crystals, and for a fleeting moment they came together to form a magnificent vermilion swirl, only to be consumed a moment later by the rock, the divine body of Maammo herself. This is what is meant at funerals with the words 'Ashes to ashes, dust to dust' – and with that the coming of the Truth had drawn one step closer!

'*Ea lesum cum sabateum!*' he proclaimed and fidgeted restlessly, but checked himself almost immediately, quickly made the three holy marks of Maammo and lowered his head; for this he had to do in front of Maammo, even though he was her chosen one – the earth spirit – a force from beneath the ground; a force greater than that of any human being; a hybrid of angel and priest. He was the daughter of Maammo – or the son – depending on which form Maammo herself had chosen.

'*Vibera berus, quelle villaaum est,*' he added, his voice strangely tight, as though he had not used it for a long time and it had rusted fast in his throat. He gave off a strange smell; it was not quite stale, but like the smell of stone that blew against the faces of people going down into the underground. He placed his hands next to one another on the railing and caressed its rough surface, corroded by decades of rain. Then he raised his eyes.

And the look in his eyes was such that if anyone had met his gaze at that same moment, their legs would have given way beneath them.

His city was right there, on its knees before him, not a dark spot in sight. In the back of his head he could hear the gentle rush of power, silver sand shaking within its golden rattle, and the power he held in his hands was so strong that he could feel them warming. Again he had to control himself, for this was not entirely of his doing – it was an expression of the infinite grace Maammo had bestowed upon him – and he contented himself with looking out over all that was his.

In front of him lay Pasila, Alppila and Laakso, and beyond that the city centre: Kluuvi, Punavuori, Eira. To his left, humbly biding its time, was Eastern Helsinki, Herttoniemi, Myllypuro, Vuosaari – how well he knew his kingdom – whilst Ruskeasuo, Munkkivuori and Meilahti sprawled out on his right. Behind him were more districts than anywhere else, but he had not turned his back on them. Their thousands upon thousands of lights shone like a sea of blue and orange. No, he had not forsaken them, for his task was to redeem them; this Maammo herself had decreed.

Killing was not a sin. Neither could it then be considered a crime; this is nothing but the falsehood of those who do not understand. The fifth commandment was a perfect example. Three letters had been added to its original form: N, O and T, thus turning its meaning around. The same applied to God and the Devil, both utterly foolish creations, one supposedly good and the other evil. What nonsense! There was only one true and holy god, and it was Maammo, Maammo the Merciful, and her three incarnations: the Holy Big Bang, the Holy Sun and the Holy Iron Heart, which was geographically the closest of all, for there it lay right beneath his feet. There it glowed, a mighty molten mass at the heart of the earth, waiting to explode and to be conjoined with the Holy Sun and the Holy Big Bang – this was the Truth. A new Big Bang would one day inevitably come, but it could not come so long as the world was filled with evil and filth, and it was to this end that Maammo required sacrifices, and blessed with her grace the pious beings who brought them to her.

He closed his eyes and took a deep, devout breath. The air tasted of the city and the spring evening. It smelt of his apostles: of movement, of inexorable forward motion, of hot metal and electricity, the blue milk of Maammo. The apostles drank it through their snouts directly from the cables in the air. He crouched down to take a closer look: even now there were five of them on the move. One of them rattled past at the foot of The Brocken, and now that it was dark and the lights were switched on he could even make out the people inside. A man fiddling with his mobile phone; a boy guzzling a hamburger; a woman reading a newspaper. Each of them believed they were simply sitting on a train, travelling home, on their way to work or to visit someone. None of them had the faintest idea that they were riding upon his apostle, or that they were the subjects of a fervent conversion process. For the apostles were constantly at work; they shaped those ignorant people's minds with a fine radiation, so fine in fact that people were only rarely aware of its presence, and even then it manifested itself as a sort of drowsiness, forcing people to yawn or take a little nap. He smiled with joy, and eventually he gave a hoarse chuckle: his work was advancing even while he was at rest.

'Maammo, Merciful One, Beloved One,' he whispered and looked upwards. There were stars in the sky, envoys of the Holy Big Bang, and as he stood there staring at them he could feel the powerful presence of the Spirit; it was as though he had a fever, though only in his palms, his fingers and earlobes. Generally this meant only one thing: Maammo was calling to him, perhaps intimating that she would appear to him that night. How ardently he wished for this, for it was magnificent. It was the greatest thing life could offer. In its sheer glory it would be too much for ordinary humans, too wild and mind-boggling, and for this reason Maammo revealed herself only to her chosen ones, to her beloved earth-spirits.

He had a feeling that, if Maammo were indeed to appear that evening, it would happen in the Apostolic Tunnel at the point where it intersected with the underground tunnel near the Central Railway Station. There he would be able to follow how the holiest of all, the Great Orange Apostles, went about their conversion; below ground for the most part, close to Maammo's heart, just like he was. He turned and, in the almost pitch dark, steadily walked down the steps from the concrete platform. He was no longer young, he had reached middle-age, or rather there was something dry and pallid about him, like an elderly person, and he did not have a particularly big build; he was short and rakish.

From the bag on his belt he slipped a key-ring into the palm of his hand, pressed it, and a thin beam of light shone out between his fingers. It was plenty for him, though deep in the underground caves he would often use a faint headlamp too, for in Maammo's temples the darkness was exceptionally dense. A larger lamp, a floodlight, would have been troublesome; it could have betrayed him to the heathens, though at night he very rarely encountered them down in the tunnels.

'At Hakaniemi?' he asked amidst everything, for the thought had suddenly entered his mind – Hakaniemi – and the thought would not have occurred to him unless Maammo had wished to steer him in that direction. But there came no reply. Not yet, at least, and he began to wonder whether this time Maammo would appear as a man or a woman, as this would determine which sex he himself was to assume. He arrived at a ledge on the eastern face of The Brocken and came to a stop at a curious looking contraption made of chicken wire.

It resembled a great umbrella, its shaft wedged into a hole in the rock and projecting up through the shade, stretching several metres into the air. However, if someone had examined the contraption closer, they would soon have understood its purpose: the umbrella-like section could be raised up and down along the shaft. There was a hole in the shaft and on the ground, attached to the end of a long rope, there lay a metal peg, just large enough to fit into the hole. All he needed was a handful of seeds, then he could lie in wait for the pigeons to arrive. One small tug of the rope and that was it.

'*Tipa tipa*,' he called softly, and now his voice was not rough in the slightest, but gentle and calming. '*Tipa tipa*. My little pigeon…'

He noticed that he secretly wished Maammo would appear as a woman. This would be more impressive than if she stepped from the wall as a man. Immediately he felt ashamed, for Maammo could read everyone's thoughts, and who was he to place the incarnations of Maammo in an order of merit? He would have to pray for forgiveness without delay: '*Maammon. Esculentae nutale sorbit ooli, aamen.*'

He knew instantly whenever Maammo was to appear as a woman, for then a blue-green shimmer came upon the rock, the kind of light given off by welding work at night; the light stretching from the floor of the tunnel right up to the ceiling. And then, without warning, the rock face would split open like a curtain of granite and Maammo would step forth. She was almost three metres tall, a fulsome, naked woman hewn from the rock, yet alive, and beneath her skin shone that same beautiful green light. It shone most intensely from her nipples, though even more powerfully from between her legs, her vulva half-open, gleaming, ready to receive the holy seed. And when Maammo took the form of a man his divine skin shone bright red and his glorious member stood tall and erect, ready to cast the holy seed out into the world. If he had so wished, he could have impregnated every woman on earth in a single night.

In front of both these incarnations of Maammo he would fall to his knees. Never did he look Maammo in the eyes – this was forbidden. The light radiating from her face was so bright that it would have burnt the eyes of any such sinner to dust. Not even the pagans dared look directly at the Holy Sun. As he crouched before Maammo his mind was filled first with a divine peace, then with joy, and he felt no worry or fear – such things simply vanished. All that remained was the state of bliss Maammo had imparted to him.

'*Tipa tipa,*' he uttered as he flashed the beam of light towards the centre of the chicken wire cage. And there it was: inside the cage was a single pigeon. He had set the others free straight away, but this – this one was not merely a grey weakling, it had flecks of white and brown, like chocolate; it was a web-footed pigeon, a breed that nested in the city centre and sometimes even in Kruununhaka. The blood of these pigeons was very good indeed, surpassed perhaps only by that of the golden-beaked pigeon.

'My little pigeon,' he sighed calmingly. The pigeon remained curled up for the night, only its eye blinked. He opened a hatch on the side of the cage and slipped in first his finger, then his wrist, and moved like an anaconda towards the pigeon. And there it was in his hand. It felt much smaller than it looked, it was almost the size of a sparrow, and he could feel its little heart throbbing frantically like a motor: *prr!* He removed the pigeon from the cage and with his free hand he performed the marks of blessing above it, reinforcing them with the words: '*Alcueera cum pica lotus est.*'

He stood up, slipped the pigeon into the large compartment in his belt bag and closed the zip. At first it flapped around a little – they always did that – then it began to calm down and found a comfortable position. Generally they would remain like this right up until the sacrifice. He quickly performed all the holy marks in each direction, calming the city around him and, surprisingly nimbly and briskly for a man his age, began climbing back up towards the corrugated iron hut halfway up the mountain.

Graffiti amused him. Or rather, he was amused that three different groups of boys battled to see whose scrawls could claim possession of the hut. There were seven boys altogether and he allowed them to play at peace, though he could have shooed them away easily enough as the hut rightfully belonged to him. But he had played such a cunning trick on the boys that they could not imagine what lay in store for them. For, in fact, he had transferred each of their souls into a small white pebble, a large collection of which lay in a bag dangling from his belt. Sometimes when the mood took him he would take out one of the pebbles, lay it on the rock and crush it with a larger stone. And lo and behold: somewhere an unexplained accident would occur, a car would crash into a wall or mount the pavement for no apparent reason, and the person whose soul had been inside the pebble would die.

The hut was situated in the middle of a patch of dense thicket. He walked towards a spruce tree with a trunk the width of his thigh. On closer inspection it looked as though its branches had been pruned at random, but this too had been carefully considered. He took hold of the cut branches and began climbing as easily as if it were a ladder. Almost three metres up he was level with the roof of the hut; he needed only jump a short distance and he was on top of the construction.

There he listened for a moment. Traffic hummed through the city, playing out its own steady symphony. The tracks screeched at the bridge across Pasila – probably a commuter train from Espoo, one of the Red Apostles, and a helicopter could be heard chattering somewhere in the east. None of these sounds was any cause for concern.

He crouched down, took hold of the handle of a hatch on the roof with both hands and yanked it. The hatch had been positioned very carefully indeed: from the ground it was impossible to know that it existed, the hut simply looked like a pile of corrugated iron. He opened the hatch fully, sat on the roof and began searching with his feet for the top rungs of the ladder. By this point, even an inexperienced person would have been able to guess that the journey down was long; that beneath there gaped chasms of empty space, tunnels and more tunnels, entire networks, perhaps as much as three hundred kilometres long.

Inside it smelt precisely the same as the earth spirit. And he could hear that same soft, eternal murmur.

5. *Daddy*

Harjunpää held his mobile phone against his ear and wondered for a moment whether it was radiating anything dangerous or not. Perhaps it was one of the patterns in the wallpaper that got him thinking; the paintings had all been removed, leaving only the nails behind. He could hear the usual background noises on the phone: doorbells ringing; low, muffled speech, a voice explaining something over the squad radio. Inside the apartment all he could hear was the faint whistle of the freezing wind and the rasp of bugs dying a slow, poisoned death, like moths madly striking against a lamp. Then there was the tapping, like a distant drum, coming from the cupboard in the hall. He had the constant feeling that something was wrong, or that something terrible was about to happen. It was a niggling feeling, as if his shoes were a size too small and his heels covered in blisters about to burst.

He couldn't pin down quite what had caused this unease; whether it was the body, which he had given only a cursory glance and hadn't yet had a chance to examine thoroughly, or Jari, the man standing silently next to him in a dress. Was it something else entirely? Something at home?

'Harjunpää, you still there?'

'Where else do you think I'd be?' he growled quietly.

'I've double-checked and they're all on their way, a doctor too. You know what the morning traffic's like.'

'OK, we'll wait here.'

'I'll tell the squad to get a move on if you think it'll help. I told the ambulance not to rush though, it's not as if anyone's life is at risk.'

'All right, just sort it out. There's no real emergency here, but I can't do anything until someone else turns up.'

'Got it.'

'Thanks,' he added and for a brief moment something approaching weariness flashed across his face, but his expression soon returned to normal: it bore the look of a man who was used to waiting, who had seen too much.

Harjunpää glanced at his watch: it was almost half past seven. He had already been at the scene for three quarters of an hour but still hadn't been able to do anything except assess the situation and try to speak to Jari. He had no reason not to believe Jari's story, but hadn't dared leave him unattended for a second.

Out of the corner of his eye he took another look at Jari: his expression was still the same. It was like a knot, a painfully tangled knot. Harjunpää could sense that same pain in his eyes and his mouth, particularly now that Jari had bitten his lips together into a tight groove. He looked as though he thought he was drowning or that he was trying desperately to bite something in two. On top of this, patchy stubble covered his face, disconsolate like the plague.

Jari already looked like an old man, though he was only just over forty. He seemed to be constantly listening to a murmur deep within himself, his head tilted slightly to one side, shivering. He hadn't wanted to put on the tracksuit Harjunpää had found in one of the wardrobes and was still standing there wearing only a thin summer dress and a pair of nylon tights wrinkled around his ankles. The doors were all wide open – they had to remain open, only now could they breathe without feeling nauseous. The breeze came in through the stairwell like something living, tugging at the hem of Jari's frock and making him tremble with cold, then gushed out of the balcony door, taking with it ton upon cubic ton of the nightmare inside.

Suddenly it dawned on Harjunpää and he gave a start – it was as if someone had whispered to him: it was the hall cupboard. That's what was bothering him. He still hadn't looked inside it, partly because Jari had become almost hysterical when Harjunpää had touched the handle. He thought back to what had happened to one of his colleagues last winter. A caretaker had alerted the police to a flat in Eira because of a smell in the corridor. The patrol had discovered an old woman, who seemed to have died of natural causes, and had taken care of everything like normal, with the routine of having done it hundreds of times before. Only when the undertaker Stenberg had gone into the bathroom to wash his hands did he discover the other body: the old woman's husband sitting on the toilet with a pistol in his hand and a bullet in his forehead.

'What's in there, Jari?' asked Harjunpää, his words booming as if they had been standing in a cave.

'What do you mean?'

'The cupboard.'

'Daddy.'

'You told me there was a dog in there. And you said that your daddy died when you were a little boy.'

'I was ten. And he told me to take good care of Mummy, and now she...'

'Your mummy's dead, Jari. She was a very sick old lady and you took care of her as best you could.'

'Is she dead?' Jari seemed confused and for the first time he looked Harjunpää in the eyes. A restless muscle at the corner of his mouth began to quiver.

'I'm afraid so. And we both went up to the door and had a look. Now put on that tracksuit or you'll catch a chill. Some more people will be here soon.'

'Who's coming?'

'A doctor, just like I told you. And some policemen who are going to take your dog to the vet's until we get you back on your feet again.'

'You can't take the dog!' Jari's scream rebounded against the walls in the empty flat, its echo reverberating down the stairwell. His hands flew up to his forehead and his fingers looked like gnarled branches with which he was trying to hold his head together. 'Daddy'll be furious! If you open the door he'll go straight for your throat!'

'Listen to me, Jari,' said Harjunpää gently waving his hands. 'It's only a dog. A Great Dane, just like you said.'

'Well, that too,' he conceded, then hesitated as if he were about to impart a terrible secret. 'You see, he's still Daddy. His spirit came down from Heaven when Mummy... I know that look. It's Daddy's look and he's very angry with me. He's come to take his revenge.'

'All right, Jari,' said Harjunpää trying to calm him. 'All right.'

Only now did he fully understand that there was absolutely nothing he could do but wait. Time passed so slowly, like watching an endless freight train crawling carriage after carriage over the level crossing. From the street below he still couldn't hear the slamming of car doors that he so anxiously awaited.

At least this gave him a moment to think about the body: she looked at peace, lying there in a normal sleeping position. Her right hand was beneath the pillow, the left lay beside her face. A grey woollen sock had been pulled over her left hand, according to Jari because her hand was cold and ached, and to Harjunpää this indicated heart disease of some sort. But the body was already badly decomposed, blackened. Fluids had seeped through the bed on to the floor and around the face were the first signs of drying and mummification. She must have been dead for well over a month; numerous porridge bowls lay strewn across the floor and on the window ledge stood a row of air fresheners.

Harjunpää couldn't work out the layout of the flat, because it simply didn't exist. The only remaining item of furniture was the bed with the body lying on top of it. Only the lighter patches on the wallpaper indicated that other furniture had once been in place: presumably a large bookcase and maybe an armchair against the far wall, and there were indentations in the cork flooring where a sofa had once stood.

'Everything all right up there?' came a voice from the stairwell and Harjunpää realised that someone had heard Jari's scream. The bright morning sunlight shone in from behind the voice and all Harjunpää could see was a dark figure that he decided must have been a woman in her dressing gown.

'You're not manhandling him, I hope.'

'Don't worry, I'm a police officer,' he replied and moved towards the corridor. Dead bugs and bluebottles crackled under his feet like small, crisp pieces of boiled sweets. The woman took a step backwards and tightened the belt around her waist.

Harjunpää didn't actually hear anything behind him; he merely sensed something, a sudden movement or a flicker of the shadows. He ducked swiftly, rolled over and stood up again. But he had been mistaken; Jari was moving in the other direction. He was already halfway across the living room, bounding towards the gaping balcony door.

'Jari, no!' Harjunpää yelled. He was already in motion; he wrenched impetus from the doorpost, and everything else seemed to happen by itself; it was as though his whole life he had been practicing for this very moment. His shoes pounded against the floor, the patterns on the wallpaper blurred in streaks around him and the open balcony doorway grew larger at an incredible speed, like a camera zooming in. Jari had already made it out to the balcony and his dress flapped in the wind like a giant tail.

He had gripped the railing and was now trying to lift one of his legs over the top as if he were mounting a horse. The wind caught one of his socks and it flew off like a bird shot down in mid-flight. Harjunpää had reached the balcony, he stood in the doorway and stretched out his hand. A single thought spun in his mind: *what floor, what floor?* Somehow he noticed a broom with no handle and a multicoloured sock lying in the corner of the balcony. He grabbed hold of Jari's shoulders and, shifting his centre of gravity, pulled him down as hard as he could – the smell of sweat hung in the air. He then thrust his knee into the back of Jari's thigh, there came a bony click and Jari was securely wedged in between Harjunpää and the railing.

Jari removed his left hand from the railing and began scratching at Harjunpää's fingers, but it was no use. They stood there panting, writhing like a many-limbed monster. Harjunpää instinctively looked down. At first all he saw was Jari's bare leg dangling like a loose object through the railings, then there was nothing. Emptiness, more emptiness, and behind all the emptiness, unfathomably far away, he could make out the ground. In his stomach he could feel the downward acceleration, his jacket flapping in his eyes. Would there be enough time to feel pain? Or would it be nothing more than a single, astonishing blaze of red?

'He'll punish me because Mummy's dead!' Jari wailed. This statement seemed to give him a surge of renewed strength and he managed to clamber further up over the railing. A pen he had got from the museum fell out of Harjunpää's pocket and shot downwards like a bullet, without even a quiver. Then it disappeared. It was only then that Harjunpää really felt afraid: something hot ran through him, in his temples he could feel his heart thumping, pounding, the image of his family flashed through his mind – how would they cope? Then he thought of Jari: did he have any chance of recovery, even with the best care available? For a short, horrifying moment he wondered whether to release his grip.

'Nobody's going to die today!' he shouted, his mouth almost level with Jari's ear. In a flash Harjunpää became almost frenzied, tightened his grip and pulled, and at that same moment Jari seemed to give in, his body almost limp. They quickly stumbled backwards across the balcony. But of course, of course, Harjunpää knocked his heel against the door and began to fall. Everything happened surprisingly slowly, as if time were a viscous, defiant mass, and he had just enough time to press his chin against his chest before his back slammed against the floor.

Bugs crackled beneath him. Jari lay on top of him, heavy and bony, but Harjunpää managed to slip out from underneath, sprung to his knees and rolled him on to his stomach. Jari no longer tried to resist. Without any trouble he pulled Jari's hands behind his back and groped for the handcuffs on his belt. He could already feel their cold, calming steel, but eventually decided to let things be. Instead he kept a firm grip on Jari's right wrist, placed the palm of his free hand between Jari's shoulder blades and sighed: 'Easy does it, easy does it.'

'*Oy*, you!' a voice yelled. Harjunpää started and raised his head. In the front doorway stood a bulky man in a boiler suit, presumably the caretaker, restlessly beating the air with an ominous-looking rubber baton. The woman in the dressing gown stood behind him, her hands covering her face in horror.

'All right, leave him alone. That's assault, you know.'

'I'm not assaulting him. I'm a police officer.'

'Right, and I'm the prime minister. If I were you I'd stay right there on the floor, the real police are on their way.'

'Have you called them?'

'Of course.'

'Well call them again and tell them to get a bloody move on. My badge is in my jacket pocket…'

'And what if you're lying? What if it's a gun?'

'I give up,' he sighed, though under different circumstances he would have herded the onlookers out into the corridor. In any case he was certain that JP's squad would arrive at any moment. He took hold of Jari's arms, helped him into a sitting position and leant him against the wall. He could feel the man quivering all over, very slightly, from head to toe, as if he were crying deep inside. Harjunpää stood up, walked over to the balcony and shut the door. He felt relief as the howl of the wind finally ceased.

'Fuckin A!' came a voice from the stairwell. Harjunpää knew immediately who it was – there was only one man in the whole police force who after all these years still greeted him with those same words. He was right. Rummukainen from Central had already chivvied the caretaker and the woman in the dressing gown out into the stairwell and stood in the doorway in a position that had become very familiar to Harjunpää over the years: legs apart, his hat pushed back on his forehead and his thumbs tucked in behind the belt carrying his gun and other equipment. It had been said that Rummukainen only had to step out of his car and stand like this for a moment to diffuse any situation. Like Harjunpää he had seen almost everything, and even now his expression was calm, not shocked in the least, but still his eyes watchfully scanned across the room. Even if he hadn't been in uniform, this at least would have given him away as a police officer.

'He just tried the quick way down,' Harjunpää whispered. 'Off the balcony. We had quite a wrestling match.'

'So I see. Your trousers are still covered in crap.'

'Yeah, thanks. So,' Harjunpää began decisively, but suddenly realised that he didn't know what to say or do. His mind was blank; it felt almost as though he had woken up in strange surroundings and couldn't for the life of him remember where he was. 'So...'

'The doctor's arrived,' said Rummukainen, nonchalantly twiddling with his moustache. 'And an ambulance, but I told them all to wait in the corridor. Best fill the doc in first, then get this guy and everyone else out of here.'

'Right,' Harjunpää mumbled and for a brief, rare moment something approaching a smile crossed his face. After this short pause he could once again feel the blood begin pumping through him; his thoughts cleared, the machinery inside slowly jolted into motion. Immediately the plan of action became perfectly clear to him: Jari out, dog out, body out; schedule post mortem for the next day and seal off the flat. If necessary get forensics in to take a look around after the post mortem, then get the place disinfected.

'Keep him company for a minute,' he instructed Rummukainen and walked out into the hallway. The front door was still wide open. Outside, in addition to the doctor and the firemen stood the caretaker, the dressing-gown woman and, judging by the way they were dressed, a few other people from the same building. Their confused, low muttering came to an abrupt halt as Harjunpää appeared in the doorway. The smell of fresh coffee wafted up the staircase and behind closed doors a few floors below came the shrill yapping of a little dog.

'He did tell us all that his mother had died.' The caretaker seemed to speak for everyone; he was almost defensive. The rubber baton was carefully hidden behind his back. 'But none of us realised she was still in there.'

'When did he first mention this?'

'It was March the 21st, I remember it clearly because it was my birthday and I remember thinking I ought to have flown our flag at half-mast.'

'He gave me one of those double lamp-stands,' said the woman in the dressing gown.

'But we all thought he was just moving to a smaller flat and getting rid of some stuff. He even gave the Lönnbergs his piano.'

'And I saw Mutanen's eldest son carrying the telly out of there.'

'The video and the microwave ended up in the rubbish downstairs.'

'Thank you,' said Harjunpää and raised his hand. 'I'll be contacting you and everyone else in this block either today or tomorrow. I'll leave my card on the notice board downstairs in case anything important comes to mind. Once again, thank you.'

He indicated for the doctor and the firemen to follow him inside, shut the door behind him and crouched down to listen. He could tell that the neighbours were finally going from the sound of their voices and footsteps becoming quieter and quieter. Then came the sound of a door closing. This was what he had wanted. It would be better as far as getting Jari out of the flat was concerned.

'Living with a corpse isn't enough to warrant sectioning him. It would be a bit extreme,' said the doctor. He was a youngish man with a round face, but despite his age he gave off the natural authority of someone capable of rational thought and who had implicit trust in his own judgement. He walked up to the living room door, looked around for a moment, then came back.

'Neither is being a transvestite.'

'That has nothing to do with it,' said Harjunpää, running his fingers through his hair – there too he found a dead fly. There was something about the doctor's attitude that bothered him. 'Ever since he was a little boy his mother has been telling him she had hoped for a girl and that life with a girl would have been much easier. When she died, if I've understood right, he thought he could bring her back to life by being a girl.'

'Aha.'

'He's your typical mummy's boy. When his mother died, everything fell apart.'

'I see.'

'Yes, I know I'm only a policeman, but as far as I can see he's completely incapable of looking after himself. You heard them say how he's given away everything he owned. And just before you got here he tried to jump off the balcony. It was a close call – for me too.'

'I'll examine him,' said the doctor. His voice was different now, there was something almost disparaging about it. He turned and marched into the living room with the firemen close behind him.

'He's been feeding the body all this time. With porridge,' Harjunpää added, but immediately wished he hadn't. Still, it was a fact nonetheless.

Harjunpää decided not to follow the interview but instead crept into the corridor between the kitchen and the living room. At that moment he couldn't hear any tapping, just heavy panting. Perhaps Daddy had sensed the new arrivals in the flat and was assessing the situation. At least Jari had been taking some care of the animal: on the floor there were a dozen or so empty tins of dog food. Harjunpää didn't stay there for long, but quietly continued towards the bedroom door and pushed it open with the tips of his fingers.

The body looked exactly the way he remembered it. The only thing he had forgotten was her mouth: her lips had dried away to reveal her teeth in their entirety, almost as if this grin were her final grotesque gesture to the world.

As many times as Harjunpää had witnessed scenes like this before, this time, for some reason, he couldn't help thinking that this used to be a living person, Hilja Maria. Once Hilja Maria had been a little baby, suckled in her mother's arms, with everything to look forward to: life and all its beauty and horror. Maybe Hilja Maria had once been a little girl with pigtails, skipping with the other girls in the playground, the best of them all at hopscotch.

Hilja Maria had probably been a very slim young lady who marvelled at herself, at the woman she had become, at the breathtaking power of creation that womanhood brought with it. At some point a man called Simo had appeared – the same man who had been dead for over thirty years – and they had told each other how much they loved one another.

Because of their existence and their love a son appeared, Jari, whose hoarse crying could now be heard from behind the wall and for whom the doctor was currently writing out a referral to a mental hospital. Harjunpää couldn't quite understand where it had all gone wrong. Perhaps after becoming a widow Hilja Maria couldn't understand that Jari had not been born simply to be there for her, but also for himself - and even then only for a short time. Or perhaps she truly believed she owned something: a child, a son, and through that another person's life and freedom. Still, Harjunpää couldn't bring himself to believe that Hilja Maria really wished she had had a girl. It was all just talk, a way of teasing Jari.

'Timo.'

'Yes?' said Harjunpää turning around.

Rummukainen had appeared behind him and was sizing up the body, though even now he refrained from commenting on the scene in front of him.

'No use talking to him. He got an injection up the arse and now they're taking him off. Eränen's squad is waiting downstairs and they'll take him. Listen…'

Only then, from the echoes, did Harjunpää realise that the crying was coming from the stairwell, and perhaps it wasn't crying after all but an agonised wailing: like frayed steel wire, lacerating everything in its path.

'OK, let's get that dog out of here,' Harjunpää said finally. He remembered only too well how high and how heavily the dog's paws had thumped behind the door when he had arrived, and he had not forgotten Jari's blind fear and his claim that the dog would go straight for the throat.

They stopped outside the cupboard door: the smell of urine and excrement hung in the air and the tapping behind the door resounded back and forth like a distant drumming. Daddy was probably more restless now than earlier, it must have smelt and heard all the strange people in the apartment. Harjunpää instinctively brought his hand up to his throat and looked at Rummukainen. His eyes seemed uncharacteristically fixed on the floor. Even his shoulders seemed to be drooping slightly.

'I don't know,' Harjunpää hesitated. 'Can something like this really make a dog go mad too?'

'Well, if it's enough to make a human go mad…'

'I've never seen anything like it. I once had to deal with a boxer dog that had eaten its dead master's backside, but that was only out of starvation.'

'Timo.'

'Yes?'

'If I tell you something, can we keep it between ourselves?'

'I don't see why not.'

'You see,' he began and raised his eyes from the floor. His expression was no longer that of a policeman carefully registering the details of a room; this was a side of Rummukainen he'd never met before. 'We once went to my aunt's place in Pälkäne – I must have been about six at the time. Their garden backed on to a graveyard, you could see all the crosses and gravestones over the wall. They had an outdoor toilet back then and I used to be terrified of going out there because of this graveyard...'

'And?'

'Well, they had this big dog, some sort of Alsatian. It used to be a stray. And well... Once it wouldn't let me out of the toilet. It stood there growling and baring its teeth and had me cornered up against the stone wall. I must have been there for about an hour before any of the adults noticed. And believe me I was scared.'

For a moment both men fell silent and tried to avoid looking each other in the eye. With the tip of his shoe Rummukainen scraped dead flies into a pile. The doors of at least three cars could be heard slamming shut outside.

'I can take anything else in this job, but not dogs,' Rummukainen finally broke the silence. 'But nobody knows that.'

'And they still don't know. Where's your squad partner?'

'Out in the car. He's still young, almost parted company with his breakfast when we got to the door.'

Harjunpää was silent. Part of him was still following what was happening inside the cupboard. He could hear panting, whining, the dog crying, but not growling, which he thought must be a good sign, as he vaguely remembered hearing that dogs only growl when they are about to attack.

'I'll open the door and grab it,' he said finally. His mouth was dry and he didn't like it, because he knew that dogs smell fear. He licked his lips and reached into his jacket for his revolver, but decided to leave it there for the time being. Instead he walked over to the coat rack in the hallway and picked up the leash hanging there. It was a robust piece of material, clearly made for a large, powerful dog.

Harjunpää stepped right up to the cupboard door. He slid one of his feet along the edge to stop the dog from bounding out and placed his hand on the handle – his palms, by now, were sticky with sweat. There came a sharp click as Rummukainen cocked his gun. Harjunpää glanced behind him – the last thing he wanted was to be struck by a stray bullet – but Rummukainen nodded reassuringly and pointed his gun at the floor. He was obviously preparing himself for the worst. But now his expression was resolute once again, and the six-year-old boy who had just a moment ago peeped out through his eyes was nowhere to be seen.

'And how are you, Daddy?' said Harjunpää trying to make his voice as friendly as possible. Something told him it would be wise to keep talking. 'Come on out of there, boy. No, it's not nice in there, is it?' He pulled the door handle down and the padding stopped. The dog was clearly standing right by the door. Harjunpää still couldn't hear any growling.

He pulled the door wide open and the smell intensified. The dog was incredibly big. It had to be a cross between a Great Dane and another large dog, because it certainly wasn't a pedigree – even with its head slightly drooping it was still level with Harjunpää's chest. It was completely black, and perhaps this made it seem even larger than it actually was.

'Come on out Daddy, you old mutt,' said Harjunpää, trying to coax it out of the cupboard. The dog sniffed the air loudly and suspiciously, then took a few steps forwards.

'Come on, boy, and we'll take you for a walk.'

With slow, heavy steps Daddy finally plodded out of the cupboard and cried, whining constantly. Harjunpää thought how terribly sad it looked, almost as if it knew precisely what had taken place: its mother had died and, in a way, so had its master. It began sniffing Harjunpää's hand, patting it with its dry nose, and finally licked his fingers.

There came another click as Rummukainen replaced the safety catch on his revolver.

6. M.M.M.

Someone called out his name; rapidly, over and over, as if they were thrashing him over the head with a twig. 'Mikko! Mikko!'

But he didn't answer. He didn't want to.

'Mikko!'

He didn't want to be Mikko again, clutching terrified at someone's legs or round their neck; he didn't want to keep watch at the door any longer, because it was nasty and said bad things.

He read through the opening again very slowly, thinking about every word, but it was pointless. His eyes saw the words in front of him, saw the rest of the text, but he couldn't hear it in his soul. His soul was broken. He had lost count of how many years it had gone on. His sense of rhythm had vanished, and when it came to writing prose, rhythm was everything: it dictated the words, their length and order, the form and structure of sentences, paragraphs and chapters, their size and relation to one another – an ear for rhythm was vital.

His soul had a good ear for rhythm. But now it felt castrated, a pile of rust and rubble, and in a hushed but persistent voice it argued against everything he did, making things seem shameful and bad and ugly, and simply not allowing him to be good.

Yet again he felt a strange sorrow slowly awakening within him. Though normally he would have quickly run from it, this time he decided to listen for a moment. It was still the same anxious feeling that made his shoulders tremble, that made him feel like weeping. He sighed heavily and let it pass, grabbed hold of his papers and began once again to read from the beginning.

But he was too exhausted. All at once he felt the fatigue of a sleepless night and years of futile attempts at writing. He gave in, cast his papers on to the table and sat there staring at them, his head bowed.

That night not only had his stomach been tense – he had spent the early hours running to the toilet every fifteen minutes – but his hands had been restless too. His fingers had left sticky dents on the sheets of paper. If paper were snow, someone might have thought a stubby-legged creature had plodded across it. He wondered what it might have looked like and decided that it must have been like floor dust rolled up into a ball. Suddenly he could almost see it: it had a wicker tail covered in thin hairs and a pair of deep red eyes as round as pearls. In the middle of all this he remembered the slipper - and the red-eyed creature died in a flash.

It was made of brown checked material and had fallen off Father's foot. There was a hole in his sock, right at the heel, though it didn't look like a hole at all, but rather like an object. It looked like he'd stood on a ping-pong ball, which had become stuck there forever, never to bounce again. Its only function was to remain there and be crushed little by little into nothingness, under Father's immense weight.

'Damn it,' he hissed and stood bolt upright. He was covered in sweat, droplets fell out of nowhere on to the lenses of his glasses, and he glanced furtively through the morning darkness surrounding him, scanning the corners and turning to look at the floor behind him. Eventually he noticed the soothing colours of the familiar painting on the wall. He was home. Safe.

Or rather, he was in the place he called home: a tiny bedsit in the middle of town, amongst unfamiliar people, almost directly opposite Kallio church; so close in fact that its bells plagued him. The walls in this room had seen other peoples' lives, but not his; the ceiling didn't know how to protect him while he was thinking, creating new worlds back when everything was still fine; the floor didn't know his feet, couldn't steer him on to the right path, a path that would bring him life: people, people's deeds, the mindless chaos that one day becomes a novel.

Besides living in a false home, he was somewhere else too, a place he despised. He despised that state of mind. Six years on the trot, and on the door to this state of mind hung a sign bearing the word HELL.

In his profession he ought to have been able to describe it well, but he could not. If he could have painted it, he would have depicted how a person can fall by the wayside, being sucked further and further down, engulfed in an abyss of murky water; how moss covers even the tiniest glimmer of light and water floods into the chest. How you hope against hope that a hand will reach out from somewhere. But no hand ever appears – nothing but eyeless fish swimming around you, their round white mouths shouting: 'Shame on you! You are guilty and should be ashamed!'

'Dad?'

'What?' he gave a start, as if he had been caught in the act, up to no good, and immediately he could feel the anxiety draining into his hands, and they began to quiver as though he were ill.

'Is… is everything all right, Dad?'

'Yes. Why do you ask?'

'You were puffing and blowing again,' said Sanna, her voice thick with sleep. 'And swearing.'

'I'm sorry. Did I wake you?'

'I have to get up now anyway. Have you been up all night?'

'No, only since three o'clock.'

'And you're sure everything's OK?'

'Yes, I'm sure. I was just thinking through a really exciting chapter. With a very nasty man.'

He stood up and walked the few metres to the end of the screen. Its frame and slats were made of unvarnished wood but otherwise it was nothing but white, transparent paper. They had bought it in a shop near the ring road, to split up the room.

'Try and sleep a while longer,' he said and only then realised how empty it sounded. The important thing was that he had walked across the room and now looked his daughter in the eye. 'I'll wake you before I leave. And I'll make you a cup of tea and a sandwich.'

'OK,' she sighed and rested her head on the pillow. 'Don't forget to leave me some money for the bus. Mari and I are going to look at that flat today.'

'Wouldn't it be nice if you liked the place… I'll leave the money in the hall cupboard. Have a good day then.'

'Dad?'

'Yes?'

'Have you seen Matti at all?'

'Well… you know how he hates me.'

'No he doesn't, not really, it's just that he's been hurt so badly, that's all. You have a good day too.'

'Thanks.'

He went back to his desk and hopelessly picked up his papers, knowing that nothing would come of reading them again. It suddenly struck him how much he missed his son and his real home in Kulosaari; he missed the life he had lost, the years when Sanna and Matti were still little and everything was just right. With uncomfortable certainty he suddenly felt that nothing like that would ever happen to him again, that from now on grey days would follow, one after the other, and that soon the weekend would be no different from a Thursday. Another grey morning was dawning. Soon he would trudge down the hill to Hakaniemi, take a rattling underground train to Kontula and shut himself inside the even smaller rented room he called his office. The years went by as quickly as ever – four years of a state grant behind him and he hadn't been able to write a thing. In less than a year's time he would have no choice but to return to the post office and the drudgery of his job in the sorting office.

He glanced drowsily over the first page and somewhere deep inside him, almost beyond his reach, he could sense that perhaps this was good prose after all, but the cold fact remained that it was of absolutely no use to him whatsoever.

He turned and stared at the bookshelf: there in a row stood his eight novels. The words Mikko Matias Moisio appeared on the spine of each book, leading his colleagues at the post office to tease him incessantly. Some of them had given him the nickname the Three M's.

His novels formed a series and they had brought him considerable renown both in Finland and abroad.

It was a series about a happy family.

7. Jam

To be absolutely specific, the vehicle was one belonging to the arson unit of the Violent Crimes Squad of Helsinki's municipal police. Not surprisingly it was known as simply the 'Fire Engine', even though this particular one wasn't red but white, just like all the other police Transporter vans, containing nothing personal that could identify the owners. Only a sharp eye would have noticed it was a police vehicle, from the two flashing blue lights hidden behind the cooling vent.

Officers from other squads were allowed to use the cars as necessary, and this time it was Harjunpää's turn to borrow it. He approached the car from behind, almost dragging his feet. At this Elisa would certainly have noted that her husband wasn't in the best of moods. Harjunpää took a deep breath. Though he could already sense the exhaust fumes drifting in across the Western Highway, he enjoyed the scent of Lauttasaari in the spring. It was a pleasant mix of budding birch trees, lawns slowly awakening and the sea finally released from the grip of ice. The air smelled and tasted of life.

In one hand Harjunpää was carrying a case file and in the other he fumbled with the car keys. As he pressed a button on the key ring the Transporter's lights flashed and there came a small click as the doors unlocked. He threw the file on to the passenger seat, climbed up into the seat, flicked on the police radio and stuck the key in the ignition. Only then did it hit him: sweat began to drip from his brow and armpits, and his hands trembled so much that his wedding ring began tapping repeatedly against the steering wheel.

'Good God,' he sighed heavily. Deep in his stomach he could feel the acceleration through the fall, and the images of all the dozens of balcony suicides he had dealt with flashed before his eyes; all the brain matter and shards of skull he had scraped off the streets throughout the city.

Now that he was no longer outside but shut inside the confined space of the car, he realised that his clothes and hair stank of death, of a decomposing body, and of the nightmare he had just witnessed. The thought of the flies and the larvae filled his mind and soon his back began to itch, then his arms, and soon afterwards his legs too. He hurriedly got out of the car, went round the back, wrenched the sliding door open and jumped into the interview space at the back. The windows were darkened and no one could see inside. He tore off his jacket and shirt and rolled up his trouser legs. There was nothing there – of course.

He remained on the bench, resting on his elbows, and sighed. For a while he sat there motionless. It occurred to him that back at the station there was a sauna, warmed round the clock, and that there was a decent set of spare clothes in his locker. He gave his shirt a thorough shake, put it back on, and ran his fingers through his hair for a final inspection.

'*Anyone from Violent Crimes on the line?*' came the voice of the duty officer over the radio – it sounded like that of Joutsen – and Harjunpää knew immediately that that meant only one thing: another job. 'No, there's no one on the line,' he muttered to himself.

'*All officers: is there anyone from Violent Crimes on the line?*'

Harjunpää slammed the sliding door shut and walked back towards the driver's seat. Just then his work mobile began to ring. He let it ring three times before picking it up, glanced reluctantly at the screen, then finally relented, pressed the button and raised the phone to his ear.

'Crime Squad, Harjunpää.'

'Hi, it's Pete,' said Tupala. He was the sergeant major who ran the Violent Crimes office and delegated all the assignments. Tupala never lost his nerve, no matter how awful the matter in hand. He always managed to sound jolly, almost amused.

'You're on mornings, right? Free?'

'I just got back from a pretty nasty job.'

'*All officers, I repeat: is there anyone from Violent Crimes downtown?*'

'Something's come up.'

'Where's Base?'

'Taking that rape-victim from the ferry down to the lab. Both duty sergeants are in Uutela fishing round a lake for a body, and everyone else is at staff training.'

'*The switchboard still needs someone from Violent Crimes. Is there anyone on the line?*'

'What's the location?'

'Hakaniemi underground station,' said Tupala. 'Someone's gone and topped themselves. Completely mangled up apparently, jammed in along the undercarriage, so they're having a hard time getting him out.'

'I'll take it. Send forensics down there, and Mononen too.'

'They're already on their way. Mononen's coming in with your previous man, then heading straight off to Uutela.'

'Thanks. Over.'

Harjunpää shoved the mobile back in his pocket and grabbed the microphone from the dashboard. 'Copy. This is 198 and Harjunpää. If this is the Hakaniemi job, then I'm on my way.'

'Excellent. How far are you?'

'I'm still in Lauttasaari.'

'OK, this is fairly urgent so get down there as soon as you can. The entire underground service has been stopped and it's chaos at the station – thousands of people milling about.'

'Over and out.'

Harjunpää leant over and began winding down the window. The feelings of emptiness and helplessness were long gone, though he wasn't quite sure how he had managed to dispel them, they had simply vanished. Everyone in Violent Crimes could dispel feelings like that, and those that couldn't soon disappeared from the force. He picked up the blue flashing light from beside his feet, stuck the black cable dangling from the dashboard into the back of the dome and held it out of the open window. There came a soft thump, a metallic kiss as the strong magnet clamped the flashing light to the roof.

He shifted himself round behind the steering wheel and a map of the city centre began to form in his mind. The most direct route would have taken him through the downtown area, but this would not necessarily have been the quickest. The area around Kansakoulukatu and Simonkatu was always heavily congested. He was about to settle for an alternative route, taking him around the bay at Töölönlahti, then along Helsinginkatu and through the streets of Kallio, when he remembered the tram lines: that would allow him to drive through the traffic and take him straight from the Central Railway Station to Hakaniemi underground. He had to give it shot.

He turned the ignition and the engine roared into life. From the sound it made you could tell it wasn't your average motor. He switched the gear-box to D. The Transporter was an automatic, which made it a lot easier to drive, particularly in an emergency, as it allowed him to concentrate more on the other traffic. He glanced in the rear-view mirror, turned on the sirens and sped off.

A few metres before the junction of Meripuistotie and Lauttasaarentie he reached down and flicked the furthest of four upright switches on the dashboard, and a red light came on. The light on the car's roof began flashing and regular, electric blue pulses beamed from the cooling vents. When he pressed the switch again the sides of the car let out an excruciating wail – *wee wah wee wah*.

He passed easily through the first junction – the traffic lights were green – then he put his foot down and headed towards Lauttasaari bridge, the sirens' blaring now long and high-pitched. One part of his mind was going through all the things any motorist should remember: not too fast, speeding only caused accidents. Calm and controlled driving, through narrow openings that always appeared as long as you were patient enough. One thing he had to bear in mind was that, although inside an emergency vehicle the sound of the sirens seems to fill your entire head, it often sounds muffled and muted to other drivers and it is difficult to judge which direction it is coming from.

At the same time another part of him realised that dealing with death on the underground was just as straightforward as dealing with people run over by trains: interview eye-witnesses and breathalyse the driver as a routine check. After that they would have to start moving the train back one segment of track at a time to ensure that all human remains and pieces of clothing stuck to the undercarriage were retrieved. The firemen would help them with that. Then they would have to check through the security videos and identify the body. And that was just for starters.

To his astonishment he passed along Ruoholahdenkatu and Malminrinne without any trouble – perhaps this was because the lights at the front of the car were so effective: they were at just the right height so that other motorists could see them easily in their rear-view mirrors. Only on Kansakoulukatu did he get stuck in traffic. On the left side of the street, next to a row of parked cars, was a lorry unloading its cargo. Harjunpää turned the steering wheel to the right and so did the silver Micra in front of him. Only as the Micra drew level with the back of the lorry did the driver notice the flashing lights in his mirror. He panicked. He hit the brakes – and so did Harjunpää. There was a screech of wheels, and as they came to a halt there was barely ten centimetres between the two cars.

At this point the driver of the Micra became even more flustered and tried to restart the engine, but for some reason it had stalled completely. Then he got out of the car, a young man with headphones and a portable CD player on his belt, and waved his hands helplessly at Harjunpää.

'Idiot,' Harjunpää's lips moved as the sirens continued to blare – *wee wah wee wah!* The lorry driver seemed to understand what was going on and with its back doors still open moved the lorry a few metres forward, leaving enough of a gap for Harjunpää to squeeze through and pass the stalled Micra.

He drove along Simonkatu without any trouble and the lights at the junction of Mannerheimintie were green. At this point Harjunpää managed to manoeuvre the Transporter on to the tram tracks. He put his foot down a little, but realised that he still had to drive very carefully, especially around the tram stops. Pedestrians weren't always expecting a car to come racing along the tracks, they might think the sirens were coming from somewhere else and absent-mindedly step out in front of him and end up under the car. This had happened once in the past, but that time the vehicle in question had been an ambulance.

The Transporter sped across Long Bridge and, once the tram coming towards him had passed, Harjunpää could see in front of him a number of Emergency Service vehicles and a tide of flashing blue lights. They had gathered at the entrance to the underground station on the pavement along Siltasaarenkatu. There were at least four cars: the fire chief's, a patrol car, an ambulance and another that looked like it was for the paramedics. There were two police Mondeos and another Transporter parked on the square outside the underground entrance. Harjunpää blinked, more out of satisfaction than anything else, content that the area had been successfully cordoned off.

Harjunpää did a U-turn outside the circular building on the corner. A van from forensics stood parked in front of the building, as there was another underground entrance on that side of the street. He gently drove his Transporter up on to the pavement and switched off the sirens. If not the silence, then at least the fact that he could hear again seemed almost miraculous: the roar of traffic, the urgent clatter of footsteps on the pavement, the screech of the trams as they turned the corner.

Harjunpää picked up his case file, stepped out of the car and opened up the sliding door on the right-hand side. He opened the lowest drawer of the interview cabinet, took out a handful of rubber gloves and stuffed them into the file – his own supply of gloves had run out back in Lauttasaari. He removed his jacket from the hook and drew it over his head. On the chest was a lion, the police coat of arms; on the back stood the word POLICE in large reflective letters and beneath that, in much smaller print, Crime Squad. He slammed the sliding door shut.

Seagulls squawked in the air and the square was swarming with people – some were even wearing T-shirts – and life went on as if nothing had ever happened. That was exactly how it should be, he thought, the end of a particular world had taken place deep in a tunnel underground. He'd had this same thought before: the death of a person was always the end of a world, of the one world in which that person had been *me*, in the world where they had experienced everything else in the only way they could, the only way they knew how. And yet other worlds were bound to theirs: a lover, children, parents, colleagues. The end of one person's own world also shook the worlds of all these other people.

The path downwards was not blocked because the first underground level in Hakaniemi station consisted of a small shopping mall full of little boutiques and customer service offices. On the stairs leading down an elderly and, for some reason, very agitated woman came up to Harjunpää. She had long, flapping, silver hair and a beret pulled down almost to her eyes, and she was clenching a pile of papers to her chest. She held out one of these flyers to Harjunpää, but his eyes were cast downwards. There must have been about a hundred or so people milling about and the air was filled with a dull, uncertain and disquieted murmur.

'Take it!' said an urgent, demanding voice beside Harjunpää: the woman with the flyers was doddering alongside him. 'Take it!'

'No, thank you. They're waiting for me down there.'

'Take it! You of all people will soon find yourself praying for mercy! And the Lord shall grant it to you, but even more mightily shall the Lady!'

'Give it a rest!'

'To deny the existence of the divine Lady is an affront!' croaked the old woman. Harjunpää was becoming annoyed. The last thing he needed amidst everything that had happened that morning was the save-the-planet brigade. For want of anything better to do, he stretched out his hand, took the flyer, pretended to look at it, folded it and stuffed it in his jacket pocket.

Blue and white police tape had been drawn between the ticket machines and the escalators, preventing anyone from going down to the platforms. 'POLICE LINE: DO NOT CROSS' it read again and again. Behind the tape stood two uniformed policemen, and Harjunpää recognised one of them as his old friend Rannila from his student days.

'Morning. Murder Squad's on their way,' he said, quiet and sober.

'Hi. What's the situation?'

'I just heard on the radio that they haven't managed to get him out yet, just some body parts. And it is a he, apparently.'

'Thanks,' said Harjunpää as he lifted the tape, crouched underneath and made his way briskly down the escalator. By now he could clearly make out a smell that he couldn't quite put his finger on – it was simply the smell of the underground, a blend of stone and slowly seeping water.

Upon reaching the intermediary level he noticed that the incident had occurred on the eastbound track, where a glowing orange train now stood stationary. Just then he sensed another smell: the smell of a mutilated body, of blood. The train's carriages had been separated from one another, leaving a gap of twenty or so metres between them. At first Harjunpää didn't quite understand what was going on: every time he had dealt with underground cases in the past the body had had to be extricated from the front of the train.

Nonetheless it was at this gap that the firemen were working and one of them had crawled so far under the carriage that only the glow of his lamp could be seen. The paramedics had already begun gathering their equipment and were clearly getting ready to leave. This was the final confirmation that no one was going to be brought out from beneath the train alive. There were a number of constables from the division standing on the platform, amongst them DS Viitasaari, who was wearing the field director's vest. Kivinen from forensics was crouching down beside a body bag laid out on the platform. From a distance the body bag looked empty, or so Harjunpää thought.

'Hello, Harjunpää,' Viitasaari nodded and glanced down at his notebook. 'This is looking pretty bad. Not a single eyewitness, or if there were any they were long gone by the time we got here – probably in too much of a hurry to get to work. And here's the funny thing: this guy's managed to get himself stuck *between* the carriages.'

'What about the driver?'

'That woman over there. We breathalysed her, she's clean. Didn't notice anything out of the ordinary coming into the station, just crowds of passengers waiting. It was only when she was about to pull away that she noticed people waving to her in the mirror and someone running up to her compartment.'

'Let's hope there's something on the security tapes.'

'We've taken them in. You can collect them before you leave.'

'So maybe it wasn't suicide after all, perhaps he just stumbled.'

'That's what we've all been wondering.'

Harjunpää brought his hand up to his forehead and rubbed his temples with his thumb and forefinger. He would have to interview the driver himself and arrange a time for her to come down to the station, but his real hope lay with the security tapes: he guessed that all in all there must have been several hundred cameras dotted around the station. No doubt they would have to put a notice in the paper asking for witnesses to come forward. Identifying the victim was another priority, though he most likely had a wallet in his pocket containing the relevant papers. Next of kin, if there were any, might be able to shed some light on this.

Harjunpää trudged over to Kivinen and the body bag. Kivinen was focussing his camera on something at the bottom of the bag and Harjunpää bent down to see what it was. Before him lay a human face ripped from the skull, like a limp, rubber mask; through the mouth and eye sockets all that could be seen was the black at the bottom of the bag. It was clearly the face of a man – a young man at that. He was cleanly shaven, and through everything else Harjunpää thought he could make out the faint smell of a familiar aftershave.

In addition to the face, the bag also contained a hand, sticky with blood. It was the left hand, severed at the wrist, and on the fourth finger gleamed a flat, golden ring. Harjunpää sighed and reached into his bag for a pair of disposable gloves – they were the new kind that could even withstand needles, to a certain degree – then he crouched down, took the severed hand into his own and gently began wiggling the ring loose. It came off surprisingly easily, perhaps because the hand had already bled dry. He wiped the ring on his other glove and peered at the inside.

Jaana, read the inscription. In the dim light he couldn't make out the date.

8. *Maestro*

He liked calling it composing, and when he was at home by himself and could put the music on full volume it was like flying. In some ways they were one and the same thing, they gave him a chance to forget all the crap things in life – like Roo, or the fact that his mum must have been a bit mad to break them all up like that. And then there was the fact that his dad didn't seem to give a fuck about him.

He gave a start and quickly looked around to the left and the right; he didn't have to look behind him, because all that was there was the cafeteria wall. He couldn't see them yet. He gave a soft sigh: he couldn't see them because it was only the first break. It usually started after lunch, then continued all afternoon and on the way home too, if he forgot to wait behind the coat rack until they had gone. Janne was the biggest bastard of the lot.

But even this he could forget about when he was composing. He would start by staring at an object, like the sand in the playground, and gradually he would notice that it wasn't just sand, it was a whole collection of tiny, individual crystals. Each one of them had a shape and colour of its own, and light reflected off them in different ways. And even though they appeared to be in random positions, by the laws of nature they were exactly as they should be. It was truly magnificent!

Then all of a sudden it was as though he no longer simply saw these crystals, he could *hear* them – they were like sublime music, the swell of a great orchestra. At times like this his hands rose up of their own accord and began conducting the orchestra. This had even happened in school once or twice, and that's why everyone thought he was a fucking nutcase. That's where it had all started.

Even his mum said he must not be right in the head, and she hated him for it. So did Roo – but he hated Roo back. He didn't know whether it was a mental illness or not, but he was afraid it might be and the thought that he was different from everyone else frightened him. He'd never belonged to anybody's group or gang: everywhere he went, he was always alone.

Trembling slightly he took a deep mouthful of air, then another, and his mind was filled once again with the sensation of flying, and it was even better than composing; when the music was already playing, everything happened much quicker. Straight away he began conducting the orchestra, and a moment later he noticed that the shoes lined up beneath the coat rack weren't just sitting there, they were chattering away to one another. One of them was explaining how it had stepped in some chewing gum, another had stepped in dog's droppings, while a third recounted how, in a queue at the checkout, it had met such a wonderful pair of high heels that it had fallen in love with them in an instant. And as for the green rug in the living room, it was no longer a rug: it was a raft, a slice of the jungle, drifting upon the ocean, and only it knew where it was heading.

A moment later and everything had turned into a great dance: his legs moved supplely as though he had springs in his knees. He soared across on the jungle raft, flew from one room to the next, finally flying above all the furniture – or at least so he imagined. Nothing else existed, just the flying, not a single one of those bastards or his frightening thoughts. How he loved this!

By now the grains of sand had turned into a great horde of people, a choir singing a hymn, like the beginning of the waltz theme of *Also Sprach Zarathustra: tada-diti-ti-tii!* The strings began to weave their melody upwards, then a violin appeared and swiftly took the lead, and like a thief his hands slipped out of his pockets and rose up into the air – and that's when it hit him.

This time it struck him on the temple. It really hurt, like fire. He let out a silent 'fuck', and he could feel his lips trembling; he knew that tears were not far away. The sand was once again just sand, and he stood there, his shoulders hunched up, surrounded by the noise of the playground at break time.

They appeared from behind the games wall. That's where they had thrown the stone. They came straight towards him, first that shit-head Janne, then Stenu, and all of a sudden he felt a desperate need for the toilet.

'How's Matti shit-for-brains?' Janne began. Then they were around him in a semi-circle and he was trapped: behind him was the wall. 'What's with the hands? Having a wank?'

'No.'

'Have you got such a big dick that you need both hands?'

'Give it a rest.'

'Lend us your phone,' said Stenu. The expression on his face was so demonic that Matti knew what was coming next.

'No.'

'Why not? You afraid I'm going to nick it?'

'No.'

'Then why won't you lend it to me?'

'I haven't got one.'

'What? Did you hear that? He hasn't got a phone!'

They all burst into laughter. It was always false laughter at first, but when they saw how crap he felt, and that he could do nothing but stare at his shoes, it turned into real laughter. Then they all took out their mobile phones – Rike had one of those fancy new ones that can do almost anything – and held them up to their ears. Then it started:

'Hello? Hello? Can Mummy's boy Moisio hear?'

'Pick up! There's a lot of people calling you!'

He turned and stared at the wall with numbed eyes, but the bastards wouldn't let him be. They grabbed hold of him and spun him back round.

'Been looking at pussy on the net again?'

'He won't even look you in the eyes! Look!'

'And why haven't you been on the net? Say something, you little shit!'

'I haven't...'

'I'll tell you why: 'cause you haven't got a computer!'

'Fuck! He hasn't got a computer! Do you think he's got a dick?'

'Let's have a look!'

'Piss off, leave me alone.'

'And what if we don't? Going to tell your dad?'

'Shit-heads!'

'No you won't. And do you know why? 'Cause you haven't got a dad either, you fucking poof.'

'You're the…'

'Jesus Christ,' said Janne; he sounded almost amazed and started stretching his arms. Matti was so afraid that it felt as if his hands were swelling. 'Did you hear that? This poor tosser just called me a poof.'

'I heard him.'

'Me too.'

'I heard him call you an arse bandit too.'

'Fucking hell,' Janne said stretching his arms again. He came right up to Matti and grabbed the scruff of his jacket. He could smell the smoke on Janne's breath. 'Right, gay boy, you know what's going to happen to you after school?'

'Don't, please…'

'You're dead. Next break I'll come and see if you want to apologise. And you can say sorry by kissing my arse. But if you don't want to…'

At that moment someone came up behind them. It all happened so quickly that he couldn't tell where she had come from, but she shoved them so hard that they all stumbled and fell over. For a moment he thought it might be the girls' PE teacher, but it was Fat Leena from Year Eight. Some of the other children called her the Hammer Thrower. She had Janne by the ear and twisted it so hard that he fell to his knees.

'What the fuck are you doing, you fat cow?' Janne cried out, but this time his voice was trembling too.

'Just thought I'd show you what it's like,' said Fat Leena. She had already stretched her hands out towards Skate, but he legged it and only stopped when he realised Fat Leena wasn't following him. The others moved back, as though they were going to help Skate, even though they too were running away.

'I'll report you to the police!' shouted Janne. 'This isn't the last you'll hear of this, fat bitch! And you'll pay if my phone's broken!'

Only when they were far enough away did Janne dare raise his middle finger at her.

'Suits me fine!' she shouted back. 'Whenever you're ready. But you'll never win.'

The bell had obviously rung, though Matti hadn't noticed when. Everything had happened so fast, and now there was no one in the playground but the two of them. He could feel his shoulders heaving – he had learnt how to cry without making a sound. He felt bleary and ashamed, the shame thick like porridge in his head, and he felt that he simply didn't dare go to his next lesson.

'Get a move on,' shouted Fat Leena abruptly.

From the footsteps he could hear that Fat Leena was leaving, but he couldn't bring himself to follow her.

'Leena,' he finally managed to say. All he could do was stare at the ground, embarrassed and bowing his head, but he could hear that Fat Leena had stopped walking.

'What? Thanks?'

'Yeah. And, um… Could you walk home from school with me today?'

'When do you finish?'

'Three.'

'Me too. See you at the front door.'

'Thanks a lot,' said Matti, though he wasn't sure whether Leena had heard him or not, because just then a medicopter appeared from behind the trees, its blades chattering, and flew low over the school. There had been an accident somewhere: perhaps a car crash, perhaps someone had been in the wrong lane and smashed into a lorry.

Or even tried to kill themselves.

9. *Murmurings*

Sinikka was warm and happy – even though she was upside down, but she didn't know this. In any case, this was precisely the position she should have been in. She kept one of her tiny thumbs in her mouth and sucked on it. She very often did this, particularly when she heard the now familiar murmuring: *If you go down to the woods today, you're sure of a big surprise…*

This murmuring made Sinikka feel better than any other. It was like a murmuring all of her own: it was so close that it caused something to flicker gently, deep within her.

For every bear that ever was, will gather there for certain because today's…

Ding-dong!

That was a noise Sinikka had heard many times before, and though she hadn't really worked out why, she knew that the ding-dong meant that the world would begin to bounce slightly quicker than usual, and that would be followed by more murmuring, first the familiar, strong one, then another, fainter murmuring.

Ding-dong, came the sound again, and at that Sinikka and the rest of the world began to bounce, much faster, and soon afterwards Sinikka could make out her own murmuring: 'Good morning.'

'Good morning. I'm DS Timo Harjunpää from Helsinki Police.'

'Oh? Ah yes, you must be here about the break-in. I simply haven't got round to making a list of everything that's missing.'

'No...'

'Don't worry, you can look at it. Quite a handsome bump, isn't it? It's our first baby.'

'I'm sorry, I didn't mean to... Do you know what it is yet?'

'No, we didn't want to. We'll find in when the time comes. So what does bring you here then?'

'May I come in for a moment?'

'By all means.'

'Perhaps we should sit down.'

'I'd rather stand. It's good for the back, you know.'

'Do you have any friends or relatives who live nearby?'

'No. Why do you ask? What's this about?'

'Your husband is Tero Yrjänä Kokkonen, is that correct?'

'Yes.'

'I'm afraid I have some terrible news,' Harjunpää finally stammered. 'Your husband has been involved in an accident and I'm afraid to say...'

'No! It isn't him! Good God, what a fright you gave me... That motorbike is still registered in his name, but someone else was driving it. We only handed it over once the payment had been settled. He sold it two days ago.'

'I'm terribly sorry. This wasn't a motorbike accident, this happened in the underground.'

'Good God! No, God, no... what happened? Which hospital is he in?'

'I'm afraid he's dead, madam.'

'Oh Jesus, no! He can't be! He took the underground because it was so much safer... Tell me it wasn't Tero!'

'There's nothing we can do. There's no doubt that it is your husband. Madam, please, come and sit down here.'

'No! No!'

'I'm so sorry; please, let's sit over here. Please…'

These were strange murmurings, Sinikka had never heard anything like them before. They made her feel suddenly very bad indeed – her heart beat so frantically that it hurt, she became very restless and started kicking with her little fairy feet and waving her arms around. Then something even worse happened: something pressed against her, all around her, again and again – Sinikka felt like she was about to burst.

Her own discomfort meant that she no longer paid attention to the murmurings, but they continued, she could feel it, and she soon heard a very strange murmuring indeed: wee-wah-wee-wah! Soon afterwards Sinikka's position changed again. In this position the world was still for a long time, and she couldn't hear murmurings of any sort. Only now Sinikka no longer felt calm, as she always had done in that position. All she felt was that she was being pushed from every direction, that something wanted her out of there.

10. *Nook*

If you were to lift the stiff hatch in the corrugated-iron roof of The Brocken and edge your way through the gap, you might be in for a surprise. Right in the middle of the hut's stone floor gaped the mouth of a shaft, about two metres in diameter, and a sheer drop leading down into the darkness. At first glance it resembled the hungry jaws of an ancient monster. If you dared move closer, at the western side of the shaft you would notice the top of a pair of steel rails, and if you inched your way towards these rails you would see, in between the rails, steel rungs leading down into the earth's invisible core.

And if you had the courage to grip the rails, place a foot on the first rung and lower yourself down, it would be another twenty-five rungs before your feet once again touched something firm. If, however, you were to shine a torch at your feet, you would notice that the firm ground was not so firm after all – it was a platform fashioned from an iron grille and covered only half of the shaft. It would turn your stomach to look down between your feet into who knows what; if you should drop something small through the grille, there would be no reassuring clatter or splash to indicate that the object had arrived somewhere.

Along the other side of the shaft the top of the next set of ladders could be dimly made out, leading down and down, and a faint upward draught would catch at your trouser legs, giving you goose bumps.

At this platform, along both the northern and southern sides of the shaft, were two doors – or rather, two openings. To the left gaped an empty room, a couple of metres wide and about five metres long, with concrete facing along the walls. However, the room was not entirely empty, for along the floor jutted a number of rusted mounting bolts, rather like those on the cemented floor outside but considerably sturdier and with two rails attached to the floor running between them. Along the ceiling ran a massive pipe, several metres long, which had once led somewhere and had perhaps served a very important function.

It was impossible to say with any certainty what had been in the room many years ago – a winch of some sort, a crane, or perhaps some kind of ventilation pump that had later been replaced by something further down, newer and more efficient. The opening to the right was covered from the inside with a green tarpaulin – the kind that you often see gently rustling in the wind, covering boats tethered up for the winter.

Behind the tarpaulin was a room all but identical to the one opposite, but this room was far from empty: on the floor along its far wall lay a foam mattress and upon that a sleeping bag left open to air. At the head of the mattress stood a wooden box, one that once had been used to transport apples. Upon the box there was a storm lantern and an alarm clock without its glass cover – even in the darkness you could feel the hands of the clock and see what time of night it was.

Near the door opening a nylon rope had been stretched from wall to wall across the room and this clearly served as a clothes-line. On clothes hangers to the right hung women's clothes, for the most part loose skirts and caftans reaching almost to the ankles, a few blazers and a floral woollen cardigan. To the left hung men's clothing: different coloured trousers, a pair of jeans, jackets and shirts and a hefty leather jacket from the 1950s. All this clearly served another purpose too: if you drew the clothes together they formed a handy inner door to cut out the draught.

Along the walls were a number of cardboard boxes, and in the two outermost boxes was presumably a selection of underwear: one box for women's underwear, one for men's. At least, on top of the left-hand box were various men's hats and baseball caps, whilst upon the right-hand box sat two berets, one blue and one green, and with them a brimmed hat and a straw hat with a plastic flower stitched into the ribbon.

In addition to this there was a folding chair – like the ones often found on terraces during the summer, the kind that are particularly uncomfortable to sit in – and opposite the chair a Trangia stove and an old burnt pan. Beside them stood a neat row of full water bottles, and behind them a row of empty ones.

Books lay in piles on almost every free surface. If you were to take a closer look at these you would notice that the majority of them dealt with different religions and astronomy – and that every last one of them had been stolen from the city library.

The only item that might have been considered a luxury or a decoration was a poster hanging on the wall above the bed. The poster showed an image from the furthest reaches of space, nebulae joining together to create another Big Bang, a new universe, or perhaps it was simply a far off galaxy – it was impossible for any layman to know precisely what it displayed, but you might guess that the photograph had been taken by the Hubble Telescope.

All in all, looking around that southern room, it contained everything that an ascetic person needed to live their modest life. That person's spirituality must surely have been far richer. For without a doubt this nook was someone's home, a gnome's perhaps or an earth sprite's, a cosy little nest of their own.

11. Command

'*Faustus dies,*' he puffed each time he grabbed hold of another rung. He climbed upwards with the agility of an animal: hand, foot, other hand, other foot. This did not present him with the slightest difficulty as he was used to lots of walking. Besides, there was not a gram of excess fat on him; just bones, tough muscles and skin.

'*Faustus dies,*' he panted for the last time, as his head and shoulders finally appeared above the grille at the top of the shaft. He stopped there for a moment, listening. Or rather, he was taking the scent, as he put it. He could make out the rumble of traffic in the afternoon gloaming, the wail of the wheels of a freight train, and somewhere on the station yard an engine gave him a short signal: *hu-huu!*

Nothing closer could be heard, which meant that there was no one on The Brocken or anywhere near it. He clambered up on to the grille and although a dim light still shone through from above, like the dusk of early evening, enough that you could just about see, he did not switch off his head-lamp yet. He stepped up to the right-hand opening, his very own front door, pulled the tarpaulin aside and moved his head slowly in both directions, the lamp's yellowish light caressing the walls and boxes in the room. He had scented correctly: no one had been inside his home. It would have been a miracle indeed if someone had managed to find it: not only because of its location, but because he had protected it with holy triangles painted in pigeon's blood.

He drew the tarpaulin shut behind him, lit the storm lantern and switched off his lamp. Though it had been a long day, the excitement within him had not yet abated. He could not sit still, nor could he lie down on the mattress; he could only pace the floor, back and forth, from the piles of books to the tarpaulin, then back towards the sleeping bag, all the while the hem of his skirt trailing like a flag torn in harsh winds.

The swirl was incredible! He had never seen anything like it before. That man's spirit had contained a phenomenal amount of particles, perhaps even one and a half times as many as other human spirits, and on top of that they had been large, almost the size of sugar crystals. And they had come together to form a swirl that was an unfathomably deep shade of red. In his mind's eye he could still see it. He could even hear it – it had given off a faint hum before disappearing completely. It had been sucked into the wall of the underground tunnel with such rage and power that rubble had almost flown out from the rock face.

'*Carboratum nexi datum*,' he sighed and removed the beret pulled down almost to his eyes. He then strode up to his bedside table, reached behind the storm lantern and picked up an aluminium mug containing his teeth, both the upper and the lower dentures. He popped them into his mouth and moved them into place with his tongue. His face changed dramatically. It was no longer the face of a sharp-chinned old biddy, but of someone considerably younger – and of a man. With both hands he flattened his hair back across his head towards his neck and dexterously tied it into a ponytail with a rubber band, making him look even less like the old woman who had just clambered up the rungs of the shaft.

He stood still and rested his hands thoughtfully on his hips. He had hesitated for a split second, and it had almost proved fateful: the whole sacrifice had very nearly failed. The mouth of the Orange Apostle – indeed, this time it had been Advocatus Mamillus himself – had already sped past them, but he had decided to try nonetheless. And how he had succeeded! Advocatus Mamillus had snatched the victim into his arms; barely had he managed to cry out before he was gone. He had clearly sensed Maammo's grateful smile, for she sent him a bunch of blessed beams, and this time they had been the colour of copper.

He removed his dress, placed it carefully on the clothes hanger and hung it on the line by the doorway. Then he raised his hands between his shoulder blades, undid his bra and took it off along with his breasts. Once he had put on his hooded top he looked even more like a man.

He put his hands to his groin and groped around. For a brief moment his face was empty, as though a spark had disappeared from within him. He then quickly took off his underpants – they were red and made of a shiny material with a broad strip of lace down the front – grabbed a thin leather belt, blackened with sweat, from on top of the sleeping bag, hooked it around his hips and fastened the buckle. He shifted the belt round so that the buckle was at his back and a leather sheath tightly crammed with sand lay against his stomach. It dangled between his legs and reached almost half way down his thighs.

Finally he slipped on his underwear, a pair of boxer shorts covered in pictures of Hagar the Horrible, pulled on his trousers and took a pair of thick spectacles out of his pocket – the kind that President Kekkonen used to wear. Once he had placed them on his nose there was no longer the slightest hint of the woman Maammo had commanded him to become the previous night.

He dimmed the light from the storm lantern. Of all others he had chosen that particular man because he had revealed his sinful ways. There had been a quiet smile on the man's face, the kind of smile that meant he was clearly content with his life, happy even – but immediately he had understood why. That wretched man had been wallowing in sin and lechery, trampling the will of Maammo into dirt. Perhaps that very morning the miserable creature had held his hand between a woman's legs, fondling it until it became moist with evil juices, shoved his member inside, and screwed her, teased her nipples and writhed until everything went black. Perhaps he had even thrust into her anus, or her mouth.

'*Diablo desum!*' he muttered hoarsely and a wave of disgust trembled through his hands. He flinched and his head moved like a dog shaking itself dry, but soon afterwards his eyes squinted slightly, almost as if he were smiling. And indeed he was smiling, for he knew: that man would never do any of this again. His fornication would no longer hold up the coming of the Truth, nor would he ever covet money and possessions again.

'*Ea lesum,*' he whispered, as if to bring an end to the matter. He had been so excited by the sacrifice that he had felt compelled to visit the underground platform a number of times that morning, and at several points he had been able to make out the thrilling stench of raw human flesh, like walking past the meat counter at the market. Yet not even this could satisfy him. He had felt the urge to mark out others for himself, even though he knew it was dangerous during the daylight hours. Rush hour was by far the best time for this, as people were crammed into the carriages, pushing and shoving each other, and did not notice as he secretly marked them as his own.

'Ha!' he snorted. Taking the risk had paid off, because in return he had been rewarded with a vision. Maammo had granted it to him and had commanded him to make it come true. This time the vermilion swirl had been great, but in the vision he had seen an even greater one, a swirl of giant proportions, one that would occur only when as many as ten or twenty people died at once and their spirits rose up together. And it would be a swirl so great that Maammo would take him into her embrace for all eternity.

Indeed, he already had some idea of how to realise this. Maammo had prepared him for it, though at first he had not understood. The key to everything lay beneath his bedside table. He was not quite sure whether he was to carry out the plan himself, and thinking about it now he felt that he should not. Perhaps not, though this would take him straight into Maammo's eternal embrace, for as the earth spirit he must not be selfish. Selfishness was an affront to Maammo. He was more important to her the way he was, a quiet pioneer clearing the road to the Truth.

In order to carry out the sacrifice he required someone else, a disciple of sorts. And already he was almost sure who that disciple would be. The girl did however have rather a quick temper, and for this reason he still had doubts. He felt he would have to examine her in a new light and maybe test her in some way.

'*Pica pica ecclesia*,' he muttered, concentrating hard as he folded both little fingers into his palms, tucked them beneath his thumbs and crossed the rest of them. He then pressed the tips of his fingers against his forehead and closed his eyes. A moment passed and he could see the girl – her cheeks ruddy, how she walked somewhat awkwardly due to her excess weight. It was enough, and he whispered to himself: 'Tonight, at the compass in the railway station...'

He moved his head, somewhat bewildered, as if he had suddenly come to, crept towards his bedside table and knelt down beside it. He held it round the corners, gently lifted it and moved it to the side, so carefully that the storm lantern did not so much as flicker and the water in his mug did not splash. There lay his key: four sweet, ripe sticks of dynamite, like four phalluses, caps on each one of them; and a coil of yellow and green wires inside that looked like the spilled guts of an animal.

As he beheld all this, for a brief moment he could see the coming of the Truth, the new Holy Big Bang. It would incinerate everything and make it pure, taking with it all sinners and infidels, all the wrongs and suffering endured by those who know the Truth.

'*Alea iacta est.*'

12. *Visitor*

'Jesus Christ,' Harjunpää sighed quietly – perhaps he merely thought it. His lips didn't move, but his mind sighed for the umpteenth time. He rested his left hand on his hip, rubbed his forehead with the other and marched over to the office door as if he were about to go outside. Restlessly he returned to his desk, made for the door, then back again to the desk. 'Jesus Christ...'

'Good morning to you too,' said Tupala. He had silently stepped up to the doorway and now stood there on tiptoes, bobbing up and down, his hands crossed behind his back. His expression was serious, as always, but his eyes betrayed an amused little smile. 'What happened to you?'

'This underground business. I went over there and blurted out to the victim's wife that her husband had died, and it turns out she's about eight months pregnant...'

'You weren't to know. And someone would have had to tell her sooner or later.'

'I know, I know… If only I'd thought to take Carita with me. But the woman lives just up the road in Merihaka. It seemed a bit pointless to drive through rush hour to the station and back.'

'I doubt having a priest there would have softened the blow.'

'I don't know. It's a good job she didn't have a miscarriage. What do I know - they rushed her to the maternity clinic.'

'I know how you feel,' said Tupala after a moment's silence, as if he had been wondering whether to go on or not. 'Once, this woman was only half way through her pregnancy when her husband went and hooked up a vacuum hose to the exhaust pipe and stuck it through the car window. Money problems, apparently. And this woman made me tell her over and over that it wasn't a painful death – you know the way people always want to know their loved ones haven't suffered… So I assured her that it's just like falling asleep. The next day I get a phone call from Kirkkonummi Police, because I'd given her my card. She'd driven up to their summer cottage and done the same thing. That's when I realised what guilt really is.'

They looked at each other in silence. Harjunpää decided not to mention that he had very nearly given the grieving wife the plastic bag containing her husband's wallet. It was covered in blood of course, but he had remembered just in time, and managed to stuff it back in his pocket without her noticing.

The wail of fire engines pulling up somewhere nearby could be heard, but neither of them bothered getting up to look out of the window: the alarms at the broadcasting company across the road went off accidentally at least once every other week.

'Oh, there's someone for you downstairs.'

'There can't be,' said Harjunpää, flicking through his diary. 'There's somebody called Eränen coming at two o'clock about that bread knife incident, then the next one's not until half three.'

'This one just walked in and asked for the officer in charge of the underground incident. His name's Kallio.'

'That's all I need. I've still got to come up with some relatives for our crazy dog man. Apparently they're keeping him in the mental hospital for at least three weeks, but someone's got to start taking care of his affairs pretty soon. And that dog's got to be found a home. Keeping a thing like that at the vet's doesn't come cheap.'

'I've told you, Timó, this is it. Things never change in this job.'

'You're right there,' Harjunpää muttered and forced himself up from the desk. The spring in his stride almost replaced the momentary feeling of lethargy, though he had barely managed to take two steps before his phone rang.

'Harjunpää?' he all but snapped, but his voice softened once he realised that the caller was his wife Elisa. 'What's wrong?'

'Nothing really, just feeling a bit sorry for myself, that's all. My headache's started up again.'

'Poor you. What if I massage your neck and shoulders again this evening? It worked yesterday.'

'You're not staying on late?'

'There's someone coming in at three-thirty for an interview, but that's it. I should be on the five o'clock train in any case.'

'Aah.'

'I've got some 800mg painkillers in my cabinet. Take one of them.'

'Will do. Love you.'

'Love you too,' said Harjunpää. He switched off his phone, walked towards Tupala, who had discreetly moved to one side and added, 'Elisa's going back to work next week for the first time in years. She's worried to death about it.'

'Make sure you massage her well, eh?'

'Oh I will.'

The lift jolted into motion and Harjunpää listened instinctively to the sounds it was making this time. A few months ago one of the cleaners, a conscientious but soft-spoken woman had become trapped in this same lift. It had happened late one evening. Naturally she had pressed the emergency button and a group of service men had arrived on scene. But the cleaner had been too shy to respond to their calls, and because there was no reply the service men decided that there must not be anyone in the lift after all. In the end Hush-Hush Heli, as she became known, got out of the lift the following morning - after being trapped inside for fourteen hours. It was a miracle that nothing had ever leaked to the press.

'Kallio,' Harjunpää announced from the lift door; there must have been a dozen or so people waiting to be interviewed. A man sitting by the main entrance stood up. Harjunpää gave a quiet sigh. He was a youngish man who looked generally all right, but he was apparently hampered by some terrible looking spasms. As he walked one knee rose high into the air, while he dragged his other foot across the floor, and his arms rose and fell in an odd, arhythmic fashion. Harjunpää couldn't recall the name of the man's condition, but he thought he remembered that it didn't affect a person's mind.

'DS Timo Harjunpää.'

'Santeri Kallio,' replied the man, and as he spoke his head jerked violently to one side and his mouth seemed to contort. Harjunpää found it hard to look at him – probably something he had learnt as a child telling him not to stare at disabled people. This time, however, he had no choice.

'Why don't we go up to my office and have a chat?' he suggested. The group of people in the waiting room had just watched the man awkwardly make his way across the floor and now stared in his direction, curious to see how well he could speak.

'I know... I... thrash about... a lot,' said Kallio once the lift had started moving. An unfamiliar knocking sound could be heard again, as if someone were hitting the lift shaft with their fist. 'But... I've still... got all my... marbles.'

'Absolutely,' said Harjunpää. He then looked at Kallio. Regardless of all he had suffered his eyes were gentle and somehow sympathetic. There was something else too, as if he were imploring Harjunpää to do something.

'I believe you,' he said, and perhaps this was precisely what Kallio needed. In any case his whole body seemed to relax and his head stopped twitching so frequently.

'That man. He was... pushed. Under the... train.'

'Excuse me?'

'He was... murdered. I saw.'

'Are you referring to the man who died this morning in Hakaniemi Station?'

'Yes. But... there were... people... in between. First... all I could... see was a... hip... shoving him. He... fell against the... wall of the... train. Then a... hand... pushed him by the... shoulder. The man... shouted... '*Oy!*'... and fell... in between the... carriages.'

'Are you quite sure?' asked Harjunpää. His voice was suddenly hoarse, rough as sandpaper, and his cheeks began to burn as if he had been hit with something. For a moment he questioned the man's intelligence – in some way he had to question it – but then he conceded, for there it was right in front of him, the worst and most shameful nightmare scenario for anyone in Violent Crimes: visiting the scene of an accident without realising that it was in fact a crime scene.

'Positive. There's… no way he… stumbled.'

The lift arrived, jarring to a halt as though it had struck something hard.

13. *Funny Guy*

Matti was ashamed. It felt as if he were covered from head to toe in mud, or some stinking sludge, as though his shoulders had been worn down by lead weights. Because of this he didn't look up, but just watched the tips of his shoes as they flashed in front of him, one after the other. He was also a bit scared, though perhaps not as much as normal on his walk home. He still expected them to jump out and attack him, even though they hadn't even shouted at him on the playground this time. Above all he was disheartened by everything, at the way his life had changed, so that everything good and safe had disappeared.

'Are you listening?'

'What?'

'I asked how you've got enough money to live in a place like Kulosaari.'

'We moved there when my dad was still writing. He had two jobs: delivering the post and writing books.'

'So why did he stop then?'

'Dunno. Something must have snapped. Out of the blue they told him they were moving him to the sorting office, and I guess that's when it all started.'

'What does your mum do?'

'She's at home mostly, but she's got a job at the newsagents,' replied Matti. Leena's curiosity and the fact that she talked non-stop made him uneasy; he would much rather have been quiet and continued staring at his feet. He wanted to go home, to go out in the garden and down to the shore; perhaps the swans would have arrived by now.

Besides, Leena was a bit odd. Her nose pointed upwards and she had a big chin, almost like a boy's, and there was something else boyish about her. Her hair had been cut so that she looked as though she was wearing a bowl on her head. Once, back in the days when people called her the

Hammer Thrower to her face, she hit this boy Joonas over the head with a stone, and his scalp had opened up and there was blood everywhere. Another time she smacked a girl called Pirjo in the face and gave her a real shiner. But no one called her names after that. Everybody was a bit scared of her now.

'Can I come over to your house for a while?' asked Leena. 'We could watch a video or something.'

'No...'

'Why not?'

'Mum doesn't let me bring anyone home. And now this guy Roo's moved in. He's works nights and he'd tell her.'

'Why has he got such a funny name? Roo...'

'My sister Sanna still lived with us when he first moved in. And one day he brought back a bottle opener with a handle made from a kangaroo's paw. A real one, it was dried. Can you imagine? A kangaroo's paw...'

'Doesn't sound like a very nice guy.'

'He's quiet, a bit of a sissy really. Imagine, he's got his own dressing table. Me and Sanna decided to call him Roo and whenever we got really pissed off with him we'd start singing 'Tie me kangaroo down, sport!' Then we'd fall about laughing because he didn't get it.'

They had come far enough that Matti could see his house, white behind the trees. It was a two-storey terrace, though there were in fact three floors because the garden sloped so much. Matti no longer felt the same calm and relief upon seeing the house as he had in the past. Now he just felt lousy and stale, like washing-up water left in the sink. He hoped Leena would take the hint and go home, but of course she didn't, and insisted on walking him to the door like a baby. He sneaked a look at her. From the side she didn't look all that bad, and she had bigger tits than anyone in their year. They bobbed up and down in a way that meant she couldn't have been wearing a bra.

'Why don't you come out with me later.'

'No...'

'Don't want to be seen out with the girls?'

'No, it's not that. I haven't got any money, Mum won't give me any.'

'Oh come on! We can take the underground, we don't need a ticket. We can go one stop at a time, get off and wait for the next train. That way you get to feel the excitement over and over.'

'Are you serious? That's completely pointless.'

'Oh really?' Leena retorted, as if it hadn't bothered her in the slightest that Matti thought her suggestion was stupid. Instead she started jumping up and down like a toddler, and at this Matti felt even more embarrassed, for Leena too.

'Hang on!' she said, as though she had just thought of something astonishing, and tried to grab Matti by the hand, but he quickly moved his arm to safety, behind his back.

'Well?'

'I'll take you to meet this funny bloke I know. You remember how people used to tease me back in the autumn?'

'Yes.'

'This man sort of cured me. I don't know how he did it, he just cured me somehow.'

'Give me a break. What guy?'

'Some preacher or priest. But he's not from the church or anything, I think he's with some cult.'

'I'm not interested in any of that religious mumbo-jumbo.'

'But this is completely different. He does these amazing magic tricks and he speaks some weirdo language all the time. Come on, let's go!'

'Where does he live?'

'We're not going to his house. He's always hanging around the underground or down at the railway station in town. Take this,' said Leena, and this time she managed to grab him by the wrist and push something into his hand. It was a piece of paper folded over many times, smudged from her sweaty hands.

'That's my mobile number. Call me anytime you want. Please?'

'I don't know,' said Matti. He didn't know why he was so reluctant. What he really wanted to do was fly, and even when his mum and Roo were at home it was still almost possible: he could always shut the door to his room and put headphones on, then he could conduct the orchestra again, though he couldn't properly take flight – there wasn't enough space in his room.

'Bye then! Give me a ring and we'll go out!'

'I don't know,' he said, again and again, and it was the truth: he really didn't know. He turned and began plodding towards the front door, and no matter how hard he stared at his shoes they remained just a pair of beaten-up trainers, and he couldn't make them chat to one another.

14. *Something to tell you*

'Hi. How come you're back so early?'

'To be perfectly honest I've had a really shit day. First off this morning someone ended up under a train and all the lines were down. I didn't get to Kontula until well after ten.'

'Another suicide?'

'How should I know? But it made me feel pretty bad. Even though I'm well aware that my fear of death is in fact a fear of rejection, it still doesn't help.'

'Cup of tea?'

'Yes please,' said Mikko, placing his briefcase on the floor. All of a sudden he could no longer understand why he had bothered carrying those few sheets of paper with him all day. He could just as well have left them at the office or at home that morning; he knew it all off by heart, like a poem: *"Someone called out his name..."* Maybe it was just a habit that had stuck from the days when he was able to write properly. He had had an almost irrational fear of losing his papers or that they would be destroyed in a fire or in some other terrible way, so he had always made numerous copies of everything and kept them in different places.

'We're going to take the flat, Dad. There's just enough room for two and since we'll be sharing the rent it'll be fine.'

'That's great news,' he sighed. He walked up to his daughter and put his arms around her, but a moment later that same uncertain guilt re-awoke within him, and he began to explain, or rather, to defend himself. 'You know it's not that I'm kicking you out...'

'I know, I know. Let's not start that again.'

'But I need you to understand. It's just I can't think or write with someone else under the same roof. It makes me nervous, like I'm always worried something's going to happen and I'll have to go and help. And I need to be able to walk around at night without worrying that I'm going to wake you up. And I talk to myself a lot... the characters' lines.'

'You think I haven't noticed?'

'Well, no and... To be honest, financially this is a bit overwhelming. I can only barely afford to pay rent on two flats, and then there's the travelling. It doesn't come cheap, you know.'

'Dad, I know.'

'I'm being silly; of course you know. But soon they'll be out of the way, and then I can turn this place into a proper home – with a workroom – and when I jump out of bed I can be right in front of the computer, just like back in Kulosaari.'

Sanna turned and picked up the chopping board. Her movements had suddenly become stiff and angular, her neck tensed, and Mikko had the distinct impression that everything was not quite right. Perhaps he had been too excited about Sanna's move and had offended her.

'Listen,' she began. He had been right: her voice was completely different from before; it was lower, almost as if she were holding back tears.

'Yes?'

'There's something I need to tell you…'

'Then you need to get it off your chest.'

'I can't…'

'And why not?' he asked, only to realise immediately how clumsy it sounded. He gently stepped behind her and placed his hands on her shoulders. At this Sanna spun round and hugged him tightly around the neck, the way she had done as a little girl. But something was terribly wrong. Tears flowed down her cheeks, her whole body heaving as she sobbed, as painfully as if she had just heard about the death of a loved one.

'What on earth's the matter? Are you…?'

'N-no… it's not me…'

'Well what is it?'

'It's Matti. And you…'

'You shouldn't worry yourself about our problems. He's going through a phase; it'll soon pass. I'm sure he doesn't really hate me.'

'He doesn't… But you weren't supposed to know. Matti told me that for as long as he could remember Mum's been telling him that you don't really love him, that you're just pretending, and that she's the only one that really loves him.'

'Really?'

'Yes. He misses you so much that all he ever does is listen to your writing music. Always something classical, never anything that other kids his age listen to.'

'Well now I understand a thing or two…'

Sanna lowered her arms limply, walked over to the sink and wiped her face with a towel before bursting into tears again.

'Sanna, listen.'

'You don't know! He didn't want to... he didn't dare tell you. He told me and... and...'

'And?'

'And now Mum's trying to do the same to him!'

'What's she doing?'

'You know the way she tried to smoke me out of the house because I couldn't stand Roo. Imagine: there's a strange man in the house eyeing me up and I'm supposed to act as if there's nothing wrong! And she expected me to send that oaf a Fathers' Day card!'

'Sanna. What's she doing to Matti?'

'Exactly the same. She doesn't speak to him for days, doesn't wake him up in the morning, so that he oversleeps. She takes the rubbish into his room if he's forgotten to take it out and goes off with Roo for days at a time without telling him anything, so he suddenly finds himself home alone for the weekend. Last autumn they went to Crete and left him at home for a week!'

'What in the world can we do to help him?'

'Don't you know?'

'No...'

'You need to save him like you saved me!' she shouted, her voice strange and almost angry, but in a way that the anger wasn't directed at him. 'He's got to come and live here with you, but then you won't be able to write again and...'

'Good God,' Mikko whispered almost silently. He could sense the swamp, frighteningly close, dragging him into its murky, brown waters. He saw eyeless, white fish swimming deep beneath him. He barely had enough time to bring his hands up to his face before bursting into tears; the heavy, pounding sobs of a grown man. And he cried not only because of what he had just heard, but for the sake of so many other things that had passed without tears.

15. *Aftertaste*

'He'll be over there. Take it back a couple of frames.'

'OK.'

'And make sure to print it off, in case the image is clearer on paper,' he continued, though he wasn't sure whether this would be of any use.

He and Rastas from the forensics lab had been sitting in the video room for well over four hours and it had clearly been too long. Harjunpää's eyes could barely focus, they felt as though they were covered in powder; his neck was stiff and his temples were pounding with the beginnings of a headache. From Rastas' laboured sighing Harjunpää could tell that he wasn't feeling much better.

'However you look at it, it's impossible to say what actually took place.'

'I know, it's the same on the camera by the door. There's some sort of movement, but it could just as easily be the guy himself.'

'At least now we know the exact time of the accident, down to the second.'

Rastas rolled his finger over the viewfinder. The screen clearly showed how, like a vortex, some of the people on the platform surged backwards, while others found themselves pressed dangerously close to the side of the train, which was still moving at considerable speed. Then a man in a light-coloured jumper threw up his hands and began waving them frantically: this must have been the man the driver had mentioned.

But no one ran off, nor did anyone attempt to hide. The tape revealed absolutely nothing about what had taken place: had the victim fallen by himself, or had someone shoved him?

'Huh,' Harjunpää muttered as he stretched, rolled his neck back and closed his eyes, but it didn't help: beneath his eyelids flashed dozens upon dozens of television screens, hundreds of men and women, young and old, all in a single, unified grey mass. In total there were five video recorders and eight screens in the room, though on that particular day each of them was in some way broken. The one and only video recorder that did work was inadequate because it played everything in black and white. This could prove crucially important, especially if they had to provide an official notice of the incident, let alone begin searching for someone on the basis of distinguishing features. The situation was made all the more miserable by the fact that throughout the city there were enough security cameras to provide CCTV footage of almost every crime – and yet the police's own technology let them down.

'What say we call it a day?' Rastas finally suggested. His voice was cautiously enquiring, but he didn't quite manage to hide his yawn.

'Maybe, but there's no point going over this same section again and again. We need to widen our search. Let's start from well before the incident, in case there's anyone wandering about the platform, or if anyone followed the victim when he first walked into the station.'

'We ought to check the people coming back up the escalators too.'

'Yes, but we still don't know who or what we're looking for.'

'We might see a familiar face…'

'Perhaps,' Harjunpää muttered flatly. He knew from experience that this would take hours if not days of work, while the rest of the investigation ground to a complete halt.

With a scowl on his face he reached for his work phone and pressed number one on the speed dial. The phone rang five times before someone eventually answered.

'Mäki.'

'Hi, it's Harjunpää again.'

'Just as we agreed. And what a fine day it's been. That aquarobics does a world of good, you know.'

'Good for you. Listen, Rastas and I have gone through all the tapes from the platform. We can place the time of the incident fairly precisely judging by people's reactions, but that's about it. There's nothing here to indicate what actually happened.'

'So all we've got is that nutter's statement.'

'There was nothing wrong with his head. My gut reaction says he was telling the truth.'

For a moment Mäki fell silent, perhaps he was rubbing his earlobe, something he was in the habit of doing whenever he was at a loss. He was doing a temporary stint as senior officer at the Pasila division, and over the past four months he and Harjunpää had got on well enough.

'Has the official notice been typed up yet?'

'Yes, Leppis just sent it off and it went straight on to the online news. Should be in all the papers by tomorrow. We didn't mention the possibility of a criminal investigation, but just asked that any potential eye-witnesses come forward.'

'That's fine. We'll have a meeting in the morning and decide whether to go all out on this one.'

'I've got a feeling that's what we should have done today.'

'Well, that wasn't really possible. You shouldn't worry that the crime scene investigators didn't do a more thorough job – at least a thousand people must have trampled over the place before you got there.'

'I suppose you're right.'

'Who else is coming tomorrow?'

'Onerva, and that's about it.'

'We'll draft in a few more if necessary. See you tomorrow.'

'See you.'

Rastas had switched off the equipment and placed the cassettes in a neat, labelled pile. He now stood by the door, which was already ajar, with one hand on the handle and the other on the light switch. Harjunpää understood perfectly well and stood up.

'Thanks for hanging in there.'

'It's all money in the bank. Good night.'

'Night.'

Harjunpää turned left into the corridor and traipsed towards the lift. He still had to go up to his office on the fourth floor to check whether anyone had tried to contact him. He also had to switch off his computer and remember to charge his phone. As he approached the lift he took his personal mobile out of his jacket pocket: it was an old Nokia, the kind that nowadays people considered heavy and cumbersome. He felt a quiet, sullen satisfaction that it had lasted so long – only once had he had to change the battery. He was particularly happy that he hadn't got caught up in the ridiculous habit of changing telephones once a year, or even once every other. All of a sudden everyone had to get a new mobile, learn all its new tricks and buy new calling plans with the internet, email and wap – all things he didn't need.

He pressed the speed dial and this time the phone rang only once.

'Elisa.'

'Hello, it's me,' he said. In the background he could quite distinctly hear Pauliina, Valpuri and Pipsa singing 'Hosianna' – at this time of year? – and the corners of his eyes rose in a smile.

'We're having a bit of a sing-along...'

'Sounds like it. How's your head?'

'Those painkillers worked a treat. Still, I wouldn't object if you want to massage me a bit later.'

'You might just be in luck... I'm going to try and get the train at 21.07, so I should be home by half past.'

'Shall I make you a bite to eat?'

'A sandwich maybe. And a cold beer wouldn't do any harm either.'

'Timo,' she said softly. She didn't need to continue; Harjunpää knew precisely what that tone of voice meant.

'I love you too,' he replied. 'Take care.'

'You too.'

Harjunpää slid the telephone back into his pocket and for a moment something warm and good flashed through his mind, soft as the finest wool. To have somewhere to go, to be; to be with people who cared about him and about whom he cared, was wonderful. How magnificent, how almost unbelievable it was that in life there existed such a thing as love; without it, he would probably not have been able to cope. And this, to him, was the most profound realisation he'd made that Tuesday.

Despite this, everything that had happened left a bad taste in his mouth, an aftertaste of failure and disappointment, as though he had just eaten a piece of mouldy bread.

16. *Kikka*

'I know, I know all too well,' Mikko almost snapped. It shamed him, as did the fact that he always poured all his problems on to Kikka. Helplessly he padded the floor of his workroom in Kontula. He had been unable to stay at home, not wanting Sanna to realise quite how hard he was taking everything.

'But where am I going to get help?'

'The local shrink, if you ask me.'

'Yes, but I tried that a year and a half ago when Cecilia started trying to get Sanna out of the house. I told them Cecilia was abusing her and that Sanna was at a low ebb... The psychologist told me I had to stop getting involved in my wife's business and start living my own life. She even said there was no way I could help Sanna, that I couldn't suddenly become her therapist.'

'That's outrageous.'

'I know,' Mikko sighed. He still remembered how humiliated and useless the situation had made him feel. 'To cap it all off she turned the whole thing around and asked whether this was all just a projection of my own violent sentiments towards Cecilia.'

'Really?'

'Yes. And by then I'd already had to take care of Sanna's bruises maybe three or four times, because whenever she could escape she came to me.'

Mikko stopped and stood in front of the window. He could see only one tree, the top of a pine; the rest was just identical grey concrete buildings, exactly like the one he was in.

'Still, I can't really imagine she'd start beating Matti,' said Kikka. 'Especially since he's always been "Mummy's little boy".'

'She used to beat me. I never told anyone before. I was sitting in the red chair downstairs and she just started battering me round the head with both fists. There was nothing I could do but try to take cover. She was trying to get me to hit her back, of course. Imagine the tabloids the next morning: *"Mikko Matias Moisio Batters Wife!"*'

'Of course...'

'Where can battered husbands go for help? Nowhere. Men don't even dare talk about it, because then people would think they're just wimps.'

He turned and looked around the room. It was almost the very incarnation of depression and sorrow. It was bleak and somehow harsh; he hadn't bothered to decorate it at all. At first he'd sensed that it wouldn't be an appropriate workroom, but eventually he'd been left with no option but to take it. The only pleasant item in the room was his desk: several decades old, it was sturdy and made of hardwood. Back when things had still been going well he had even painted it two different shades of green with flowers, the sun and a blossoming tree. Down one side there were four birds flying together; a single, whole family just like he'd once had. Was it such a pleasant item after all, bringing back memories of the past he had lost?

Another reason that the room was not truly a workroom was the fact that even the corridors were heavy with smells reminiscent of the earliest stages of his life, a time before he realised he could write: the smell of miserliness and penny-pinching, of tobacco and heavy drinking, the stench of quarrelling families sorting out their differences. Even if he used earplugs while trying to write, he could still make out the sound of the couple next door at each other's throats. It always ended with the children crying and the eldest son ringing his doorbell asking him to call the police. That put pay to any attempts at writing and he would remain blocked for days at a time.

'I'm sorry about always unloading the crap in my life on to you,' he said, and now his voice sounded different, pinched like an oboe; and with that he understood that there was at least some good in his office – it was a place where he and Kikka could meet in secret. He always felt relieved after seeing her. She was sitting in the chair by his desk, a green GN that he had bought with the money from his first novel. Kikka was almost a miniature person, she couldn't have been taller than 5'2", yet she was still perfectly proportioned in every way: she was thin but not too thin, and her face had the funny ability to be either angular or soft depending on her expression. Her hair was the colour of wheat, her nails unvarnished and her hands were small and delicate. So too were her breasts, and her nipples were tiny, barely the size of a small coin, yet when he kissed and caressed them they came to life and protruded like olives.

In his eyes everything about Kikka was beautiful. Her wrists, her thin white neck; the way she walked, the way her hips and buttocks came to life. Her laugh was beautiful, as was the way she coyly tilted her head when she was amused. Particularly beautiful was her profile, both her face and her body. Her smooth stomach curved gently down towards her groin, while on the other side her bottom was softly rounded.

The very fact that she was a woman was beautiful too. Mikko found that same beauty in all women, even supposedly 'ugly' women. It was this that had first captivated him about Cecilia and that had blinded him to so many things he should have seen as warning signals.

And when he looked at all of this together – the tilt of her head and her fleeting smile, almost revealing her teeth – the sense of how much he loved her began to burst within him; how he craved her, how at once fervently and wistfully he wished that Kikka were something permanent and stable in his life, a part of him. Yet then the thought began to puzzle him, frighten him even, and with difficulty, like holding in a sneeze, he would try to suppress those feelings. On one level he fully understood that he was not afraid of Kikka herself, nor was he afraid that over time she too might prove to be some kind of monster. What he was afraid of was commitment and, ultimately, love itself.

'Mikko, come and sit next to me.'

'On the bed?'

'We're hardly going to do it on the table,' she scoffed as laughter spread across her face. She had to say this, it was their little joke. The first time they had made love had been on that same table, as there hadn't been a bed in the room. The typewriter had fallen, crashing to the floor, cracking its cover. Every time he saw that crack he smiled quietly to himself.

He lay down on the bed next to Kikka and pulled himself up tightly against her side so that his head was resting on her shoulder and his face lay against her neck. He began to inhale the smell of her skin, drinking it in with his soul, moving his arm around her head and caressing her earlobe with his fingertips. They would often sit like this for hours at a time, two hours, occasionally changing positions, Kikka curling up in Mikko's arms. Sometimes they would exchange a few odd words, but for the most part they'd simply lie there, breathing together.

'Did you try talking to anyone other than that psychologist?'

'You name it... There was a man at the community office in the church, Jokinen I think his name was. I stupidly thought he'd understand what was going on, but once it became clear that Sanna was going to move in with me, the only thing he worried about was how Cecilia would deal with losing her role as a mother and how Sanna and I could support her – even though Cecilia was deliberately trying to force Sanna to move in with me because she knows I can't work properly with someone else living under the same roof.'

'So how did you work back in Kulosaari?'

'The ground floor had a room facing the sea that I used as an office. You could only get in through a door in the back garden. Down there I always felt like I was alone.'

For a moment they lay together, inhaling the same air, each breathing strength into the other. Mikko could feel an artery in Kikka's throat pulsing restlessly, expectantly, and moved his hand to her smooth stomach.

'But even that stopped working?'

'Yes. Cecilia started appearing at the door dozens of times every day, even though she'd agreed not to. She'd make a drama out of nothing, then once she'd gone it would always take me an hour or two to get back into the world of the novel.'

'Yet you were supporting the family with your writing?'

'Well... I don't know. She must have been profoundly envious, jealous even. Once we'd already decided that I would move out she suddenly announced that she would stop the divorce proceedings if I signed a written agreement never to write again. When we went to the social services things couldn't get underway because Cecilia just didn't turn up. At least there they understood what a terrible situation this was for Sanna. They started talking about placing her with foster parents – my own daughter! I walked out of the office and Sanna moved to Kallio the following week.'

Kikka tightened her arms around him and moved her leg across his thigh. Mikko closed his eyes and tried to close his mind too, to concentrate on that single moment, on Kikka lying there warm beside him, her hair gently tickling his forehead. But his thoughts still turned to his son, and all at once everything was perfectly clear to him: as soon as Sanna had moved out, Matti would have to move in.

'Mikko,' she whispered, like an agreed signal. Mikko propped himself up on his elbows; their lips met and they kissed, rapidly, over and over, as if they were tasting one another, and he slipped his free hand beneath her blouse until he felt her bra strap.

What happened after that was the most beautiful thing he knew. It wasn't simply a physical act – sex, a shag, a fuck – it was a gift, an act of giving and receiving, between two people who trusted each other so much that they were prepared to share something of the utmost intimacy, bringing each other the pleasure and fulfilment that alone they would be unable to experience.

17. *Sausages*

There were fourteen objects in total, and although in a mysterious way they were all very important to Matti and had been for several weeks, what was most important was that they were in the correct order. He had only realised this a couple of nights ago; this and the entire process for that matter.

From the left, in a row, there stood a spruce-green glass ball the size of a fist, tiny air bubbles trapped inside forming a universe all of their own. Beside that was a bicycle reflector, the old kind set in a tin cup with no room for a real lamp, and next to that stood a lion carved from stone somewhere in Africa. Then there was an open pine cone, and next to that a fluorescent elephant that glowed in the dark. The elephant's trunk reached out towards a pure white shell that was full of brightly glowing red glass beads, each like a droplet of blood.

The shell was followed by a rock, sparkling with amethyst crystals, then a small skull – presumably this had originally been intended as an ashtray, but despite its size it looked so genuine that anyone looking at it would have felt the hairs on the back of their neck stand on end, with a shiver of mortal fear. Next in line was a green porcelain hand holding an almost life-sized alabaster egg, while beside that crouched a goblin made of black clay, its mouth in a grimace and its arms outstretched. The bear's hand just reached the next object: a small round stone, like the earth seen from deep in space, that looked as though it could well have been spun at the bottom of a giant's cauldron. The stone was followed by a brass owl, barely the size of a thumb, while the owl was joined by a titmouse ruffling its feathers. Finally, on the far right-hand side, was a sacred white scarab made of stone, a beetle whose job it seemed was to keep the whole throng in tow.

Matti was lying on the floor, his hands propping up his chin, and from that perspective everything looked rather different from the way it looked crouching down or from above. He was wearing a large set of headphones, the kind that kept both the high and the low notes in perfect balance, allowing him to concentrate solely on the objects in front of him. In this precise order they formed a symphony of their own; not any old symphony, but one that didn't yet appear on any recordings, one that nobody had ever heard, and though at times it seemed to include parts of the alternating horn theme from *Sibelius' Fifth*, it was otherwise entirely his own composition.

When he first looked at the glass ball, the lower strings began to stir gently somewhere deep within the earth. Then a pair of tubas joined in, followed immediately by the timpani sounding a warning of their imminent arrival: *tu-rum, tu-rum*. The purring of the strings grew, rising from the depths beneath the floorboards. Finally the violas tentatively joined the choir of voices and, as if pulled by a set of ropes, he rose up to his knees and his hands floated up into the air with his fingers loosely spread out. He began conducting, beckoning new voices and instruments, calling them to join the music, the notes all the time rising higher and louder. He moved his hand towards the reflector and the oboes softly joined in. It was the third time he had conducted that same symphony and by changing the position of the objects he could create an array of different variations.

Once the music was in full swing he picked up the smooth stone and felt the rumble of the instruments flowing through it, in unison. At this he began to make out the end of the piece: it would be a bit like *Sibelius' Seventh*, the music rising to a crescendo, then thinning and drifting away at the end.

Sibelius' works seemed like rock and roll, like real heavy metal – at that point he was thundering his way through *En Saga* and the *First Symphony*. When he thought about this he felt at once shy and embarrassed, as if one day he would be able to achieve the same, or at least something similar, and that all he needed was a little support – then suddenly everything was blown to pieces. His ears burned as if someone were trying to rip them from his head. The music died away and now all he could hear was the babbling of the television and the shuddering of the washing machine. Startled, he spun around and sat there, resting on his hands like a child.

His mother stood in front of him, her hands on her hips, Matti's headphones dangling from one hand, and an expression like sour milk on her face. He knew what it meant. He was in for another lecture, complete with examples of what a little shit he was and how he was going out of his way to ruin her relationship with Roo.

'You could at least knock,' he said sullenly, amazed at his boldness.

'Oh, so now I didn't knock? You just couldn't be bothered to answer, I was imagining all sorts.'

'Maybe the music was up too loud...'

'Music? What bloody music? Don't think you can pull that same madman act like your father. You're just as screwed up as he is.'

'Dad's not a...'

'Quiet! I'm not interested in that good-for-nothing. I am interested in who's been eating Kari's sausage? I've told you a thousand times that the sausages and the whole milk are for him only. Don't touch them again!'

'I haven't.'

'Yes you have! You bit off a chunk, I can see the teeth marks. Kari had to throw the whole thing out and now he's so angry he won't even talk to me. You should be ashamed!'

'*You* should be ashamed, you shit-head,' he whispered, to his own surprise. Perhaps he only found the courage because his voice and lips were quivering, just as they had done that afternoon in the playground before he'd started to cry.

His mother lunged forward and stood, her legs apart, towering like a giant above him. Matti saw her raise the headphones above her head like a whip, but she didn't strike him.

'You'd better watch your mouth, my boy,' she shouted. 'Your father wants a settlement, which means selling this house. And that means Kari and I are going to have to move into a smaller flat. And do you know what *that* means?'

'No…'

'It means there will be no room for you! That's how much your father cares about you, he's prepared to make you homeless. He rang you again this afternoon by the way. I can't stand the way he forces his way into this house. I'm going to have that phone cut off.'

'Fucking arseholes…'

'What did you say?' She leapt at him. The headphones clattered to the floor somewhere in the background, and she started grabbing at his hair with both hands. It hurt, burning as though someone had poured boiling water over his head. There was nothing he could do but try and prise her fingers off him, but he couldn't. He tried to hit back, and may have even struck her.

'Kari!' she shrieked. 'Kari, help! He's hitting me! Help!'

Suddenly she let go of him and quickly messed up her hair; then she gripped her cheek firmly between her knuckles and twisted it, leaving a glowing red mark on the skin. Matti could hear the thud of footsteps as Roo came bounding out of the living room and into the hallway, the thud becoming louder and louder, like a stable full of horses galloping towards him.

'Kari, help!' she cried, though for no reason whatsoever. Kari strode past her with one enormous step. He only had to kick once and the entire symphony was gone, destroyed. Its different elements flew into the air and the flute – the small ruffled titmouse – lost first its beak and finally its whole head.

18. *The Marker*

'*Enuresis nocturno,*' he thought. He was so used to talking to himself in the safety of Maammo's temple that his lips moved now too, though he was around other people. They moved very slightly, as though he were sucking on something, a pastille perhaps, yet no one paid him any attention as he rode upon the great Orange Apostle – an underground train, as the heathens called it. It seemed an unspoken law that people should look around them but see nothing, only emptiness, the same emptiness that filled their mindless souls. Only he, the earth spirit, knew why this was so: the Apostle had silenced them and, unbeknownst to them, was drawing their attention and shaping their minds.

He was thinking of other things too. He was thinking of so many things at once that his mind resembled a coil of different coloured cables, almost like the one beneath his bedside table, but far more tangled and twisted. In a way his thoughts and deeds were like a fuse; above all he recalled the vermilion swirl and how he had succeeded in pleasing Maammo by carrying out her will, and a fond tingling warmed his breast. His thoughts turned instinctively to the new Big Bang. It would be similar to the swirl, yet a million times more powerful, and his function was to precipitate its coming. He thought too of the chubby girl and the compass mosaic, and the sound the Apostle made as it came to a halt: *phiuu-phiuu*. There came a whole series of these sounds, and as the Apostle jolted into motion again there came another series, only this time the sounds rose towards the end: *phuii-phuii*. It was a song of exaltation, a holy psalm chanted by the Orange Apostle to the glory of Maammo.

His mind was also filled with the revelation he had experienced earlier that day about the child disciple and the sacrifice, and now he realised that it would be better after all if the disciple were a boy; he could adopt the boy straight away by sacrificing three pigeons, at least one of which had to be a web-footed pigeon. To sacrifice his own son – that, if anything, would prove the extent of his devotion, and in return he would without a doubt be allowed to merge with Maammo and perhaps even to spend eternity as her all-seeing eye. He did not know any boys; yet the boy would surely cross his path if this were Maammo's will.

Nonetheless he still examined and considered the woman standing in front of him: this one he would mark out as his own. She would have been particularly suitable, though she was rather on the young side. She was carrying a backpack too, and perhaps she was suitable precisely because of her age: beneath her tight jeans stood her pert behind, and something wet and seething hidden beneath its folds. Her breasts were crammed inside a bra embroidered with floral patterns or lace – he noted this as she stepped on board. All this was sinful and offended Maammo. Above all it represented greed in its most obscene and grotesque form. Her entire being greedily craved men, the feel of their paws upon her breasts and their pricks inside her. This in turn awoke greed in men too: the desire to take this vamp to their beds, to embrace her soft flesh and suckle on her nipples, and finally to shove their pricks into her depths.

'*Esox lucius*,' his lips stirred quickly. They stirred out of a profound disgust, for this represented the base greed of all people; that which made them yearn for more and more, better and better. It was with this greed that the human race defiled Maammo, raped her: chopping forests from her surface, drying up lakes and rivers, melting the polar icecaps, eating away like a cancer at the atmosphere. For this reason alone the coming of the new Big Bang was essential. It would destroy the human race, burn that army of lice to nothing, and thus open the path to the Truth and victory of the kingdom of Maammo.

'*Ea lesum cum sabateum!*' A torrent of holy words gushed through his mind and suddenly he felt the power and the grace of Maammo's hallowed touch. His whole body seemed flooded with light, the fine green light emanated by Maammo herself, and he was once again certain that he was indeed her most beloved, the holiest of her earth spirits, and this in turn meant that he was like a nail thrust into a stick of dynamite. The explosion he would cause could set the process in motion and lead ultimately to the realisation of the Truth.

'*Faustus dies*,' he murmured to himself as he quietly wiped away a tear that had crept its way from beneath his glasses and down his cheek; at the same time he clasped his other hand tighter around the scalpel. However, this was no ordinary surgical knife, but a stamp blessed with the holy marks of Maammo. It was unique in that he had first snapped it in two almost halfway down and filed its jagged edges smooth so that it fitted better into the palm of his hand, ensuring that no one would notice it. He slid the knife down several centimetres, between his thumb and first finger, and removed its protective plastic cap, revealing the razor-sharp blade. How he wished to sink it deep into that woman's pert, rounded buttock! How she would squeal! Oh and the burning pain she would feel in the very part of her body that most strongly radiated her greed for flesh – and which awoke that same greed in others!

He swallowed many times, forcefully, a bobbing motion showing on his throat. Naturally he managed to control his urge because this was not Maammo's will – it came from him, from the human within him – and he could only control that urge because he was also an earth spirit. As such his purpose was to carry out Maammo's bidding, and her bidding was not – on this occasion – to make that woman squeal and cry for her wickedness, but to slice a hole in her clothes or backpack between five and ten centimetres long. This was enough, for it worked in two ways: it opened a channel through which the greed could flow out of that sinful being while at the same time it allowed the power of the Orange Apostle to work its way inside the wretched woman's thoughts.

Phiuu-phiuu, chanted the Apostle as he began to slow his speed. He noticed this himself – it was as if a great force were pulling his entire body forwards; people began moving, the hastiest amongst them standing up. His woman moved towards the door; he would have to move quickly and press himself against her. But the moment was not yet right; not until the doors had opened - when everyone was looking at the ground, at their feet, watching their step. That was the right moment.

He edged closer to the woman, so close that he could smell the stench of sin and seduction, and raised his hand up to waist-level, resting it against the bottom of the woman's bag. The scalpel pierced it easily, sunk into it as though it were butter; he jerked his hand a palm's length to the side; the channel had been opened. The woman was clearly none the wiser and no one else had noticed a thing. Only Maammo, the Apostle and he knew.

He did not make the mistake of hurrying away – this would have aroused suspicion. Instead he allowed himself to drift with the flow of people, first on to the platform, then on towards the escalators. As he approached the first rubbish bin he quickly stretched out his hand and bid the scalpel farewell: '*Sed vitae discimus…*'

And with that it struck him – the idea came from the backpack he had just slit open: the plan should be carried out in the manner of the Palestinians.

19. *Note*

Matti's hands searched, frantic and shaking, but he couldn't find it. He went through the pockets of all his clothes several times, but it was pointless. He was convinced he hadn't lost it or thrown it away. What if his mum had got hold of it? It might have had something to do with his mood – he felt oddly uncomfortable, as though a strange, faceless threat hung over him; as though at any moment something terrible might happen. Above all he was afraid that he was going to die, or rather that someone was going to kill him. Although he didn't give the matter much thought, he imagined that it would be a relief. Never again would he feel that niggling shame that he was somehow different, nor would he have to worry that someone might throw stones at him or humiliate him, pull his hair or threaten to throw him out of the house – after that he would never have to fear anything again. All he had to do was walk across the back garden and out towards the shore, wade out until he reached the steep drop in the sea floor and swim. He had read somewhere that it was easy: first you feel light, almost as if you were floating, before falling into a deep sleep.

'They probably wouldn't give a shit,' he mumbled, barely audibly. The sobbing that followed came in violent bursts – the kind that a dog locked in a dark cupboard might make. Tears formed a wobbling pearl at the end of his chin, droplets every now and then falling on to his T-shirt. Eventually the crying broke his resolve. He slumped slowly to the floor, like a burst balloon, and a new wave of sobbing wrenched him. His orchestra lay strewn across the floor, smashed to pieces. The flute was missing a head, and the head a beak; the black goblin's arm had broken off and the shell had cracked, showering red beads all around like blood.

The water in the sea was probably so cold that it would lead almost instantly to hypothermia, and though he wasn't quite sure what it was, he imagined it might bring some kind of numbness, making it easier to die.

Then he spotted it: the note was on the floor beneath his desk; precisely the same white mass of paper the size of a sugar cube that Leena had given him. He crawled towards it, his hands and knees moving nimbly; he took the note between his fingers, clenched it in his fist and pressed it against his forehead. Instantly he felt better, as though there were still a chance for him; perhaps he wasn't so terribly lonely after all. He sat up on his knees and hurriedly began to unfold the note, but a moment later he froze, puzzled. In a flash his cheeks felt red and hot, as if he had been running fast.

At the middle of the note was Leena's mobile phone number, but around this there was something else. Hearts. They couldn't have been anything else. Hearts drawn in red felt-tip giving off little rays all around them.

'What's she playing at?' he thought, and after a moment's pause continued: 'Surely she doesn't think...?'

His mind seemed blurred, this time in a different way, and it occurred to him that he simply couldn't bring himself to call her; that she would think the call was a response to these hearts, and for a long moment he sat there motionless, quietly whimpering to himself. He slowly stood up, as though he were still half asleep, and as if by a will of their own his legs began to carry him towards the living room.

He was alone. Mum and Roo had gone out somewhere again, secretly, without mentioning anything. No doubt they had gone shopping again. They bought all kinds of useless stuff; weed clippers and bread machines, electric whisks and other contraptions they only ever used for a few weeks before forgetting about them altogether. Even so, they still wouldn't buy him a mobile phone of his own. Nothing much had come of the argument earlier that evening: lots of shouting, but none of the punching and shoving against the walls Sanna had once gone through. Roo had stood in the doorway puffing, but hadn't said anything and hadn't seemed prepared to attack him physically.

He placed the note on the table – it was the same veneer table that he and his father had once used to play chess – and though he had already picked up the receiver he hesitated for a moment longer. Then, his fingers stiff, he started dialling the series of numbers. The telephone only rang once before someone slightly out of breath picked up: 'Leena!'

At first he couldn't say a thing, then he stammered: 'Leena, is that you?'

'Yes. Who is this?'

'It's me, Matti,' he whispered, and the relief he felt was so sudden and so strong that he started to cry again. He couldn't help it – it was the same barking sound as earlier, but now he felt embarrassed at the thought that Leena might tell everyone at school.

'Has something happened?'

'Ye-yes.'

'Did those guys beat you up? I'll fucking show them.'

'No... no, my mum...'

'Shit. Your mum? Do you want to come over?'

'No.'

'What do you want then?'

'Could we go and... see if we can find that... that guy you've been talking about?'

'OK,' she said, straight away - as if she hadn't had to give it a second thought. 'I reckon he'll be down at the railway station. See you at the underground at half past.'

'Oh, OK.'

20. *A Moment Shared*

Harjunpää kept his eyes closed; the stream of images had stopped for a moment. It had been like a corkscrew spinning furiously: his mind had been filled with the sight of the eyeless face lying limp at the bottom of the body bag; the pen falling from his jacket pocket and spiralling down from the balcony out of sight; Jaana, heavily pregnant, her round stomach, the shock on her face, the tears. Then there was the bloody hand and the wedding ring he had twisted from its finger. All this had spun through his mind the whole train journey home, but now it was over.

He lay on his back on the bed breathing calmly; he could feel Elisa's side warm against his own, and the ebb of her breath – he could tell she was not yet asleep; it was as though she were waiting for something. He could hear the splash of water running in the shower – one of the girls, probably Pauliina, was still washing her hair. Every now and then came the faint sound of whistling: it was a song that had been on the radio all day.

In a soft, mellow way Harjunpää felt good – or rather, content. For once he was where he belonged, in his own world, surrounded by his loved ones. For him, home was far more than a place one simply lived: it was a spring, a source of energy, imperceptibly strengthening him for the day ahead.

He rolled on to his side and softly placed his hand on Elisa's stomach, moving it gently along her bare skin, beneath her shirt, and cupping it around her right breast, at once both protective and questioning. But Elisa didn't react the way she normally did, didn't take a deep sigh and press her body tighter against his. Even her nipple seemed in a world of its own and didn't begin to harden like a cherry.

'Timo…'

'Yes?' he slid his fingers back towards her stomach.

'I've got a million things going through my mind.'

'Nervous about going back to work?'

'Not exactly nervous. It's just got me thinking.'

'You're worried you won't be able to cope? Is it leaving the girls at home?'

'They're young ladies already. When I was away doing that course they learnt to take care of things by themselves. The laundry was always done, the rubbish taken out and everything hoovered. And whenever I left them some money and a list one of them would always do the shopping.'

'I know.'

'And after the course… it struck me that I've got a real vocation now. I'm a bookshop assistant.'

'And that proves you'll be just fine.'

'Yes, it's not really that either, it's this change.'

'It is a big step, but we'll get through it. And think of the financial benefits it'll bring.'

'Sorry, it's just my faith… I feel as though I was meant to get this job at the Christian bookshop.'

Harjunpää didn't know what to say, but continued gently stroking his wife's stomach and listened as a freight train rattled past on the nearby track. He had been happy for Elisa when she had discovered her faith. In every way it had seemed perfectly natural, there had been nothing fanatical about it, no revelations, no preaching, no speaking in tongues. Elisa had quite simply found some kind of inner peace, something that had had a calming effect on the whole family.

'Are you worried because you're only covering a maternity leave?'

'No, it's not that either. Somehow I feel that the future will sort itself out when the time comes.'

'You're right. And the commute into Helsinki isn't all that bad, it only takes half an hour. After a while you learn to think of the journey almost as time out from everything else.'

'So you've said.'

'Come here,' said Harjunpää as he turned on to his back. He held his wife's head on his chest and placed his arm around her. He held her like a small child, rocking her gently from side to side. Ten minutes later Elisa was fast asleep. He could tell from her breathing and the faint movement of her limbs. But he could not sleep – his wife's million thoughts had transferred themselves into his mind, and they troubled him. Something new awaited them, that was clear, but he didn't like it and had an unnerving feeling that what was to come was something utterly unknown.

The strip of light around the door frame disappeared as Pauliina switched off her lamp.

21. *Frog*

Matti couldn't help thinking that Mum had deliberately driven Sanna out – and Dad too for that matter. But why not him? He felt guilty, as though his mind were covered in thick scales like a bream, and he wished so much that the journey was over, but they had only come as far as Sörnäinen. More than that, he wished he had never agreed to the meeting in the first place. When Leena had first told him they weren't going to buy a ticket, it had seemed right and even a bit exciting, but now he couldn't stop worrying that the ticket inspectors in blue uniforms would come along and catch them. Imagine what a row it would cause at home! He knew his mum wouldn't fall for the same excuses again: a month ago he had locked his bedroom door and gone out through the window. His Mum had somehow worked out what he had done, and had locked the window and put the double lock on the front door so that he couldn't get back in. He'd had to sleep on the floor in the bike shed.

He let out a small wimper: took a few short breaths then breathed out slowly and heavily. Leena grabbed hold of his hand and held it in her lap. Her expression was one of true unhappiness – and it was all his fault.

'He'll think of something to help you,' she said suddenly. 'He's a real guru, you know.'

'But what if he's not there...?'

'He'll be there, I can feel it. He'll be at the station, either where that Estonian guy's always playing the flute or down a level by the compass.'

Matti didn't reply. He sighed again and tried to pull his hand away, but Leena was holding on to it fast. Her fingers were sticky and she placed her other palm on his hand. Matti relented and stared out of the window. Now that they were in a tunnel it was completely black outside and the glass reflected everything like a mirror: both Leena and him. For a startling moment he imagined that his reflection was a more real Matti than he himself was, and that when the train came into the lights of the station the reflection would disappear and he would die.

'Look,' said Leena, trying to cheer him up. 'We're in Hakaniemi already and not a Smurf in sight.'

'Maybe I'll be OK after all,' said Matti, but he didn't dare look at Leena. His voice had changed too, as if his throat were a size too small.

'What? You mean your mum's going to throw Roo out for good?'

'No...'

'What then?'

'Dad rang me,' he lied, but couldn't for the life of him understand why. The idea suddenly popped into his head and seemed strangely real. 'He's writing again and once he gets the down-payment on his book he's going to apply for a mortgage and buy a bigger flat so I can move in.'

'No way!' Leena gasped, her voice like a balloon deflating. 'Whereabouts is he going to move?'

'Maybe Kruununhaka or Katajanokka.'

'Fuck, that means you'll have to change schools,' she said, loosening her grip on his hand, only then to clasp it even tighter. Neither of them looked at the other. The loudspeakers announced Kaisaniemi as the next stop.

'Listen,' whispered Leena, bending down closer to him. Only then did he notice she was wearing a soft-smelling perfume. 'If you want, you can feel my tits – under my shirt.'

Matti couldn't say a word, though he could feel his ears shining and a cough tickling his throat. He managed to slide his hand free and mumbled something indistinct that didn't really mean anything. Leena didn't seem particularly bothered.

'Well, some other time then,' she said, her voice neutral once again, though her cheeks had now become red and blotchy. 'Come on, this is our stop.'

They stepped out of the train. The air smelt of damp stone, the way all underground stations smell. Leena suddenly seemed fired up. She shot to the front of the queue and sped past the people standing on the escalator. Matti lagged behind her and the breeze through the escalator shaft tousled his hair. Rarely had he been in the centre of town this late at night and he was surprised at the number of people coming and going; youngsters too - boys barely his age carrying skateboards.

The escalator came to an end and they reached the gates. Leena stopped sharply, as if something had startled her, and those coming up behind bumped into her. She took Matti by the elbow, dragged him to one side and whispered, 'Over there. That's him over there.'

'The one handing out those leaflets?'

'Yep.'

The man was standing at the centre of the compass mosaic on the floor, in such a way that everyone walking past was forced to notice his presence. No one took any of his leaflets, dodging instead to one side and walking around him as if they hadn't seen him. He was standing with his back to Leena and Matti. From beneath his cap flowed wisps of grey hair. He clearly wasn't a down-and-out, but his clothes were worn and made him look poor. He certainly didn't look like the guru Leena had described.

'Wait.' Leena yanked at his sleeve and held him back. 'He knows we're here.'

'What, even though he can't see us?'

'Yes, look at his hand.'

The man raised his free hand level with his shoulder, pressed his thumb and forefinger into a circle and began to turn, very slowly, as if he too were part of the compass. He stood sideways to them, brought his hand across his face, turned some more, stopped and stood there staring at them through the telescope formed by his fingers. He was wearing thick-rimmed glasses, his face was wrinkled and strangely pale. Matti suddenly felt rather odd, as if he were trapped in a dream, unable to escape. His feet seemed stuck to the ground.

'I don't like this,' he whispered. It felt somehow terrifying that the man knew they had come up behind him, unless he merely did this same trick every now and then.

'Keep your hat on,' said Leena; she too was clearly nervous. 'It'll be OK. Look at his hand! When he does that it means he wants us to go over by that pillar.'

'How do you know all this?'

'I just do. Come on.'

They walked towards the left corner of the compass, where there was a thick glass pillar with a bench around it. This often served as a meeting place, but now the only person there was a gnome-like tramp rattling a stick and gathering up his bags, ready to leave. The man in the glasses didn't follow them or watch them, he just carried on handing out leaflets. Still Matti couldn't rid himself of the feeling of the man's eyes on his back. The throng of people seemed blurred and the noise had subsided, as if someone had turned it down with a remote control.

'Come round the back,' said Leena, and he did as he was told. Her closeness felt reassuring.

'Leena, I really don't like this. What if he's some sort of perv?'

'Him? He's never tried anything on. I reckon he really is a priest, but he's just gone a bit schizo and got himself kicked out of the church. You get these amazing vibes when he looks you in the eyes. It kind of makes you respect him or something.'

'But what if he...?'

'Hello,' said the priest. He had appeared out of nowhere, though only a minute ago he had been standing at the centre of the compass, and he greeted them as if he had known Matti for years. His voice creaked like a new pair of shoes. He was about the same age as Grandpa Onni, and close up he didn't look as past it as he did from a distance; he was even wearing a black bumbag. He was staring Matti in the eyes, and though Matti tried to avoid his gaze it was no use: he felt compelled to stare back. It was almost as if through the priest's eyes he could see far off into the void beyond. His face began to tingle the way his leg did when he had been sitting in an odd position for too long.

'You do not seem too well,' said the man, more as a statement of fact than a question. 'Are you having problems at school? Or at home perhaps?'

'At school mostly,' Leena began, but the priest lightly moved his hand – his fingers seemed to have a life of their own, like the fingers of a musician or a blind person – and Leena immediately fell silent and lowered her eyes, almost in shame.

'I believe your parents are divorced and you are suffering because of it.'

'Yes...'

'Is there perhaps someone you miss?'

'Yes.'

'Who?'

'Sanna. My sister,' Matti added, and now he knew precisely what Leena had meant by 'amazing vibes'. Matti felt as though he were standing in front of the president, or a bishop, or even the Pope. It was as if the man with the glasses were connected to him through an invisible channel of light.

'*Sabra laude scolae,*' muttered the priest. 'And are you being bullied at school?'

'Yes,' Matti gulped, and all at once he was deeply ashamed of the bullying and of the fact that it showed like an enormous boil on his forehead. He tried to lower his eyes but simply could not; he was transfixed by the priest's gaze.

'And you wish you were strong enough to put an end to it?'

'Yes, but...'

'But you are not a body builder.'

'And I'm always the last to be chosen for the sports teams.'

'Would you believe me if I told you it is still possible?'

'I know, but...'

'I shall ask you again. Do you believe that there exists a force that can help you?'

'Well... if you say so.'

'Do you believe me?' asked the priest. He all but commanded Matti to concede, and at this he became even more distressed. He felt the same as when, in a recurring nightmare he had, the house was on fire, he tried to call 999 but always dialled the wrong number; and whenever he did manage to dial correctly the person who answered spoke a language he didn't understand.

'Do you believe me?'

'I believe you,' Matti uttered, for there was nothing else he could say. The edge of the priest's lips crept into a smile, not a triumphant or cunning smile, but a perfectly normal, kind smile.

'What have we here?' he said, and thrust his hand into his jacket pocket – it was made of a small checked material that would have shimmered terribly on a television screen. He rummaged in his pocket for a good while, as if he were looking for something specific amongst an array of different objects. When he finally pulled his fist out of his pocket he opened his fingers, and there in the palm of his hand lay a pebble. It was a perfectly ordinary, little grey pebble, the size of a lump of chewing gum.

'What do I have in my hand?' the priest asked as if he were talking to an idiot.

'A stone. A small stone.'

'Really?' he smirked, as he closed it in his fist and said something in a foreign language. Then he cast the pebble to the floor and asked:

'What is it now?'

Matti flinched and took a step as if to run away, but Leena grabbed him by the wrist; and though he was terrified he was forced to look down at the floor. And there was the pebble! Just a moment ago it had been a frog, he could have sworn it, and it had been alive because he had seen the underside of its jaw moving as it breathed.

'Calm now,' said the priest. 'Pick it up.'

'No. What if it's something else...'

'It is a pebble,' said the priest, and with that Matti crouched down and reached towards the stone. Fumbling tentatively he picked it up, and sure enough it was a hard little pebble, ordinary except that it was slightly warm from being in the priest's pocket.

'It is your pebble now,' said the priest, and spoke once again in that strange language. 'It is your magic pebble. Keep it with you always, in your pocket.'

'Thanks...'

'And if anyone bullies you again...' he continued, raising his hand aloft. 'First, tell me what is happening at this very moment.'

'We're here, now.'

'And my hand is raised,' added the priest, lowering his hand once again. 'And what is happening now?'

'Your hand's down again.'

'Precisely. And if you are bullied, squeeze the stone and think of what the moment truly means - the bullying will have already stopped; you will have won.'

'Thanks a lot.'

'I shall require something in return.'

'What?'

'You must tell me,' said the priest, and now his gaze was once again so intense and strong that it felt as if their eyes were connected by a steel pole. He began to speak the priest-language again, and this time it sounded as if he were saying a prayer. He continued to stare at Matti, his eyes in some strange way holding him prisoner. He then raised his hands and quickly prodded him on the forehead, and Matti could feel himself falling to the ground.

It was an ordinary wooden rowing boat, except that the bottom was painted red and the sides white, and it had a name too: *Summer Idyll*, painted in black across the bow. Matti was alone in the boat, sitting on the middle seat, rowing occasionally, allowing the boat to drift gently forwards. The lake was so wide that he could not see the shore, and the surface of the water was so calm that he could hear bubbles bursting at the bow. He stopped rowing and, as if by a miracle, he was able to see deep within himself, into the back of his head, at the centre of which was a vault of dazzling light leading into the unknown. In the middle of the vault stood a motionless golden figure, with its hands clasped in prayer. Matti realised that it was an angel, his very own guardian angel, or else it was Jesus, and just as he was about to ask everything disappeared, and all at once he found himself sitting on the bench at the foot of the pillar, on the underground level of the railway station, and he could feel someone holding his arm tightly.

It was Leena. She looked confused and even somewhat shocked.

'You were out for at least half a minute,' she said, but when she realised Matti didn't understand she began to explain. 'He pushed you over. You know, the way they do at church meetings. I held on to you, so you just slumped down here and didn't fall and hurt yourself.'

'Come on...'

'And I could see your eyeballs moving even though your eyelids were shut.'

'What did you see?' asked the priest, kneeling down closer to him. It was as though the priest were stalking him, watching his every movement.

'A kind of golden figure...standing with its hands clasped...in the back of my head.'

'Hands clasped?' urged the priest. 'In what way?'

'Like praying.'

'Was it a man or a woman?'

'I think...it was a woman'

A wrinkle twitched rapidly on the priest's cheek. He then lowered his eyes and for a moment he stood staring blankly at the floor. Finally, his voice hoarse, he said: 'You are mistaken, son. You saw wrong.'

He said nothing else, and neither of them could make out the expression on his face; except, perhaps, that he was not overjoyed. Then he simply turned and walked away, and after only a few steps he had vanished into the mass of people – they could no longer make out as much as his cap.

'I wanted to thank him,' said Matti. He was still dizzy and tired. 'What if I want to see him again?'

'He'll find you,' said Leena, suddenly almost bitter. 'You can be sure of that.'

22. *Not very good news*

'Yes, that's perfectly understandable,' Harjunpää said into the telephone, realising that he had already succeeded. All he wanted was to bring matters to a swift conclusion. He had been right not to force the issue, or to try to call all the shots – as things were he had no grounds on which to do so – instead he had decided to listen, and gradually steer the caller at the other end.

A little red wooden spinning top whirled on the desk next to the telephone. He had picked it up a while ago at the market hall in Hakaniemi. One spin was enough to send it travelling in a circle about thirty centimetres in diameter a dozen or so times before slowly falling on its side. Harjunpää dearly wished that the present telephone call would end before the top stopped spinning.

Onerva was standing behind him by the door, he could sense it, perhaps simply from the faint, barely perceptible smell of her perfume, the one that Harjunpää thought suited her best. The window was ajar and he could hear the same kind of scuttling sounds the bugs had made in Lauttasaari: he had attached Rastas' printed video frames to the wall, but because he had only taped them at the top edge the breeze caught them and they fluttered like snakes, rustling against one another. His work phone started ringing in his jacket pocket – typically, the previous owner had set its ringtone to some ridiculous *diddly-dee diddly-day* – and from behind a closed door further along the corridor came the sound of inconsolable weeping.

'Let's say one o'clock. Come down to the police station. On the right there's a reception desk where you can tell the duty sergeant you've arrived. He'll call me down to fetch you. And if I've had to go out for some reason, I'll leave the keys at the desk in an envelope with your name on it,' he explained in such a way that the person listening couldn't possibly disagree. He listened to the caller repeat his instructions, agreed that the matter was now settled and hurriedly replaced the receiver.

'Harjunpää,' he snapped into his mobile.

'Hi, it's Piipponen.'

'Morning.'

'I hear you're in charge of the Hakaniemi incident.'

'That's correct.'

'If it's alright I'd like to have a few words with you about it.'

'Come over now if you want, we're just about to sit down and try to work out what this is all about.'

'Great.'

Onerva approached him, her shoes delicately tapping the floor, and the scent of the perfume he had sensed a moment before intensified, but not a bit too much. Onerva knew the bounds of good taste. Mäki walked in behind her. He had undergone only three years' training as superintendent and was considerably younger than Harjunpää, but he was certainly no rookie – neither were any of the younger officers for that matter. The new generation was calm and collected; they knew how to run an investigation and look at matters from all perspectives, and most of them had excellent people skills to boot.

'Right, looks like the Lauttasaari case is going to sort itself out,' Harjunpää said to both of them. 'The closest relative I could find for Jari was a cousin. Thankfully he's a lawyer.'

'What about the mutt?'

'It gets better. This lawyer cousin's got some friend who'll take it in until Jari gets out of the mental hospital.'

'Have they opened up the mum yet?'

'Yesterday – Vilonen rang from the coroner's office. They've ruled out external violence, apparently it looks like a heart problem. Of course, we won't know for sure until they get the test results, because she was so badly decomposed.'

'Sounds like that's coming along nicely. But what about yesterday's underground fatality?' asked Mäki and began fiddling with his earlobe. Harjunpää and Onerva exchanged a brief glance. They were not the only ones who were puzzled, and Mäki had been brought up to speed the previous night.

'Definitely not suicide,' said Onerva. 'Seems everything in his life was just as it should be: happy marriage, first born on the way, no money problems, everything fine at work. Everyone I've spoken to confirms he was far from being a manic depressive, more like the life and soul of the party.'

'No one would top themselves like that, in between the carriages. The risk of being left a cripple is too big. We combed the tracks to see if there was a suicide note or anything, but no.'

'So we can safely close that line of enquiry?'

'With the current information, yes.'

Mäki changed hands and began pulling at his other ear.

'So what we're left with is either an accident or a deliberate act.'

'I believe Kallio, our witness. And I asked Tarja about those spasms. Although they're probably the result of some form of cerebral palsy, she says they don't affect people in any other way.'

'And why would he make up something like that anyway?'

'Right. And on camera three you can make him out quite clearly because of the way he walks. The tape shows him taking precisely the route he mentioned in the interview room.'

Piipponen had appeared and was leaning against the door frame holding a blue folder under his arm. He was something of a jack-of-all-trades, always coming or going, and generally making such a fuss that people couldn't help noticing his presence or the fact that he was going off on a case. At other times he could be quiet enough to pick up on all the latest gossip from behind closed doors. Above all he had the ability to disappear without being noticed, like a thief, and not even his closest colleagues knew where he had gone. True, his nickname Piip was a shortening of his name, but more to the point it came from the days when pagers were still in use and people constantly had to search for him by beeping him.

'But what if he saw wrong?' said Piipponen, as if he had been part of the conversation since the beginning. 'What if the hand he saw wasn't pushing after all but trying to grab hold of the victim?'

'That's a good point.'

'Maybe you should go and talk to him again. You know, just to go over the details. One of you does the talking, the other can watch him.'

'It'll be useless,' muttered Harjunpää. 'But we could do it.'

'On the other hand, if it was deliberate then where's the motive?'

'Precisely. And why do it with so many people around when the risk of being caught is so great?'

'The victim had a clean record,' said Onerva, and Harjunpää noticed himself deliberately trying not to look at her right hand, the one that had been badly damaged in a car crash. Regardless of the fact that the operation had been a success and that the scars were only barely visible, he couldn't help noticing that the index finger didn't move at all and he knew that two of the others were partially paralysed. Onerva had given up knitting. Since her recovery she hadn't even tried it, but she didn't want to discuss it with Harjunpää and he didn't want to pry. Nonetheless, with great determination she had learnt to shoot with her left hand and had clearly channelled her creativity in new directions; since coming back to work she had become something of a computer genius.

'I checked through all the national registers and he only appears three times: once as a witness in a car crash and twice as the plaintiff. In the first instance his phone had been stolen and in the second someone had wrecked his motorbike.'

'His motorbike?' said Piipponen, stretching in a way that left no room for interpretation.

'Yes, but he was a loner, with no obvious connection to any gangs. Central intelligence checked their records.'

'What else do we know about him?'

'He was a perfectly average citizen. In the mobile phone business.'

'Mobiles?' Piipponen grew suddenly more interested. 'I suppose you all remember that case when...'

'Yes we do,' Onerva interrupted him. 'But our man was the coordinator of a bona fide company in Vuosaari and as far as we know he hasn't been up to anything on the side.'

'His wife's statement corroborates that. That's why he sold his bike, for a bit of extra cash.'

Harjunpää stood up and closed the window. The rustling of the paper snakes stopped.

'So far only two people have come forward in response to our appeal,' said Harjunpää. 'One of them sounds like it's worth looking into, about someone seen loitering around Hakaniemi. The other one's something along the lines of, "I saw a man in Ruoholahti sniggering to himself last summer".'

'Have they checked his clothes for fibres?'

'No such luck, you can imagine the amount of blood they were covered in.'

'So all we've got is the rather vague statement of one witness?' Mäki asked. 'Anything else?'

'Miles of CCTV footage.'

'OK,' Mäki muttered. He had stopped rubbing his ear and resolutely clasped his hands together. 'Let's divide it up by place and time and start going through it systematically. We need to liaise with the underground staff and check out anything they might know. And thirdly, go through our records for any underground-related cases and analyse them thoroughly.'

'There'll be thousands of them,' said Onerva somewhat apologetically. 'There are so many complaints filed about trouble-makers, drunks, pick-pockets...'

'Then get on to IT and ask them to sort out some sort of word search programme for us. What else?'

No one said anything, for the simple reason that they had nothing to add. Everyone had plenty of work, and it was all from the dullest end of the scale: sitting in front of a video monitor or a computer screen.

'Ahem, sorry,' said Piipponen hesitantly, clearing his throat. 'I've got some news, but I'm afraid it's not very good.'

'Well?'

'I'm sure you all remember when old Lörtsy had a brain haemorrhage back in November?'

'Has he died?'

'No, he's still in a coma. But all his open cases are being divided throughout the division. And, well... you know how it is when you get handed a whole pile of new cases and old ones get left hanging around...'

'Get to the point.'

'Well, I got assigned some of his cases too and... one of them is almost identical to this one. It happened at Kaisaniemi underground station and there was an unconfirmed sighting of someone being tripped up. There was even a fairly large-scale search for a grey-haired old woman, and Lörtsy eventually brought someone in for questioning. You remember the one they called Cranky Kaija?'

'The one who hit people with her walking stick?'

'That's the one, but she had a water-tight alibi. She was in the nick that night and they only let her out five minutes before the incident, so even if she had wings there's no way she could have been in Kaisaniemi in time.'

A number of heavy sighs could be heard across the room. None of them dared utter the words that had come into each and every one of their minds. It sounded so absurd: *serial killer.*

23. *Problem*

What did it mean that the boy had seen a woman at the centre of the vault?

He pondered this question. He was sitting on a rock rubbed clear of moss, almost exactly at the top of The Brocken, perhaps slightly towards the eastern side, surrounded by high thicket, alders, birches and a few dwarf pines. He sat there thinking, and he was certain that what the boy had seen was some sort of sign, though he was unsure quite what it meant. Was it a command or a warning?

He held a rope fifteen or so metres long and passed its knots through his fingers like a rosary, though the rope could not have been less like a rosary – it was a hunting rope. He laid it along the ground towards the east, down towards a suitable opening in the thicket, and tied it at the other end to a cotter bolt at the top of a steel pole several metres high. Suspended from the bolt was a contraption fashioned from chicken wire that resembled an old umbrella. At the foot of the pole a generous handful of breadcrumbs lay scattered on the ground.

'*Sumo cesi Virgilicius Maria?*'

He was searching for the most opportune moment, and that was why he hoped this was it. The boy had claimed to see a woman radiating light – one of the two incarnations of Maammo; the boy was simply a heathen and could not have known this. If it were indeed true then the boy's vision represented an indisputable message to him.

'*Quelle villeum a mundo condito.*' He made the holy mark of Maammo three times and looked to the sky, but still he could not see any pigeons. This too was strange, for normally he only needed to wait ten minutes at most. Perhaps this time they too sensed that this was a monumental occasion, and therefore it was of the greatest importance which of them flew down to take their final communion. Around him the city hummed its familiar symphony, somewhere to the west the sound of sirens slashed through the air. At least this time it was not of his doing – he had not crushed a single pebble from his bag.

'*Sumo cesi Virgilicius Maria?*' he asked and contemplated the other option, one that was simply not as good. If the boy truly had seen the Virgin Mary, this may have been something sent by the heathen God to defy him – and Maammo. But how could he have seen the Virgin Mary, since neither she nor their God truly exist, and are nothing but a fanciful tale from the pages of books, distorted beyond recognition over the centuries. Only the Holy Big Bang and the coming of the Truth were true and real – countless scientists had been able to prove it. And if the boy had indeed seen a vision of the Virgin Mary, an instrument of the heathens' false God, then to use the boy to set the New Big Bang in motion would be an act of extreme holiness and of the utmost devotion to Maammo. '*Ea lesum!*'

Whatever the truth of the vision was, the boy was the right choice. The boy belonged to him, and through him belonged to Maammo, and was therefore suitable to precipitate the coming of the Truth. Indeed, there was something unusual about the boy. For a brief moment he had seen an aura shining around him. At least, he had most certainly sensed something, as the hairs on the back of his hands had stood up the way one's hair stands when a flash of lightning strikes nearby. In addition to this the boy had swooned far easier than anyone else, and had remained unconscious for almost forty seconds. That - if anything - was proof enough.

The pigeons had arrived! At first he heard the thrilling whoosh of their beating wings, almost like a squeal, then they appeared overhead in a great curve. There were dozens of them, probably the same flock that lived in an old dead birch near the broadcasting company. They turned once more in the air, then lowered themselves to the ground, to the same place on the rock as always. Their heads jerking forwards, they hopped greedily towards his bait. Already he could see that at least one of them was light brown – a webfoot! He held his breath and waited patiently, then he yanked the rope and the bolt came away with a metallic ping. The chicken wire cage fell crashing to the ground. The pigeons burst into flight, but only one, two, three, he counted, only three had escaped, leaving the rest fluttering wildly inside the cage.

He did not approach them straight away. He had to let them calm down first, for perhaps an hour or two, so that they would not associate him with their fear, and he could become their saviour. Only at that moment would their blood be in perfect equilibrium, ready for the sacrifice. He quickly made the holy marks of Maammo, and extended a blessed gesture towards the horizon, thankful for the magnificent sacrificial birds it had sent him.

24. *Another Problem*

Mikko always kept his phone on silent whenever he was in his office. There were two reasons for this. Firstly, if the phone rang he had to drag himself out of the world of the book and into an entirely different reality. Far more laborious than this, however, was to get back into this imaginary world after the call had ended; to recreate the characters in his mind and begin to think and act like them. This would waste at least an hour, though generally it took two, and so a few telephone calls were enough to ruin an entire day, leaving him unable to accomplish a single line.

The other advantage to this was that, once he had finished trying to write for the day and was beginning to make his way home, he could see whether anyone had called him. If Sanna or Matti had called him that usually meant that something serious was happening, because they at least had learned not to call him while he was working.

It was only by chance that he happened to be standing by the window, leaning his forehead against the cold glass and staring at the telephone which lay on the window ledge, when the screen began to flash the name SANNA in a dim green light. He didn't hesitate for a second.

'Sanna?'

'Hi dad... How come you answered? Sorry I...'

'It's all right. I wanted to answer. Work's not going particularly well right now.'

'Well... this might sound really odd.'

'Then it should suit me fine.'

'It's just that... What does it mean if someone dreams... or has a vision of a long tunnel with bright light shining and a golden figure standing waiting for them at the end of the tunnel?'

'A vision with light shining at the end of a tunnel?' he repeated, if only to gain time to think, as he could hear from her voice that his daughter was clearly upset, worried even.

'And you dreamt about this last night, did you?'

'Not me, someone just asked me about it.'

'A friend?'

'Not really... just a guy at work.'

'You see, there's no one right way to interpret dreams and visions, they're so personal. Don't tell your friend this, but I've read a number of books about people who have been near death or who have actually died and been resuscitated. A tunnel leading into the light and someone standing there waiting for them seems to be common in those cases. In one of the descriptions I read, the man standing at the end of the tunnel was the person's father, who had died years before. The father wouldn't allow him to go any further and said that it wasn't his time yet. And then he was resuscitated!'

'Oh God,' Sanna whispered, and fell silent. Mikko sensed a cloud appear over his mind and he suddenly felt the need to lighten the tone of the conversation.

'Cynics say it's just the lights in the operating theatre… Remember that television series *Iron Age*?'

'Not really, isn't it really old?'

'Oldish, you can borrow it from the library. Have a look at that, especially the scene where Väinö tries to solve all his problems. He goes and lies down under a boat…'

'What, a rowing boat?'

'Some kind of boat. Anyway, he sees the boat turn into a tunnel just like the one you described and the person he meets at the other end is himself – dead. It's all very well put together. Then at the end he realises that he's found what he was searching for upon the River of Death after all… Sanna? Hello?'

He glanced at the screen – they were still connected – and quickly moved the telephone to his other ear. 'Sanna, are you there?'

'Yes.'

'What happened?'

'Have you spoken to Matti at all?'

'I called him yesterday, I think it was. Your mother said he wasn't home. I guess I should get the extra cash together to buy him a mobile of his own.'

'She always does that – says he isn't home. She used to do it to my friends too. Matti called me really late last night, he couldn't get to sleep…'

'And?'

'He's in danger,' she said, and although Mikko couldn't see her, he knew that her lips were quivering, the way they always did when she was about to cry.

'Would you care to explain?'

'Matti had the vision. He's the one that asked me about it. Some priest or magician hypnotized him or something… He's being dragged into some weirdo cult!'

'Sanna, calm down. I'll come home straight away and you can tell me exactly what he said, OK?'

'I'm… at work.'

'When do you finish?'

'Four.'

'Right, I'll be home by then. Trust me, we'll sort this out and I'll take care of him. OK?'

'Ye-yes.'

Mikko ended the call and his hand dropped.

'God help me,' he whispered. 'Now I lay me down to sleep, I pray Thee, Lord, my soul to keep...' Then it was as if he woke up, and his thoughts began flying back and forth, yet always returning to the realisation that he had neglected his son. In his defence he told himself that he couldn't have done any more, that his own struggle had been too overwhelming. Nonetheless, leaving the children with Cecilia had been the wrong decision, despite the fact that she had convinced them to stay by calling him a monster. And what a ridiculous settlement he had agreed to - simply because the children had stayed with their mother he had given up his share of the house! Where was Matti right now? What did he know about Jehovah's Witnesses? The Pentecostalists? He knew nothing about them. What about Satan worshippers?

Everything came to an abrupt halt, as though he were somehow paralysed. A moment later he was filled with the urge to set off right away. His intuition was telling him something, he was sure of it. He felt a strange force within him. He had to find Matti, wherever he was; he'd even take him out of school if necessary. He slammed the door behind him.

He too had been down that tunnel once, back when everything had fallen apart – and he had held the barrel of a pistol in his mouth.

25. *Flash*

Harjunpää pressed a button by the door of the video room, switching off a row of monitors and dozens of different LED lights. He returned to the control desk and began gathering up cassettes, discs and reels of tape. The day's achievements were as much of a mess as the pile of equipment in his hands, he thought to himself. There came a knock at the door; not even the normal security keys could open it. Harjunpää dropped the material back on to the table and cursed – something he rarely did – as he was sure it was Piipponen, who was supposed to have arrived several hours ago to look through the rest of the tapes. Typical that he should turn up just when the job was finished. 'Hi,' said Onerva quietly. She had probably knocked the same way as she had a thousand times before, but he had been too worked up to recognise the familiar rhythm. 'What's eating you?' she asked.

'Everything. There's something seriously wrong here, and I mean our method of working too. We're stuck here in the dark wading through thousands of video tapes and a whole load of old cases and complaints when we should be out there interviewing people in and around the underground stations - shopkeepers, security guards...'

'Mäki's arranged for some internal enquiries to be conducted amongst the staff at the security firm. I'm sure they'll come up with something in the next few days. He also sent a more strongly worded notice to the press. You'll just have to cool it, Timo.'

'And where the hell is Piipponen? We agreed to split this job up and now I'm left with a pile of things I still haven't done.'

'He went to the post.'

'What, to send a letter?'

'Ha ha,' she smirked. 'Our D.O.A. Kokkonen, but you never know with him...'

'Listen,' Harjunpää sighed heavily and sunk back into his chair. 'The fact is I haven't got anything off these tapes.'

'Kirsti and I have had slightly better luck,' Onerva tried to buoy him up, laid her pile of papers on the table and sat down next to him.

'First of all there's Lörtsy's old case. In the report the driver of the train and one of the passengers both mentioned seeing an elderly woman rushing along the platform and accidentally knocking the victim in front of the train. Either that or the victim bumped into the old woman.'

'Is any of this on the video?'

'Sadly not, the camera facing that end of the platform was out of order that day.'

'Of course.'

'However, we did get a fairly good description of the woman; but the photo-fit was in the papers so many times they eventually stopped printing it altogether and instead started making snide remarks about how the police weren't able to get hold of one old woman.'

'That's right, I remember now.'

'Lörtsy and his partner spent a good two weeks hanging around the underground during rush hour, just riding back and forth, keeping an eye on Kaisaniemi in particular.'

'And came up with nothing.'

'Right, but I still think they did everything they could. The lack of results certainly wasn't from lack of trying. Still, Piipponen doesn't appear to have taken the matter any further, though there were a number of questions left unchecked.'

There was another knock at the door. This time it sounded as if someone had kicked it, someone in a hurry. Piipponen appeared in the doorway, quick and nimble as the finest acrobat. In one hand he was carrying a bulging paper bag, while in the other he had managed to pick up three paper cups of coffee without spilling a drop.

'Give us a hand, Harjunpää. These cups are hot as hell. I reckon we've more than earned our coffee break today. These doughnuts are from the bakery across the road,' he explained as he sat down and began ripping open the paper bag. His annoyance aside, Harjunpää felt a faint glimmer of a smile creep through his mind. If for no other reason, this day would be remembered for the fact that Piipponen had treated everyone to coffee and doughnuts.

'That was quite an autopsy, or should I say patching together. Severe crushing and mutilation is the official cause of death, but they'll be able to tell us more once they get the results back. No other obvious problems with his internal organs; blood alcohol level zero.'

'That was quite a long post mortem…'

'Tell me about it. On the way back I stopped and had a chat with a few snouts I know, they said they'd keep their eyes peeled.'

'Perhaps it's not such a good idea to get the underworld involved in this,' said Onerva. 'If these are premeditated crimes we have to assume we're not looking for anyone sane.'

'Oh I agree, just thought I'd be on the safe side.'

Onerva picked a few sheets of paper from the top of the pile and tapped them with her fingernail.

'This might seem a bit far-fetched,' she said. 'But we're going to check them out. Kirsti dug them up on a cross-reference search. In the first case the plaintiff felt a slight pain, but then assumed they'd been struck by a young boy's skateboard. In the other one the woman in question was already on her way up the escalator at the Central Railway Station when the person behind her noticed that blood was dripping from her hand.'

'Shit,' Piipponen snapped. 'I had a feeling during that post-mortem that we were going to end up going through every assault on the underground.'

'In both cases the victim had a slit in their clothes about a centimetre long and beneath that a superficial skin wound.'

'You think they were cut with the tip of a knife?'

'Maybe. Maybe even a surgical knife. Then there's a whole wad of damage claims where people's bags – and in particular leather jackets - have been slashed without their noticing.'

Harjunpää picked up a complaint from the top of the pile, Piipponen grabbed the one underneath. They weren't very long, and understandably they had been filed as miscellaneous complaints or alleged assaults, because there could be no certainty as to what had happened. In another file the plaintiff himself had suggested that the wiring of another passenger's bag might have been responsible for the cut. Onerva closed her eyes and rubbed her temples with her fingertips.

'You're right,' said Harjunpää after reading through both files. 'We need to talk to these people again. Both damage claims date from between the two fatalities. Both took place during the afternoon rush hour, while the fatalities occurred during the morning rush hour.'

'Wait,' said Onerva and raised her hand as if she were in primary school. 'I've just had a thought.'

'You're kidding,' Piipponen smirked. Harjunpää remained silent. He knew from years of experience that Onerva's flashes of inspiration often reaped great rewards.

'We need to get hold of all the video tapes from Hakaniemi taken yesterday too.'

'Because?'

'If this is some kind of a psychopath – which it clearly is – then they'd have gone back to the station some time yesterday and had a look around, at blood stains, you name it.'

For a moment no one said anything. None of them really quite believed that perpetrators always return to the scene of the crime, but gradually their expressions began to soften, and finally something approaching a smile spread across their faces, as though they had just invented a car that ran on water.

'Well done, Onerva. Most pyromaniacs do that too.'

'I'll get the tapes sent over today,' Piipponen enthused.

Some people joked that Piipponen was only ever keen to do the cushy jobs, like setting up camera surveillance, or when he had the opportunity to take some kind of glory. What did glory mean in a profession like this? Simply doing one's job?

Once they were in the corridor Onerva strode along briskly, leaving the others slightly behind. Piipponen sidled up to Harjunpää with an air of confidentiality.

'Timo,' he whispered. 'Been thinking of getting a new set of wheels?'

'No. Doubt I will for years.'

'There's this top-notch Merc going. 1999, only one previous owner, barely 50K on the meter; MOT done and all the paperwork in order; doesn't rattle, doesn't choke. Tell them I sent you and the price will drop five percent.'

'You've been for a test drive.'

'Too right I have!'

They continued along the corridor towards the lift, and only then did Piipponen realise what he had said. 'Yesterday, I mean…' he spluttered.

26. Experiment

'*Vasces et libera bombardus*,' he muttered under his voice, and though he was accustomed to the dusk, to the dark even, for once he wished there was a little more light. He was at home, kneeling on the floor beside his only chair. The storm lantern dangled from the back of it, its flame so tall that the lantern gave off a thin tail of black smoke, and the smell of burning petrol filled the air. In addition he had pulled the tarpaulin which served as a door halfway across the opening, allowing a pallid grey light to filter in through the hatch above.

'*Carboratum vitilea bodulis*,' moved his lips. His fingers moved too; they were surprisingly nimble and flexible, as though some of his joints were made of rubber, and this dexterity meant that he had almost finished. In front of him on the chair was a pair of small-handled tongs, a pocket knife, a needle and a tiny screwdriver – and, of course, the alarm clock itself. However, this was not his own, but one he had stolen from a shop, one with a proper nine volt battery. The clock had partly been taken to pieces, and beside it lay his head lamp, though this time he could not rely on its light, for it too was part of the experiment, which was why he had removed its battery.

He had visited the library in Pasila and in less than half an hour on the internet he'd found what he needed. The majority of the instructions were nonsense, little boys' silly fantasies that could not possibly have worked. This one, for instance, he remembered word for word: "Drill a small hole in the base of a light bulb. Pour petrol or gunpowder in through the hole and cover it with tape. Go into your enemy's room and exchange your light bulb for his. When he switches on the light – KABOOM! Your enemy's head will be gone!" How can one drill a hole through the thin glass of a light bulb? It is as fragile as an eggshell; and how can one pour petrol through a hole the size of a pinprick when the air inside will not be able to escape?

Of course, he had found plenty of information about different chemicals, instructions on how to handle them and in what quantities to mix them, but he did not care for this. He already had his bomb, the sticks of dynamite lying there beneath his bedside table, and now all he needed was a reliable detonator. And for this he had also found the necessary instructions: the classic alarm clock trick.

At once he had understood how it worked, but only a moment ago had he realised that if he attached the fuse to the minute hand the bomb could be detonated at any time. However, if he attached it to the hour hand it could tick away in peace for up to twelve hours. Still, he – or rather his Piggy Back, as he had begun to call the boy – would need only half an hour at most, and thus the minute hand was the obvious choice.

'*Bona spes cum flammen alere,*' he whispered, as he checked that the screw he had mounted in the clock face, at twelve o'clock, was raised high enough for the minute hand to strike it firmly. Sure enough, it was in the right place. He turned the clock around to check that the cable attached to the screw was securely in place. He needed only one battery, the one that ran the clock; it would provide more than enough electricity to ignite the primer.

With the tip of his knife he carved a small hole in the edge of the clock's back cover, so that it could be closed properly while still allowing the cable to snake its way out; then he replaced the cover and turned the minute hand to eleven o'clock – giving himself five minutes. He double-checked the wires attached to the head lamp, then simply allowed the clock to tick, though it did not really tick the way clocks did in the olden days. It was more of a quiet hiss, like a hedgehog sipping milk.

'Piggy Back,' he said, his voice full, tasting the words - it felt good. He was content now that he had reached final certainty about the boy; he was not a trap, he was a son sent by Maammo herself. And the sacrifice of his own son was an act that would please Maammo so vastly that it might even begin a chain of events culminating in the Coming of the Truth: the birth of the New Big Bang.

He ought to have understood this earlier: after all, it was he who had summoned the plump girl to his side and she had unwittingly brought him precisely what he needed. But final confirmation of this had come only once he had sacrificed the first of the pigeons required for the adoption: its blood had created a particularly beautiful pattern on the rock, almost like the swirl of the spirit as it leaves the body. Not only this, but it had also tasted exceptionally good, and was so thick that he had allowed himself to imbibe two whole spoonfuls of it.

The minute hand had only a few seconds to go. It did not jolt forward showing each minute separately, rather it flowed upwards. Is it possible to flow upwards? No matter, this minute-hand did so, and it only had to flow a drop or two more before it touched the screw. With his tongue he restlessly realigned his lower teeth, over and over again, all the while staring fixedly at both the clock and the head lamp. The moment was nigh.

At last! The lamp flickered and lit up, shining even more strongly than with its normal battery – it worked! Maammo's grace was with him. By coincidence the beam of light from the lamp shone directly towards his bedside table, as if it had known that there, hidden away, lay his beloved sticks of dynamite. In a frenzy he raised his hands in thanks and prayed, almost shouting: '*Ea lesum cum sabateum, torea borea in loco parentis! Ea, ea, ea!*'

His voice rebounded off the walls in a hollow, stony echo.

27. *Knock*

Since finally moving out Mikko had only once visited his former home in Kulosaari Park, to help Sanna move her things to Kallio; and he had no reason to visit now either. He was filled with a strange anxiety, like something thick and viscid heaving within him, mercury, or maybe cement. He had been gripped by this same sensation all those months ago during the divorce proceedings.

But there he stood, staring at the light brick wall that once had brought him such a deep feeling of contentment. The house was one of eight in a terrace. He stared at his former front door, and the familiar bronze lion-head door knocker stared back at him. Its expression seemed dead now; before the divorce it had followed him everywhere, and had been on the front door of every house he had lived in during his adult life, but now it belonged to a woman from whom he was entirely estranged, and who lived with a man he did not even know. Ironically, it was his writing that had bought them the house in the first place.

The bushes in the front garden had been pruned, castrated, leaving nothing but stubs, and on the side of the pine – the pine that had once been so dear to him, his power source; when embracing it he had always felt a mystical energy coursing through him – a dartboard had appeared; several darts hung dangling from the tree's bark. Even his stone labyrinth had disappeared. He had taken the idea from the poet Pentti Saarikoski, although his labyrinth had been much smaller. Every one of its stones had been unique, they were individuals that he had collected over the years. Still, the space had not been left empty: in its place there now stood two pink plastic flamingos balancing on wire legs, swaying quietly in the wind.

And on top of everything came one last humiliation. His cheeks furrowed as though he were chewing something, and his breath came fast and shallow. Despite this he picked up his mobile for the third time, pressed number three on the speed dial, and a few seconds later the telephone began to ring on the other side of the door. It made a shrill metallic sound - it was an old, black telephone he had bought at a flea market and restored, and it had always sat on the table in the hallway. It rang a third time, spitting out its harsh cry, and when Cecilia couldn't bear it any longer she picked up the receiver. This confirmed that she was merely playing with him - for if she had wanted to she could have unplugged it altogether.

'What is it now?'

'Cecilia, be reasonable, open the door. I've brought something for Matti.'

'You've got no business coming here, trying to be all chummy with me.'

'Come on, Cecilia, please…'

'And I think I remember telling you he's not here anyway,' she said.

'Yes you did, but I've already been round all the places he normally hangs out and he's not there either.'

'How am I supposed to know where he is every minute of the day? And even if I did it wouldn't make any difference, because he's changed, he's become violent. He attacked me, and Kari had to pull him off; then today I got a phone call from the headmaster saying he's given some kid named Janne a black eye, and now I have to go in and talk to him.'

Mikko didn't say a word. He couldn't, he was entirely unable to speak, for he was so utterly astonished. Somewhere beneath his bewilderment he was certain that she was lying. None of this sounded even remotely like Matti.

'That's all the more reason for me to see him. And I could go to the school instead.'

'If things carry on like this we'll have to put him in a foster home.'

'Now listen to me! You... First you smoked me out of the house, then Sanna, and now you're trying to do the same to Matti. He's your own son!'

'Oh I did, did I? I can't do anything about it if neither of them wants to live here any more. I can't force them to stay.'

'Listen. As part of the settlement we agreed that you could keep the house specifically so that the children could live there with you. Is that suddenly no longer the case?'

'Do your papers say something like that? Mine certainly don't.'

'But for crying out loud... We had a verbal agreement!'

'I don't remember anything of the sort. Were witnesses present?'

'God almighty,' Mikko hissed almost silently. He ended the call, took one step, then another, each like a violent gust of wind, then grabbed the bronze knocker hanging from the lion's mouth and began hammering on the door. He realised it was senseless, but perhaps his problem was that he had always been too sensible. More than that, he simply felt that the situation was unbearably malicious and unjust.

'I'll take out a restraining order on you!' Cecilia hollered. She too had put the phone down and was now standing behind the door. 'You mark my words - a restraining order!'

'They're for abusive spouses. And if anyone in this family has ever resorted to using their fists it certainly wasn't me!'

'If you don't leave this minute I'll call the police!'

'Call them for all I care! Call them all you want!' Mikko bellowed, but at that moment it was as if he began to wake up; suddenly he burst through the surface of his momentary rage and felt ashamed of the whole episode, the depths to which he had demeaned himself; and he shuddered almost instinctively, shaking the remnants of the episode from his body.

'Fine,' he said. 'I'm going. But I've bought Matti his own mobile. I'll leave it here on the step. It's all paid for with a prepaid deal. Wait five minutes then pick it up so no one pinches it.'

'Is it new?'

'Second-hand.'

'Of course, your son isn't worth a new one, is he?'

Mikko didn't reply. He took the telephone and its charger, the instruction manual and the SIM-card and placed them on the top step. Then he took a few panicked steps, like a little boy caught doing something naughty. A moment later, incredibly, he almost burst into tears, but managed to stifle them. It finally occurred to him to go to the shopping centre at Itäkeskus, just in case Matti had ended up there.

28. *Decisions*

Her face in the mirror –
how pained the sight;
how keen the girl there feels your spite.
Lips pursed in a smile, tight and long,
breasts large and strange and wrong.

Leena sat at the edge of her desk, her head propped in her hands, reading through the first verse on a smudged and frayed piece of paper, though she knew it off by heart. It was her favourite poem. With the end of a compass she picked absent-mindedly at the corner of the desk, scraping away small white shards of laminate. Her stomach was swollen for the second day running, her abdomen ached every now and then and her breasts were sore – her period would start again any time now.

Turn away from the mirror,
and shut tight your eyes,
only the room's darkness feels your cries:

105

how could anyone love me,
miss me, touch and kiss me?

Everything seemed so strange. She had read about a boy who could see the beauty in everything, who could imagine fairies living by the edge of the lake, could speak to animals and understand the language of the birds. How she wanted to be like him. But the first time she had seen Matti in school she had finally understood: Matti was the boy, and she had fallen in love with him, making her head spin; she had never felt so intensely about anyone before. It was as if her dreams had finally become real.

But no matter how hard she tried Matti had barely noticed her. And why should he have noticed her, he probably hadn't even wanted to know her: a fat girl, the Hammer Thrower, with a face as bloated as a baseball glove. And now that he *had* finally noticed her and had become something of a friend, he would have to move to another part of town and go to another school.

She blew her nose and wiped her eyes, and pieces of laminate began to fly again. And then there was the priest. She wasn't sure whether it was jealousy or envy, but whichever it was she had a nasty feeling about it all – she had realised that, despite his odd behaviour, the priest had taken a shine to Matti. He had even made the holy sign three times for Matti, and only once for her. Matti was his favourite, and she would have to settle for second place. She sensed the sheer darkness of her thoughts, black as liquorice spit. Another tear dropped from the end of her nose.

But hush, good friend!
for someone awaits for you,
in prayers soft and tender whispers: love me too:
for he loves you – not just the shell;
your beauty is more than he can tell!

Sobs passed her lips and she slumped her head on to the table, whimpering. After a while she sat up again, sucked her upper lip between her teeth and thought to herself. It was quiet. Mum had gone to aerobics again, or yoga, or whatever it was she did, and Dad was away on one of his countless business trips. All she could hear was the distant hum of traffic from the Eastern Highway and the occasional sounding of a foghorn from the harbour in Sompasaari. But then something occurred to her. She went into the living room, found a row of novels by Matti's father standing in the bookcase, removed one of them, placed it in her small pink bag and threw it over her shoulder. A moment later she was in the hallway; she pulled on her shoes and grabbed the keys from the shelf.

29. Hit

Harjunpää was crouched on the floor of his office, a newspaper spread out in front of him and a pair of disposable blue rubber gloves on his hands. Again he found himself holding that same waterlogged leather wallet between his fingers. By now it had dried out, shrivelled and gnarled, but the job was still as frustrating as ever: none of the wallet's various compartments yielded a piece of paper or a card that might have borne a name.

The wallet had belonged to a male body fished out of Tokoinranta the previous week. The body had clearly been in the sea through the winter, drowned last autumn, and Harjunpää still hadn't succeeded in making a positive identification of the victim. A notice in the newspaper hadn't resulted in as much as a phone call and his features didn't match those of any listed missing persons. Harjunpää hadn't been able to do anything about the body for a few days and even now he prodded the wallet merely to soothe his conscience.

He could hear Onerva approaching – nobody else's shoes clip-clopped in the same way, like soft jazz. He stood up, stretched his back and peeled the gloves from his hands.

'Timo,' she exclaimed. She had rushed along the corridor, there were red blotches on her cheeks and she was smiling in a way that immediately caught Harjunpää's attention. She was holding both her hands in the air and from each of them dangled numerous sections of video tape. 'I think we've hit something…'

'Really?'

'I think so. These are from the tapes taken after the incident. Look at that.'

Onerva lay the tapes out flat along the table and Harjunpää reached for his magnifying glass. It was the same one he had had throughout his career, its original leather case was worn and shone like metal. Painstakingly he began moving the magnifying glass along the tapes, and in each frame the same figure could be made out, sometimes immediately after a train had left, when no one else was standing on the platform.

'She goes back there a total of seven times,' said Onerva. 'At precisely the spot where the incident took place. Look at this one – she peers over the edge of the platform and moves her head back as if she's sniffing something.'

'A woman. Not a very young one either, see that long flowing skirt.'

'It's blue; the monitor decided to show colour for a change. And that beret is a deep burgundy.'

'It's almost pulled down over her eyes.'

'But what on earth would make someone like that shove people in front of a train?'

'*If* he was pushed, that is... Still, this woman had better have a pretty good explanation.'

It was as though something inside him came to a halt; he grasped at the thought, the way one grasps at fragments of a dream that reappear throughout the day, and suddenly he was absolutely certain.

'I've seen that woman...'

'Really? Who is it?'

'I don't know. It was yesterday when I arrived at the underground station. That woman was standing in a crowd of people on the upper level. She seemed very agitated and started shouting something at me.'

'Something to do with the case?'

'No, she's one of those religious folk, said something like, I'll pray for mercy yet.'

For a moment they stood looking one another in the eye. It had always puzzled Harjunpää, the way her eyes were each a different colour. Then they began to smile, together, each knowing what was going through the other's mind: like a silent shout of yippee, they both felt the same sense of joy and satisfaction whenever an unfathomable case edged ever so slightly forward.

'Shall we go today?'

'Hang on.' Harjunpää scratched his chin; indistinct, blurred thoughts suddenly spinning through his mind. 'We've got to plan this properly... We haven't got any hard evidence against her. She might say she witnessed the incident and was so shocked by it that she was compelled to go back to the scene again and again...'

'You're right.'

'In any case – we're not even sure if there's a crime to suspect her of. We're still only investigating two miscellaneous fatalities. We can't apprehend her...'

'Damn it.'

'I know. And there's no way Mäki will turn them into murder investigations on such insufficient evidence.'

'Damn it.'

30. *Disturbance*

'*Armor cumbator?*' he wondered all of a sudden. Perhaps he even said it out loud, for something was disturbing him. To be more precise, something was disturbing his thoughts - and they were good thoughts. He did not feel threatened – this was a passing disturbance. Could one of the people going down into the underground be a priest? Priests were the envoys of the infidel and their presence always caused him some sort of disturbance; this he had experienced many times before. He scrutinised the people around him, those going down and those coming back up the other side of the escalator, but no; none of them gave off the same negative aura as a priest.

He quickly shook his head and this seemed to help: he recovered the thought that had so warmed his heart. Only an hour ago he had sacrificed the third pigeon required for the adoption and its blood had been potent, a beautiful red. In accordance with the law of Maammo the boy was now his son, and with his own son he could do as he saw fit. He wanted nothing more beautiful than to sacrifice his son, and through this to surrender his own spirit, his flesh and blood, to Maammo for the sake of the New Big Bang. But he did not yet call the boy to his side, for not everything had become clear to him.

He was not sure where the event was to take place. Should it be in a church midway through a Sunday service? On the one hand this would have been highly impressive, but it did have one weakness: far too few people attended Sunday services. This time he wanted to create a truly massive swirl. Perhaps a department store would be a better choice, on a Friday or a Saturday during the busiest shopping hours. Indeed, this would be particularly apt, as those covetous people would meet their end surrounded by the very Mammon of their fornication. The third option was naturally an ice-hockey stadium: they were almost hollow and the force of the blast might cause the building to come crashing down upon those who survived, thus creating an even greater swirl.

'Take it! The Truth shall come!' he shouted to a man who dared walk close enough to him, but to no avail. That day not a single person seemed interested in the Coming of the Truth, and this if anything proved how depraved humanity had become and how profoundly it deserved what was coming. 'Take it! The Truth shall come!'

Then he felt it: the disturbance was behind him, perhaps a hundred metres away or as close as the newsagents. He raised his free hand, pressed his first finger and thumb together forming a telescope, then raised his hand up above his shoulder so that the person behind him knew he had been seen. He then moved his hand in front of his face and slowly began to turn around.

Framed in his fingers was the plump girl. What could this mean? He had not sent her any message, let alone an invitation. And why was she not with his son? Her expression was worried, sad perhaps. She had looked the same when he had first saved her; it had either been the 1st of May or the city festival – a celebration of debauchery nonetheless – and the girl had been sitting on a bench at the railway station, drunkenly sobbing out of sheer loneliness. He had approached her and saved her, made her one of Maammo's children: he had touched her forehead, sending her his powers, and she had stopped crying and begun to sober up in front of his very eyes. Since then her soul had belonged to him, and through him to Maammo herself.

'Hi there,' said the girl joylessly, standing out of either shyness or respect about ten metres away from him. This was indeed the way to behave in the presence of the earth spirit. With his fingers he made the first of Maammo's holy signs and she understood that this meant she should come to him. She began to waddle closer. She was carrying a rucksack, or at least something with straps resembling those of a rucksack, and she clung to the straps with both hands as though it contained something very special.

'Good evening, my girl.'

'Hi. Sorry for turning up like this. I knew you'd be in the middle of your work.'

'Why, that is all right, my child – or should I say young lady? No work could me more important to me than that which I can do to help you.'

'Thanks. Um, well…'

'Shall we move out of the way? Over by the wall, perhaps?'

'Yes.'

He walked ahead and the girl tottered after him. He already knew that she was going to ask him something, something which to her tiny mind was very important. He was no longer upset that she had caused him a momentary disturbance, and he suddenly felt most merciful. There was no reason he could not help a poor creature like this. They stopped by the wall.

'Well, you see…' she stammered, as she began slipping the rucksack from her back. It was pink, a pig, it even had eyes and a snout. Two little piggies back to back. 'It's Matti…'

'The boy who went rowing?'

'Yes, that's him.'

'So his name is Matti…'

'Yes. And, you see, I… To me he's… His dad wants him to move in with him, and then he'll have to leave Kulosaari.'

'And you like him?'

'Yes! Couldn't you do something about it?'

'And where exactly will he and his father be moving to?'

'All the way to Tampere! Then I'll never see him again!'

'*Mortuus percecae!*' he exclaimed. That would not do at all. This would ruin his sacrifice. It would deny him the opportunity to serve Maammo in the most divine way, and could even jeopardise the Coming of the Truth! Restlessly he shifted the position of his legs and looked at the girl, who clearly thought that he too was upset at the prospect of her losing Matti. It was for the best that she thought this.

'And when is this move to take place?' he asked, and this time he managed to control his voice and his state of anxiety. This may have been a test sent by Maammo to see whether he could overcome great difficulties in order to fight for the Coming of the Truth.

'I'm not sure, but he said it might be very soon. Maybe in a week or two.'

'*Sabre dantum!*'

'I don't understand…'

'So you would like me to do something to prevent this?'

'Right!' she exclaimed and frantically began opening her rucksack. 'I thought you might be able to change his dad's mind so that he won't want to move to Turku… I mean, Tampere… or so that he won't take Matti with him.'

'I see. You would like that too…'

The girl finally opened her rucksack, she had been fiddling anxiously with the knot, and removed a book with three large M's on the spine. After the final M, in almost microscopic lettering, stood 'oisio', forming the word MOISIO. She opened up the book to reveal its inner jacket flap.

'There's a picture of his dad. I thought it might be easier to send him thoughts if you know what he looks like…'

'You are a wise girl. And where does his daddy live?'

'Somewhere in Kallio, I think.'

'Does he work?'

'Yes.'

'Where?'

'At the postal sorting office. It's somewhere in Pasila.'

'Well well, Pasila indeed. And how does he travel there?'

'He's not there at the moment. He's got a year's leave and he's living on some scholarship. But he has got an office in Kontula and he goes there on the underground.'

'Morning and evening?'

'Yes, and he always travels during rush hour, so it feels like he's really going to work.'

'So he travels between Hakaniemi and Kontula?'

'Right.'

'Verily I will help you,' he said ceremoniously and made all three holy signs before the girl's face. This clearly did her a lot of good, for an expression of contentment appeared on her lips.

'Thanks a lot. Really.'

'It is nothing. It shall be my pleasure.'

'You're the best… Could you…?'

'You would like something more?'

'Erm… could you give me the vibes again?'

'For you, certainly. Go and lean your back against the wall.'

He approached the wall behind the girl, placed the fingers of both hands upon her temples and began to concentrate: '*Ea lesum cum sabateum…*'

He wanted to give the plump girl good vibes, very good vibes indeed, for she had earned them. Perhaps she had unwittingly rescued the New Big Bang. He raised his head and stared with all his power right into her eyes, watching her like a hawk, then quickly moved his fingers from her temples to her forehead – and this time she fell down straight away.

Her eyeballs almost rolled all the way back, with only the slightest strips of her irises still showing; then her eyelids closed and began twitching as though she were dreaming intensely. The whole length of her body pressed against the wall and slowly she sank first to her knees, then to a sitting position. She came to just as her bottom touched the floor. She shook her head in bewilderment, her eyes scanning around her, as if she did not quite know where she was – for a moment she probably didn't.

'Wow,' she panted, thrilled, and started pulling herself to her feet.

'What did you see?'

'I was on the roof of a really tall building, right on the edge. And I was really thin, just like a ballerina. I was wearing a leotard and one of those bell skirts. I was scared, but then I jumped and… I could fly! I glided very slowly through the air, hopped off the roof of the next building, and then I turned into a boy…'

'My girl, that was a beautiful vision. You were shown good things as a sign that Maammo loves you and will take good care of you.'

'Thanks a million. Can I…'

'No. Go now. Go! *Ea lesum!*'

He did not look to see whether she left or not, for surely she would leave if he so commanded it. He turned and walked in the opposite direction, and for a brief moment he sensed a slight uncertainty, a doubt in his mind, but then he remembered the face of the man on the inside flap of the book; he remembered every detail of his face, even the overgrown hair around his neck. That this man should dare try to steal his son!

He was filled once again with a fighting spirit, that same unshakeable will, the strength with which he doggedly carried out his work from day to day, and he was no longer in any doubt as to who next would be sacrificed to Maammo through the Orange Apostle.

31. *Hide Out*

If anyone were to walk along the thin dirt track around the edge of Kulosaari Park in the direction of Naurissalmi, before long, if they looked carefully, they might just make out a small clump of rushes. It wasn't particularly big, barely even a hundred square metres, but it was high and thick: the rushes grew in a dense patch and were so tall that in parts the tips of theirs flowers stood several metres high. And those with a keen eye might even notice that a narrow strip of land ran through them; not really a path as such, but a vague parting in the undergrowth, as if a very thin person had wandered through there every now and then.

The water was cloudy, the bottom was covered in mud, though the tops of a few rocks could be seen jutting out through the surface. And if someone were to walk along this narrow strip, they would soon see that the rocks formed a kind of bridge. Less than a metre apart, it was possible to walk along them to a place hidden within the rushes. At the end of the path was something of a surprise: a flat stone, polished smooth by centuries of tides, making it comfortable to sit on.

Matti sat shivering on the rock.

He sat crouched with his arms wrapped around his shins, his cheek resting against his knee, and he couldn't understand what it was he'd been thinking – or rather, he couldn't comprehend that he hadn't been thinking anything at all. He'd been in some kind of trance, and had taken off his trousers, shoes and socks and waded from the rock into the sea. Only when his underpants and the bottom of his shirt were wet had he snapped out of it; only then had he taken fright and retreated back to the rock, leaving the water barely rippling.

Had he done it because he wanted so much to get away from everything? Away, loose, free, trying to escape, though he had nowhere to go. He didn't dare think of home, he was sure a police car would be waiting for him in the driveway. And if there was no police car, then his things would be scattered around the garden awaiting his return. The headmaster had said he was going to ring his mum, and he was certain she would do the same as she had done to Sanna on countless occasions: throw all her things into the front garden, as if to say 'take your stuff and leave'. Only after a drawn-out ritual humiliation and a lot of pleading would she allow her to stay – 'this time'.

On top of that, he couldn't quite understand what had happened during the lunch break at school. Leena had been away all day, skiving probably, and Matti had wanted to ask her why she'd suddenly gone so quiet. Had he offended her in some way? The other boys had noticed that she wasn't at school and Janne, Rike and Stenu had cornered him in the playground. As soon as Janne had asked: 'Where's your girlfriend today,

Matti Shithead?' Matti had punched him. He'd been clenching the pebble the priest had given him, and had done what the priest had instructed him to do, thinking: 'This moment here and now is crap, but at the same time I'm already back home.' Then he'd just lashed out, punching him once, right in the face. He hadn't even had enough time to see where he'd hit him, but Janne fell back, landing on his arse, and the area around his left eye had started swelling so much you could see it from a distance.

They had all fallen silent. Janne had yelled a little, and the others had helped him away. Rike had threatened to go to the headmaster, and apparently he had done so. Matti was duly summoned to the headmaster's office during the next lesson. The head had said he was shocked, that he was going to call Matti's mother, and that he was going to do all he could to put an end to bullying and violence in his school. He had even threatened Matti with the police and social services and goodness knows what else. At this very moment he was hiding amongst the rushes, sitting on a rock shivering with his arms wrapped around his legs. He hadn't thought to take off his wet underpants; he felt like a little boy who had wet himself.

It was beginning to get dark, though as spring went on the darkness seemed somehow much weaker. An old-fashioned motor boat could be heard chugging in the distance: *pfut-pfut-pfut*. The air smelled of fish. He stood up, numbness pinching his legs, removed his jeans which had stuck uncomfortably to his backside, and listened. There was not a sound from the dirt track, nobody was moving around. He took a long stride and stepped on to the first of the rocks leading back to the shore, carefully pulling aside the rushes so that he could see the next rock. Somewhere deep within him grew the feeling that there wasn't anything or anybody in the world that could help him other than Leena's priest. If only for a short while the priest had made Matti feel better, and at least for the moment, the perpetual bullying seemed to have stopped.

32. *Advice*

They came at almost exactly the same time, or perhaps Kikka beat him by a second or two ;it was almost as if she gave Mikko permission to come. He didn't roll off her straight away, as Kikka enjoyed the feeling of him inside her afterwards, the way he slowly drifted away before finally slipping out in his own good time. He too enjoyed the sensation of Kikka contracting around him, slower and slower. There they lay, breathing as one, their sweat mingling, and for a brief moment they themselves were one. It felt good.

Mikko breathed in the soft perfume on Kikka's neck and with his fingers gently brushed her tangled hair behind her ears. Kikka's hand was between his shoulder blades and she delicately caressed the most sensitive part of his back. Time passed, and it was a good kind of time: not a single negative thought went through Mikko's mind; all that existed was the moment and the warmth of Kikka's bare skin. But soon it too had passed. He released his grip, slowly rolled on to his back and lay beside her. Kikka nestled her head between his shoulder and his neck and with her other hand pulled the sheets up around them. They were motionless once again; all they could feel was the gradually calming beat of their hearts.

'You're worried about something,' she said quietly, in a way that meant she didn't expect him to explain.

'A bit.'

'Because Matti hasn't called you?'

'Partly.'

'It doesn't mean something's happened to him. Kids that age can sit for hours moping about anything, especially if he really did get into trouble at school like Cecilia said.'

'It's just so unlike him… And what really annoys me is that I went there and left that telephone with her.'

'Why?'

'Because she could very well 'forget' to give it to him, or break it.'

'A grown woman?'

'Yes, I know it sounds ridiculous. All kinds of things started happening while we were going through the divorce. I used to have a green Loden hat that I wore while writing. It was a bit like a talisman to me. Then it mysteriously disappeared.'

'That's pretty low.'

'I know. And once while she was watering the flowers she managed to spill half the watering can over my typewriter, the electric Olympia, even though the nearest vase was at least a metre away.'

They lay there in silence for a moment yet, not moving, and as their passion subsided they could make out the various sounds within the building: somewhere downstairs a door slammed angrily, someone roared back and forth across the courtyard on a sputtering moped, while the couple next door were in the early stages of yet another argument, just beginning to raise their voices as if they were looking for a suitable reason to have a row. All this made Mikko feel uneasy and he tossed and turned, but no matter what position he found, nothing felt comfortable.

'What's wrong now?'

'Everything. I don't know what I'm going to do about the house; then there's this office – for some reason I just can't bring myself to like it. And I guess I feel a bit melancholic about Sanna moving out today.'

'You'll soon get used to Matti being there instead. But I'll still give you the same advice: go and talk to your parents about it.'

'You don't know them.'

'But you're their son. And this is only a temporary problem.'

'Even so...'

'For crying out loud, you're only asking for a loan. Just draw up all the proper paperwork.'

'They can certainly well afford it. To my knowledge Father gets three times as much pension as I do wages.'

'And with five leased properties – surely one of them must be empty. They could take you on as a tenant.'

'The two-bedroom in Punavuori might be vacant, at least they mentioned that they were going to renovate it. There would be just enough space for Matti and me, and I could use the room facing the courtyard as an office.'

'Go and talk to them.'

'I'll think about it,' said Mikko, wriggling on to his side, with his back to Kikka. His eyes were blank and his face was like a grey stone, his mouth an iron fissure running through it.

33. *News*

Harjunpää had walked from Pasila to the Police Station so quickly that a thin trail of sweat was slowly running down the end of his nose. For a reason he couldn't put his finger on, he was eager to get stuck into the underground case, with an enthusiasm much like when he had first joined the Crime Squad. Perhaps it also had something to do with the fact that he couldn't remember being in a situation quite as frustrating as this before: two fatalities, possibly linked, but still they couldn't ascertain whether either of them was in fact a crime. On the train that morning it had also occurred to him that they should get hold of the CCTV tapes from the upper level of Hakaniemi station and examine the point at which he had walked in, to check whether the woman who kept returning to the platform was the same woman who had preached to him.

Upon arrival he headed straight for the bathroom. He threw his shoulder bag on the floor, ran the water until it was cold and began rinsing his face. Only as he was dabbing himself dry with a paper towel did he notice that he was not alone. There was someone else in the toilet, someone who had clearly been there for some time, and there was a hint of satisfaction in his voice as he sang merrily to himself.

Harjunpää took another towel as he heard the toilet flush. Then came the sound of a belt being fastened and a moment later the door of the left-hand cubicle swung open: Piipponen appeared. The evening paper was folded beneath his arm — presumably he had been reading it just now — but when he saw Harjunpää his expression changed in an instant, as if a Venetian blind had suddenly been pulled shut.

'Christ, Harjunpää,' he puffed. His voice was serious and sharp; irritated wrinkles appeared across his forehead, and with a flick of his wrist he opened the paper to reveal the headlines. 'Take a look at this!'

The lettering was thick and ominous, only three words followed by a bulky question mark, a little touch that nonetheless revealed so much. "UNDERGROUND SERIAL KILLER?" Harjunpää hissed wearily. The question mark meant that the press had absolutely no confirmed information, only enough to come up with a suitably scandalous headline that would sell its papers. This headline meant that once again someone had leaked information – a problem spreading like a cancer through the police force.

'These guys should be strung up by the balls and have a hot poker shoved up their arse,' Piipponen growled, his moustache quivering. 'You know what this means, we'll be doing nothing but answering reporters' phone calls all day. And before you know it the TV news will expect some kind of comment.'

'Who could have done this? Surely not Mäki.'

'Hang on,' Piipponen exclaimed. He began leafing through the newspaper, trying to find the lead article, and after scanning through it for a moment he read, '"According to police sources…"'

'You know what that means.'

'Not a clue.'

'It means, "According to some half-wit mole…"'

'Shit…'

Harjunpää was already thinking frantically about who could have been behind it. Apart from himself, the only people who knew about the case in detail were Mäki, Onerva and Piipponen. Of course, then there was everyone at forensics, as well as the whole team at the Crime Squad; after all, they had all gone through the case together in the coffee room. The reality was that any one of thousands of police officers could have been responsible for the leak: all it would have taken was access to the squad's case files.

'What are you looking at me for?' Piipponen snapped and his eyes widened. He was shocked, and stood tapping his fingers against his chest, making his voice shake. 'You're not suggesting I had anything to do with…?'

'Of course I'm not. I was just thinking and stared at you by accident.'

'Harjunpää, for Christ's sake don't go spreading things like that.'

'Of course not… We're having a meeting in Mäki's office at quarter to.'

'You know what?' said Piipponen slowly, as if something very important had just occurred to him. 'There is a silver lining to all this.'

'And that is…?'

'All the chief inspectors will have got wind of this, and the ministers. They're bound to be interested. It'll give the whole investigation a boost. We'll all be put on overtime – a suspected serial killer! We'll get this case rolling once and for all!'

'Which means we can look forward to spending all our evenings and weekends here too. Thanks very much, but I'd be happy with your basic bread-and-butter policing,' Harjunpää muttered as he turned on the tap again. His mouth suddenly felt horribly dry. Piipponen slammed the door shut behind him and a moment later, echoing further along the corridor, Harjunpää could hear him singing yet again.

34. *Shadow*

'*Ecce sum cumbale*,' he groaned, heavy and frustrated. There were a number of reasons for this. Firstly he was too close to the church, which stood barely fifteen metres away. He was sitting in the park outside Kallion kirkko, as inconspicuous as the shadow of the bushes nearby; a black evil radiated from the church's grey granite walls – it was almost palpable – while the wail of thousands upon thousands of people killed in the name of Christian heresy rang in his ears.

Secondly, he had deviated from his usual routine. Previously he had always selected his victims at the underground station, at the last minute – just before the arrival of the Orange Apostle; but this time he had planned everything in advance and now lay in wait for the chosen one. From this vantage point he had an unobstructed view of the iron gate leading into the courtyard of the house on Neljäs Linja. The door of number 24 opened out into the street while all the others opened into the courtyard. There was no possible way he could miss Mikko Matias Moisio slipping off to the underground station.

'*Prate Mamolae non?*' he uttered, looking for an answer within himself. For this was the worst of his problems: Maammo had not appeared to him. He had remained awake and wandered praying through his underground temples until the early hours, but nothing had happened. Only once had he discerned a faint bluish green glimmer in the wall of the tunnel leading north east, but when he had run up to the spot it had disappeared. He could not understand what was happening. Did Maammo not wish for him to sacrifice this Mikko Matias? Not at all? Or simply not on that particular day? Perhaps Maammo wished merely to test him. Precipitating the New Big Bang was a task requiring the utmost trust and skill, and perhaps Maammo wished to test whether he was capable. He sat, pondering.

From further down the hill came the pulse of the morning rush hour traffic along Hämeentie like water running through a brook. A van rumbled along Neljäs Linja, shuddering across the cobbles; a lark was singing; on the fourth floor of Mikko Matias' building someone closed a window; and at the edge of the park an old woman appeared walking a dog the size of a cockroach. From out of nowhere a flock of jackdaws rose into flight, and for a brief moment the air was filled with their noisy squawking. Was this a message from Maammo? Perhaps Maammo had instructed them to nest near the church in order to keep an eye on the evil plotting priests. Suddenly the black iron gate of number 24 was pushed open.

A man stepped out on to the street; he was on the thin side and had bad posture. He was carrying a brown leather case; he checked his watch.

There was not a shred of doubt: this was Mikko Matias Moisio, the chosen victim – he could tell from his overgrown hair and profile; his nose was larger than average. The straggling tufts of hair across his cheeks sealed the matter once and for all.

'*Ea lesum cum sabateum*,' he proclaimed and held his breath. He waited to see which route the man would take: would he turn first into Suonionkatu then along Kolmas Linja or would he take the road straight down the hill along Siltasaarenkatu? He glanced in passing at the window of a shop on the corner. It was filled with corsets and brassieres and lace underwear, all items that lured men into sin and lewdness. On his way to the park he had noticed them and had made the first sign of the curse in front of each window.

The man continued straight ahead past the colossal church building. This too had horrified him: an entire block of flats filled with priests! The man then turned at the next corner – this was the most obvious route, as there was an entrance to the underground station at the bottom of the hill. Just before the man disappeared from view he quickly made the sign of the holy diamond. In this way there would always be an unbreakable connection between them. Even if he disappeared from view, the mark of the diamond meant he would be able to find the man again and again.

He crossed the road and made his way towards Suonionkatu. A shudder ran through him as he passed the house of priests, but once at the corner he could see Moisio again: he was already halfway down the hill. He was a writer, and he began to wonder whether a writer – an artist – would produce a swirl different from those of other people as the spirit left the body.

And despite his initial hesitation he now felt more strongly than ever before that, in good time, all this would become clear to him.

35. *Meeting*

They had all crammed into Mäki's office. Mäki himself was sitting at the edge of his desk and for once even he seemed uncertain as he flicked distractedly through the Statute Book. Onerva, Piipponen and Harjunpää were all present, as was Rantanen, the new chief of the Violent Crimes Division. He was a youngish man, apparently the youngest chief the Crime Squad had ever had, but in a short space of time he had achieved a great deal – solving a few old stagnating cases, and without stepping on anyone else's toes in the process. To everyone's astonishment he had even got the old screws to put in a bit more effort.

'These are the facts,' said Rantanen, absent-mindedly scratching his chin. 'And there are still two conflicting witness-statements regarding the first case?'

'Yes. One says the woman barged into the victim, the other says the exact opposite.'

'Whichever way you look at it, it seems to me that everything points towards it being an accident.'

'Then why didn't the woman come forward?' exclaimed Piipponen, exasperated. Harjunpää rubbed his eyes. From the outset he had sensed that, of all of them, Piipponen was the one that most wanted to turn these cases into murder investigations.

'And what if she quite simply didn't see the headline? She may not have noticed what happened in the slightest.'

'Or she noticed but felt too guilt-ridden to come forward.'

Harjunpää half closed his eyes. He was certain that what little information they had was not enough to start investigating these deaths as homicides. Their only hope was to try and obtain more evidence, but he didn't have the faintest idea how. The investigation had come to a standstill, all they could do was go over the same information time and again, just as they had done the day before, and Harjunpää suddenly had the feeling that even Rantanen was at a loss. Given the circumstances this was no great surprise.

'It can't just be a coincidence that we have two very similar fatalities and a woman fitting the same description present on both occasions,' said Piipponen emphatically, and Harjunpää remembered what Onerva had told him earlier: year after year Piipponen was always at the top of the overtime list.

'That is a point worth noting,' said Rantanen. 'But even that doesn't bring us close to what might be   considered "reasonable doubt". Timo, what's your honest opinion of our witness?'

'You mean Kallio? I do believe we should take him seriously. He's got all his marbles about him, but as we mentioned yesterday, and as he himself said, he does have compulsive spasms that affect his head, and that's why he can't maintain eye contact for long.'

'We've arranged another interview with him later on today,' said Onerva. 'We'll show him some photographs. And just for the record, I checked our databases with a number of different word combinations but there doesn't seem to be any woman matching this description on file.'

'OK,' Rantanen sighed. He looked each of them in the eye in turn. 'As far as I can see we don't have enough evidence to turn this into a murder investigation at the present time.'

Piipponen drew a sharp, hissing breath through his teeth, showing his disbelief at the stupidity of this decision.

'But let's keep our options open,' Rantanen added. 'We need to approach this on two fronts. First we need to try and get more evidence of any potential crime, let's not rule anything out just yet. That might mean talking to people travelling on the underground during rush hour, but I'll leave that up to Mäki.'

'So it's full steam ahead?'

'Yes. The other line of enquiry is to ascertain who this woman is. And if it turns out she was at the scene then we get her in for questioning, at the very least as a witness. That way this case should start opening up.'

'So that means we can put in for overtime?'

'As Mäki sees necessary at this point.'

'Yes!'

'But if I find out who leaked unsubstantiated information to the press, I'll skin him alive. You can imagine the flood of calls I've had to deal with this morning...'

No one said a thing. Not even Piipponen.

36. *Choice*

Every time he stepped into the underground station the same smell wafted towards him – damp stone, like something ripped apart – and he didn't like it. For Mikko it signified the journey to his strange workroom, the smell of hopeless attempts at writing and constant failure. But this time he barely noticed it. A dilemma spun through his mind: should he call them or not? And as he was already halfway down the clunking escalator at Hakaniemi station, on some level he had already decided not to make the call.

It simply wasn't the done thing to pop round to his parents' apartment. He had to be invited, or rather summoned: "Come round for coffee tomorrow at two." Mikko had never been able to say no; at most he may have mumbled something indistinct about having something else to do, but it was useless – by the appointed time he would always be there. Whenever he turned up of his own accord, uninvited, he was always chided for having upset their 'schedule' or their 'timetable'. This despite the fact that his parents were both retired.

His journey to Kontula was hampered by an inexplicable anxiety – all he could do was try, try, try, churning out first one page, then another; a third, a hundredth, a thousandth. Yet not a single one of them could he accept, for they all had the same fatal flaw: they lacked rhythm. They were nothing but lists of words, one after the other. They didn't ring properly, they lacked that sense of smoothness, like when you run your hand along a steel bar: it slides seamlessly. Never before had he churned out as many empty pages as now; so many thousands of pages that he had stopped counting them over two years ago.

The handrail was moving marginally faster than the escalator itself and his body stretched forward awkwardly. He adjusted his position and switched his satchel to his other hand. It was the same satchel that years ago he had taken to school, it even had an old-fashioned buckle. Another reason to make the call and go to Eira was because he simply couldn't carry on like this, living between two expensive apartments, neither of which was conducive to doing any work. It was a cold fact, but he had no other option. The bank had refused him a loan, the manager's argument being that his artistic funding was not considered sufficient income, let alone the fact that it was only temporary and would run out in less than a year's time. Even his wages from the post office had been considered too meagre.

According to the screen the next train would be arriving in four minutes: this gave him another moment to think things through. On the down side, going to Eira always unnerved him well in advance, and this time he had been nervous from the moment he had promised Kikka he would do it. After every visit he felt depressed, humiliated even, to the extent that he was unable to write anything. All he could do was sit slumped at his desk, his forehead resting against the cover of the typewriter.

Three minutes until the train arrived. Almost without realising it he slipped his hand down to the mobile phone case on his belt, but he didn't open it yet; and just then he sensed it more strongly than ever: it was as if someone were staring at him. Watching him, observing him, standing too close. He took a few steps to one side and slowly turned around. No, there was no one looking at him, everybody looked just as closed and indifferent as always. But still the feeling wouldn't go away. It brought with it a fear, almost like when as a child he needed the toilet in the middle of the night but was afraid the Cupboard Monster was lurking behind him. What was going on? It startled him: on top of everything else - the writing, the loneliness - was he now becoming paranoid?

After all, he was utterly alone. He didn't have a single colleague, no boss or staff, no one with whom he could discuss the problems of writing and how he could make it flow better. He had never belonged to writers' cliques, it was as if he dared not feel part of such a thing; on the other hand, the other post office workers had always considered him first and foremost a writer. Kikka was all he had, and he knew all too well that dumping his problems on her day after day would ultimately kill their relationship.

According to the screen there was now only a minute until the train arrived and he moved closer to the edge of the platform, perhaps even dangerously close, though he always moved back in time. He stretched out his neck and stared in the direction of the train. He wanted to see how beautiful the lights looked as they shone yellow against the tracks long before the train itself came into view. Even the sound of the wheels was pleasant: a steely cry like that of a frozen lake as a crack kilometres long sears through the ice.

Still he had the feeling that he was being watched! He spun around sharply, but didn't catch anyone looking at him. Close to him stood a woman rather like Kikka, who looked back at him, slightly taken aback, and beyond her a dishevelled old man with glasses. There were lots of others too, dozens of people in a jostling crowd just like every morning at this time, but none of them were looking in his direction, let alone openly staring at him. Seeing the woman reminded him that he had promised Kikka to deal with the problem that same day. He absent-mindedly pursed his lips together, reached for his mobile and reluctantly began walking back towards the escalators. He dialled the number.

'Moisio,' his father answered the way he always did, making certain it sounded like the name of a manor house or a royal court.

'Good morning, it's Mikko.'

'Good morning indeed. You haven't called us for a while.'

'I've been working really hard. And there are so many other things going on too… Can I come round?'

'What day?'

'Well, now if that's OK…'

'Your mother and I are going to the market for some caviar. Why don't you come over this evening and join us for some blinis?'

'No thank you. It's actually rather important…'

'We would have to change our plans entirely, of course. Wait a moment.'

He heard his father cover the mouthpiece with the palm of his hand – everything softened – but Mikko could still hear him shouting to his mother, who was clearly in another room. 'Mikko's insisting on coming round. Do you mind?' His mother replied, and although he couldn't quite make out the words he detected her familiar, somewhat irritated tone of voice. He began to feel uncomfortable, as though he were wearing a shirt that was too tight, making it hard to breathe, and he could feel his armpits dampening, streams of sweat trickling down his sleeve.

'Come if you must,' said his father. 'But we can only wait an hour. Your mother has a hair appointment at ten.'

'Thank you… Can I bring you something?'

'No, don't bring anything.'

'I'll be there in half an hour.'

'That's a quarter past eight.'

'Yes, thanks again,' he said and decided to walk to Eira so that he wouldn't have to wait in the stairwell. He decided to go past the Market Square and buy some flowers, even though last time his mother had simply left them unopened on the draining board and the time before that she had inexplicably had a severe allergic reaction to them.

37. *Waiting*

'*Arberata et constatellum*,' he thought, somewhat amazed, for surely no penniless folk could afford to live in this part of the city. What could an impoverished writer living in a tiny flat in Kallio possibly be doing in a place like this? He stopped at a pedestrian crossing at the intersection of Kapteeninkatu and Tehtaankatu and looked carefully to the left. From this vantage point he could see that Mikko Matias went into the fourth door along. The place had to be a familiar one, as he had clearly known the door code.

Who could he have been visiting? His parents, he guessed straight away. And if only one of his parents were still alive then it was his mother, as no man would take his own father a bunch of flowers. It must have been something very important – he had seen on the platform how the writer had hesitated and changed his mind at the last minute. There was something almost amusing about the whole episode – he would never know quite what a lucky decision that had been, for although Maammo had not appeared to him that night, he sensed that the situation was so critical for the Coming of the Truth that it was nothing less than his duty to carry out the sacrifice.

He stepped closer to the wall and only then did he realise why the place made him shudder: this was the same street corner where several years ago two police officers had been murdered. He felt something more, someone else had died at this crossing too, and the image of a little girl and a tram flashed through his mind, followed by a strip of pitch-dark night and bright explosions. Perhaps someone had died here in the bombings during the war, but the matter did not interest him any further.

He was only interested in Mikko Matias. Primarily this was because never before had he managed to build up such a complete picture of a sacrificial victim. For him they had been nothing but a blurred mass of greed and filth. However, Mikko Matias was gradually becoming a person to him. Nonetheless, he too lived in sin and lechery, so this would not affect his plans in any way.

In some ways Mikko Matias had the same amenable nature as his former son. He had clearly felt the presence of Maammo, but had not been able to say where it had come from. Every now and then he had glanced around as if he were looking for something, and on the Esplanade he had even popped into a pharmacy, pretending to buy something, when in fact he had simply stared out of the window to see if anyone walked hesitantly past the door, or if someone might follow him inside.

And that sensitiveness had produced a very rare phenomenon. At several points the writer's hands had been surrounded by an aura, a bright shining like those in Kirlian photographs. He had only seen this once before. He had met a shrivelled old woman who was able to cure people's ailments with herbs, or by touching them with her bare hands. Perhaps

Mikko Matias' aura was somehow linked to his profession – after all, writers quite literally work with their hands.

For the boy, the death of the man who was once his father and this sudden change of plans might be difficult at first. But he would soon recover; more than ever before he would need a father figure in his life, and he knew exactly how this could be achieved. In any case the boy would not be able to grieve the death of his former father for long. His feeling that the boy's own sacrifice would be very soon indeed strengthened with every minute that passed. He was still only missing one thing: a location, a stage. Maammo had not yet given him the smallest clue as to where it should take place. Unless this too were some kind of test through which Maammo wished to shore up his loyalty.

He leisurely walked the twenty or so metres to the tram stop and waited, looking every now and then at his watch. He was good at waiting, experienced. Nothing could be more demanding than standing in a draughty station for hours on end handing out leaflets, waiting to see an expression of interest – let alone thanks – spread across those impenitent faces.

And what he was now waiting for was something very interesting indeed: how fascinating would the swirl of the spirit be as it left the body of a writer.

38. *Visit*

The brass letter-box was embossed with the word 'LETTERS'. As a child Mikko hadn't understood what it meant, but now he realised that the gap was too narrow for the newspaper and that was why the delivery boy had always stuffed it beneath the door handle. The letter-box had been polished so that it shone like gold, and so had the handle and the bell. It had always been like this, and seemed like it always would be. How strongly that same letter-box was associated with Mikko's earliest memories.

He glanced at his watch – it was exactly quarter past eight – and quickly ran through how he should broach the subject of money. It occurred to him again that they were after all his own mother and father, not gods who decided who could and could not live.

He knocked on the door, instinctively so that it sounded neither too strong and arrogant nor too timid and quiet, and through the door he could hear his father clearing his throat and getting up from his armchair. The floor creaked beneath his feet the way it always did. Then came the sound of his father's heavy footsteps approaching the hallway. His father had always been an imposing man, and he still was; not only because of his size and manner, but because of his status too. He was an economist by trade and had spent his entire working life in the service of numerous banks, in positions so important that his word alone had been crucial in devising income strategies and even in finalising the details of the national budget.

His father pressed down the handle of the inner door. It still made that strange metallic creak which aroused an old, indistinct sense of fear in Mikko. As a child perhaps he had associated this with coming home, late for dinner yet again, and being forced to fetch the belt hanging in the kitchen doorway. The sound was also associated with his mother or father returning home; he could never tell what mood they were in, he had to read it from their gestures, their expressions. A certain type of expression could mean another night of hell, a night spent prying his father's fingers off his mother's neck, or keeping him away from the gun cabinet – or even wrestling him off the window ledge. Would he jump this time? None of their relatives or neighbours had suspected a thing, the façade had been immaculate.

'Well well,' said his father – he always said that – and proffered his massive fist. They shook hands like strangers, but still it was the closest contact they ever had. 'Come in. *Dear*, Mikko has arrived.'

His mother appeared in the living room doorway. She always seemed to be suffering and decrepit, and though there was nothing wrong with her physically, she had taken every available test at every hospital in the city. On the surface she was in tip-top shape: her blouse gleamed, it must have been of pure silk; she wore thick, golden rings on her fingers and bracelets on her wrists, so many pieces of jewellery that any sense of good taste was long gone.

'These are for you,' said Mikko as he handed her the bunch of roses. This time he had unwrapped the bouquet on the forecourt.

'Dear me, I don't know why you bring me these things. I'll only come down with some reaction or other.'

'Come on through,' his father said. He was wearing a suit, a white shirt and tie. 'Take your shoes off first.'

'Yes, of course,' Mikko muttered humbly, and he could hear his mother go into the kitchen, but couldn't make out the sound of her opening the cupboard with the vases, nor could he hear the water running. Something was gnawing away at him. He remembered that whenever he had brought his parents signed copies of his books they had never so much as touched them, telling him instead to leave them on the table; and afterwards they never even mentioned them. He wondered whether they'd bothered to read them at all.

'Sit,' his father ordered, gesturing towards the sofa. Coffee had been laid out on the round Chippendale table, the same one that as children he and his sisters had been forbidden to touch so as not to smear it with fingerprints. Only Marja had dared to touch it in secret, and because their parents had never established which of them was the culprit a collective thrashing had followed. His mother appeared from the kitchen and sighed quietly. Mikko knew why too: to demonstrate what a nuisance his sudden arrival had caused.

'You said there was something you wished to discuss,' his father began. This too was more than familiar to Mikko; they never exchanged any kind of pleasantries, and although he had planned what he was going to say in advance, he was suddenly confused, lost; perhaps partly because he had never before thought to ask his parents for anything.

'Well, I'm in a bit of trouble… It's to do with Cecilia.'

'Your father and I knew from the start that nothing would come of that marriage, but of course you wouldn't listen.'

'It did last eighteen years…'

'Your father and I have been together for fifty happy years.'

'Yes,' he stammered. He wanted to say more but kept his thoughts to himself. *You've been together for fifty years of hell, constant nagging and bickering; it's a miracle your children are capable of having relationships with other people at all.*

'Have you still not been able to sort things out with that Cecilia of yours?'

'This is about Matti actually. Sanna and her friend have moved to a flat in Vesala, so now Matti is going to move in with me.'

'And how is that possible? As far as I understood it there were clear conditions regarding this in your settlement.'

'Yes, but in real life not everyone follows those agreements…'

'I always said that woman was greedy and malicious.'

'It's not about that… The fact is that I can't live in a one room bedsit with another person and write at the same time.'

'Write?' said his mother incredulously. 'You haven't written a thing in seven years. I tell you, creativity and other such nonsense all comes to an end sooner or later. One day you'll simply have to accept it.'

'That's right,' his father croaked. 'It's the natural way of things, once you've fallen from the top it's impossible to climb back up there.'

Mikko felt very awkward indeed, so much so that he could feel a churning at the bottom of his stomach, as though vomit were rising upwards, the acrid taste tickling the back of his throat. What an idiot, why did I come here, he thought. I still haven't got to the point. *Do you remember whipping me whenever we went to the countryside, Mother? First you would strip me naked and command me to bend over a chair, then you'd start whacking me with birch branches; first on the back of my legs, then on the front. The blows would get higher and higher, and you would only stop once you had struck my penis. Did it give you some kind of satisfaction?*

'I have to move to a larger apartment,' he finally said out loud. 'But the bank won't give me a loan. I thought maybe… you might be able to…'

'Stop right there!' exclaimed his father, as if in shock, and raised both his hands in refusal. 'Your mother and I are very clear about this and we will not mix family relations with financial matters. You are a grown man and you should know how to take care of your own affairs.'

'Yes,' Mikko uttered, staring down at his hands, for he simply could not look his parents in the eye, not now and not as a child. *Do you remember how we struggled on the window ledge, Father? I hadn't even started school and it was my duty to save you. If you tried it again I'd help you with a kick up the backside!*

'But are none of your rented flats empty at the moment?' he stammered eventually.

'Now listen here, your mother and I are both of the opinion that matters relating to our investments are of no concern to outsiders. Be that as it may, all of our apartments are currently occupied with decent, respectable tenants who pay their rent on time.'

'Yes…' he mumbled in such a way that it no longer meant anything. He was beyond taking offence at his father's insinuation that his rent might go unpaid. He remained silent for a long moment, quietly sipping his lukewarm coffee. The matter had been dealt with and in his family there had never been any opportunity to argue the point.

'I saw Marja a few weeks ago,' he said finally, subdued, still staring down at his hands.

'I beg your pardon?'

'My sister, Marja.'

'Mikko. We do not want to discuss her in this house. She has chosen her path and knows full well that it is an affront to us.'

You made the decisions for everyone in this family. No – you denied us the right to make our own decisions. For Marja it all started when you forced her to have an abortion and prevented her from marrying her boyfriend. If she had been able to choose her own path, she might have been the next Helene Schjerfbeck. Now she's just a bag lady, hanging around Hakaniemi for all the layabouts to fuck. She won't live much longer.

Again Mikko bit his tongue. Everything felt hopeless, immaterial. He replaced his cup on the saucer with exaggerated care.

'Well,' said his father to indicate that the discussion was now over, then glanced at his watch to check that they were still within the designated timetable. 'It's time for your mother's appointment at the hairdresser's. I suppose I'll have to go to the market alone now, as we had to postpone our trip like this. What a shame you won't join us for blinis.'

'Try and get your life into some kind of order once and for all,' his mother said, pained. 'I doubt you'll ever understand what a terrible disappointment it is that our children amounted to nothing.'

'I see,' he muttered, barely audibly.

I'm an internationally-acclaimed author. And do you know what my earliest memory of childhood is - of life? I must have been only a few years old. I could walk up the steps one at a time holding on to the wall. Every night, Mother, you washed my penis so hard that it hurt, and once I started crying and said that I wanted to leave home... Do you remember what you did? You dressed me in nothing but a long-sleeved vest, left me sitting on the first floor, down in the stairwell, my bare bottom against the stone steps, and you said, 'Suit yourself, you can leave if you want to'. It took me a long time to climb back up to the sixth floor, and when I got there the door was shut, of course. I looked at the letter-box and tried to rattle it because I couldn't reach the bell. I couldn't properly reach the letter-box either...

'See you again, son. Be a man. We'll be in touch.'

'Letters...'

'I'm sorry?'

'We'll be in touch.'

39. *Travellers*

All year Matti had been worried about going to school and he knew perfectly well that it was all because of the other boys. He was worried now too, but in a different way; perhaps more exhilarated than worried, and for many reasons. For a start there were the events of the previous day: he had got into a fight, he'd hit another person. He had mixed feelings about it. On the one hand there was the feeling that he had done something bad and that he himself was bad, a criminal almost; both his mother and the headmaster had shouted at him, and he was still unsure what would happen to him.

The other feeling was unfamiliar to him – he was almost proud. Perhaps proud was the wrong word. It was almost as though he had risen above Janne and his friends, and above all, he felt protected from them. On top of this, the pebble the priest had given him had worked; it was in his pocket now giving him strength, or at least the faith that he would be able to get through this day too.

This very moment is a step, my left foot on the ground. But it's no longer the same moment, because now my right foot is on the ground. And whatever happens today, at this very moment I will be on my way home...

It was incredible, but at the same time it was true. He walked into the underpass, another moment; then he was halfway along the tunnel, another moment. A moment later he spotted Leena. It was impossible to mistake her, she was so much larger and sturdier than the others. What he didn't understand was why she was there at all, because she usually took a much quicker, more direct route to school.

'Hi.'

'Hi. You're better then?'

'Yeah, I didn't feel like coming to school yesterday,' she replied. She seemed distant and stared at him oddly.

'I know the feeling.'

'I heard... I know what happened yesterday; Kati told me when I rang her about our homework.'

Matti didn't respond. He didn't dare look at Leena, he was too scared. She might think he was a little brat. They walked together silently for twenty metres or so. Cars rumbled past. Then Leena gave him a friendly knock on the shoulder and said, 'Good for you!'

'You think?'

'Yes, I'm proud of you. Kati said everyone else is too. That sack of shit has been bullying other people too, you know.'

'Really?' he exclaimed. He stopped and looked at her. She was serious, her smile reaching right up to her eyes.

'I was afraid of all sorts...'

'I told you the priest was a guru, didn't I! Come on, we'll be late.'

They set off again with more of a spring in their step, but Leena's curiosity soon got the better of her and she asked nonchalantly: 'Your dad... Has he been in touch? I mean, has he said when you're moving?'

'He's got to sort out the money first,' he replied sullenly and looked at the ground. Then he remembered something, his expression became neutral again and a smile spread across his face; he thrust his hand into his pocket and pulled something out.

'Check this out!'

'A phone! That's great, where did you get it?'

'Dad brought it round last night and left it with my mum.'

'Your dad's great! Give me your number. You remembered to ring and thank him, didn't you?'

'Well I can't... yet.'

'I think you ought to thank him.'

'Yes, but it doesn't work yet.'

'Why not?'

'It hasn't got a SIM-card.'

Leena stopped and put her hands on her hips. 'You mean he gave you a phone without a connection?'

'Yes...' Matti mumbled, and now the satisfaction he had felt a moment ago was gone and he felt oddly embarrassed, perhaps because his dad was so poor. 'I don't know. He and my mum aren't really on speaking terms, she wouldn't open the door when he came round. He left the stuff on the step and Mum picked it up later. Maybe someone nicked it...'

'Yeah right! If a thief found all that stuff on the step they wouldn't take the card and leave the phone. This can only mean one of two things.'

'What do you mean?'

'Your dad's really strapped for cash, that's obvious... I doubt you'll be moving just yet. Or maybe someone else took it...'

'What?'

For a moment Leena didn't say anything; she sighed heavily, as though something had upset her, and without looking at him she finally said: 'You'll figure it out soon enough.'

40. *Realisation*

'Hmmph.' Mikko felt his throat move, but he didn't make a sound. It was almost like a whimper, after crying, but he hadn't been crying, at least not that he had noticed. But in his mind he had been; once again he felt as if he had been thrashing about beneath the surface of the marsh, eyeless fish shouting all around him. His hands dangled beside him like a pair of dead bats.

Why had he gone there at all? And of his own free will! He had known exactly what would happen: they weren't going to help him in the slightest. Perhaps he was imagining things, but he had felt as though his mother and father had in fact been pleased about his difficulties and his depression, as these things only strengthened their wishes: that in no way could he ever be good and successful. It seemed incredible that some parents wanted this for their children, but in his case it was the sad truth.

From his earliest memories, nothing he had ever done had been considered good or well done. 'We should have known,' they said, or 'You know it'll never amount to anything.' As a child and a young man those were the two sentences he had heard most often. The third was 'Shame on you!' He remembered the first time he had managed to slide a maggot on to a hook by himself and had caught his first ever fish. Excitedly he had run to show his parents, his father had merely glanced over his shoulder and snorted: 'It's only a roach. Come and show us when you've caught a real fish.' And when, after a year's hard work in the woodwork class at school, he had produced a coat hanger – or at least something resembling a coat hanger – the following spring his mother had taken it to the cottage and used it to heat up the stove.

'Damn it, damn it, damn it,' he cursed to himself, wondering why all the humiliation of the past few decades was suddenly flooding back to his mind, though the reason for this was clear enough.

His parents' message, which as a child he had accepted as the truth, was: 'You do not deserve our love'. Behind this lay another message: 'You are no good, and you have no place feeling good, because there is something wrong with you'. On one level he had tried to deal with these sentiments over the years in his diaries, but never in such a concrete way as now. He also realised that his current problems all stemmed from his past, even the fact that he was unable to write. In fact, it wasn't so much a question of ability as not allowing himself to feel good, to reap what writing and being a writer meant to him, as this would have represented a defiance of the most important authority figures in his life – and that in turn was bad and shameful.

He trudged past Johanneksen Kirkko – it was in this church that he had been baptised and taken his first communion – and he was so immersed in the depths of his own wretchedness that he didn't really notice the individuals around him; all he sensed was that he was walking in a throng of rushing people. A few times he almost bumped into someone walking the other direction. And then he felt it once again, that same awkwardness, as sharp and sudden as a pinprick: someone was staring at him! Or following him. He stopped and spun around: nothing but a crowd of people strolling past. He turned back, crossed the street and continued on his way, his steps somewhat calmer.

With each step his mind slowly began to relax. His thoughts returned to his meeting that morning; sitting there he had realised that throughout his whole life he had had entirely the wrong impression of himself. He had always thought that there was something wrong with him, that there was something inside him making him bad, preventing him from being good. He had written about this in his diaries, but now in some way it had become more real: his parents were the ones with the problem, his mother and father. Admitting this was still intolerably difficult, it felt almost blasphemous. Now it dawned on him that as a child he had denied himself the right to accept the painful truth: that his mother and father were wicked people. At the same time it dawned on him that had he not been able to suppress this thought, he would have been too afraid to live.

His parents lacked the fundamental ability to love – they couldn't even love their own children. This alone went a long way towards explaining the brutality he and his sisters had experienced as children. One of his most terrifying memories was of when he had been out rowing with his mother and father, and for some reason they had started arguing in the middle of the open lake. His father had started rocking the boat from side to side, it started taking on water, and all the time he kept shouting: 'I'll drown us all!' Mikko was so young he couldn't even swim.

He remembered everything, and the thought made him suddenly nauseous, as if the coffee he had just drunk had turned bitter and was rising up in his throat. He leant up against the wall of a house; he rested on the window ledge, staring vacantly at his hands and feet, repeating to himself like a mantra: 'There is nothing wrong with me.'

41. Solution

'*Eupatorus gracilioprnis!*' he exclaimed to himself, for now a terrific excitement grew within him. It felt as though a hot summer's day were sweltering inside him, like a storm brewing. It was the same feeling he always experienced just before Maammo appeared to him. And now that he was surrounded by people, and not deep underground in Maammo's temple, he felt a burning need to preach to them, to proclaim the Coming of the Truth. Still he managed to control his excitement, for he could still see Mikko Matias and did not want to reveal himself so soon.

'*Ea lesum!*'

How well he had succeeded in solving the problem at hand! This was not just any solution; this bordered on genius itself. For, in this new way, in conducting this sacrifice he need not usurp the authority vested in him. Indeed, he would be able to carry out an act of such grace that he would live on as part of Maammo for billions of years, wandering from one Big Bang to the next. And what could be more magnificent: with this act he would defeat the heathen God!

According to stories in the Bible, God sacrificed his only son Jesus, and this was seen as a sign of his great love towards mankind. But he would go one better, for nowhere in Maammo's laws did it state that the adopted sacrificial victim had to be a child, it could just as easily be an adult.

'*Cum sabateum!*'

Everything was perfectly clear. All he had to do was hurry back to the top of The Brocken, set his pigeon trap and sacrifice another three pigeons. In this way he could adopt Mikko Matias and claim him as his son too – and then he would show their God. He would sacrifice *two* of his sons, whereas God had sacrificed only one.

'*Res in cardine est,*' he whooped, for he had had yet another revelation. For final confirmation he would ask the Five Wise Ones for advice. They were there for all to see, but only earth spirits were blessed with the knowledge that they were in fact the Five Wise Ones and that they could answer any question, as long as you could understand their language. He could do this well, as could all earth spirits. The trick was that the speech of the Five Wise Ones could not be heard, it had to be seen.

He no longer cared for Mikko Matias and let him disappear into the crowds of people. Mikko Matias was heading towards Hakaniemi, but here their paths would separate, for now he turned and began walking towards the Central Railway Station. A moment later he noticed that he was hurrying – running as fast as he could, shoving people out of his way and scoffing at them as he passed: '*Merde essum!*' he cursed, though they knew not what he was saying.

42. *Critical Moments*

Harjunpää felt clammy and uncomfortable, so much so that it could easily have been a slushy, foggy morning in November and not spring at all. From Onerva's silence he guessed that her state of mind wasn't any chirpier than his own. It was all because the case had reached a dead-end: they had two deaths, neither of which they could categorically say was a homicide, no clear suspect, barely a shred of evidence, not even a clear line of investigation. It was almost as if they had been suddenly crippled, stripped of their professional skills.

They sat together in a car parked by the side of the Central Railway Station and wondered where to go next. They had already been to Kaisaniemi underground station, as Harjunpää had felt the need to see the scene of the first death, from Lörtsy's old case. Ultimately this had been of very little use; it hadn't given him any clearer a picture of what had taken place, and now he felt somehow drawn to the Railway Station. He had the uneasy feeling that something would soon happen there too.

'I just can't think of a possible motive,' Onerva sighed, finally bringing the long, grey silence to an end. 'Especially since there seems to be no connection between the two victims, nothing linking them to one another.'

'I know. If it is the old biddy I saw, I'd have to put it down to insanity or some sort of paranoia.'

'Another possibility I thought of...' she began, but left the sentence unfinished and pointed instead at the radio. 'Hang on. What was that?'

'I wasn't listening...'

'It was about someone preaching,' she said and a sparkle appeared in her eyes. She snatched the radio from the dashboard and brought it swiftly towards her mouth.

'Switchboard. This is unit 189. Can you repeat that, please?'

'Sure. There's a three-three wandering around on the ground floor of the Sanomatalo building; preaching to people, kneeling in front of the lifts praying and trying to force people to do the same.'

'Male or female?' asked Onerva, as she bit her lower lip and held her breath. The silence seemed to last unbearably long, spanning out across metres of time.

'An elderly man,' the duty officer finally replied. Harjunpää and Onerva looked at one another in disappointment.

'Unit 189 will take it. We've got a visual on the building. It may be linked to our case too.'

'You're not on the system... Okay. Crime Squad Unit 189 is on its way.'

'Roger.'

Harjunpää had already turned the ignition key and the car roared into life. A moment later he slipped into first gear, gently eased the accelerator and steered the car on to the road. He could already see their destination, the transparent glass walls of the Sanomatalo building rising up on the corner, bearing neon advertisements one above the other. He was forced to drive the last stretch of the journey against the flow of the traffic, but he and Onerva had worked together long enough that she could almost read his mind: she grabbed the emergency light from beside her feet, all but threw it on top of the dashboard and flicked the switch, sending its blue light flashing in all directions.

'Why did we take this job?' asked Harjunpää, who was still unsure of the situation.

'Because preachers like that more than likely know one another. Let's just calm him down first.'

'Sounds good to me,' Harjunpää said firmly, bringing the car to a halt. Despite the rush he still remembered to lock the doors – a microphone had been stolen from an unlocked patrol car only a few weeks previously.

They slipped through the revolving doors and came out into a corridor full of shops, at the end of which was the ground floor hall. There were no great crowds of people to be seen, just the odd passer-by hurrying along. In the open acoustic they could hear the shouting clearly: '*Ea Iesum! Cum sabateum!*'

'Over there,' said Onerva curtly. Directly in front of them stood a row of decorative bushes the size of trees, and from the right of the bushes came the shouting. The man had sunk to his knees and was facing the lifts, his upper body swaying. The lifts had been designed so that all their mechanisms and weights could be seen behind a glass wall. The machinery was dotted here and there with bright yellow pulleys. It was a beautiful, ingenious construction. Everyday machines suddenly formed a mobile of sorts: one lift went up, another soon followed it, while a third was on its way back down. At a glance he counted a total of five lifts standing side by side.

It seemed as though the man on his knees had sensed their arrival; he spun round to face them and caught Harjunpää's gaze. He turned immediately, as if in an attempt to stand up or run away, but before he could straighten his body fully his hands flew up to his chest, he collapsed to his knees once again and finally landed on his forehead, a dull thud resounding as his skull struck the stone floor.

'Epilepsy,' Onerva gasped, and they broke into a run. They didn't have far to go, twenty metres at most. No one else seemed to pay the man the slightest attention. Though some glanced over their shoulders before continuing on their way.

'Let's get him into the recovery position,' said Onerva sharply as they bent over the man, grabbing hold of him. At a glance the man looked slightly the worse for wear, but by no means had he reached the down-and-out stage yet. His thick-rimmed glasses had fallen off and slid across the floor; his cap had also slipped off, revealing a silvery grey ponytail tied up on the crown of his head. The man was neither whimpering nor shaking. Harjunpää placed his fingers on the man's neck, then frantically tried the other side.

'No pulse,' he whispered, then tried his wrist, remembering to put his fingers in the correct place. 'Nothing. He's stopped breathing! Let's get him on to his back!'

They each grabbed hold of the man and began rolling him over. Despite their haste Harjunpää noted that the man smelled rather stale, yet somehow strangely familiar. The man's hand fell lifelessly to the ground, like that of a body before the onset of rigor mortis.

'Still nothing. Come on old boy, wakey wakey!' Harjunpää panted and slapped the man's face, but he didn't react in the slightest. Onerva had already pulled his jacket open; she then tore at his shirt, sending the buttons flying - revealing a bony, hairless, grey chest. It wasn't moving.

'Hey!' Harjunpää shouted at a woman who had stopped further back. 'Call an ambulance! Tell them the patient is male, in his fifties. He's stopped breathing.'

'How does it go again?' whispered Onerva, her voice clearly trembling. 'I'm not sure I... wait a minute. First two breaths, then fifteen rapid compressions – quite fast, about a hundred per minute. Put your hands here. Right, just below the rib cage. A few finger-widths upwards; fingers pointing towards the throat and the other palm on top. I'll breathe first...'

Harjunpää hesitated for a moment. The man looked dirty and unkempt, and his lips were cracked. But they had no other option: the man's life was literally in their hands. He stuck his fingers into the man's mouth – he had been right: he fished out first the upper then the lower set of false teeth. They were slippery and a glistening thread of spittle dangled suspended from the man's mouth. Harjunpää quickly wiped it away, held the man's nose firmly with one hand, lifted his chin with the other and angled his head backwards, keeping the windpipe open all the time. He took a deep breath and bent over the man's gaping, toothless mouth. It resembled an axe wound in a corpse. At the last moment he closed his eyes, felt the man's lifeless lips against his own and blew as hard as he could. As if from the distance he could hear Onerva shouting: 'It's working, his chest is rising!'

He breathed into him again, it was no easier than the first time. Then he sat up dizzily, shaking as Onerva began the compressions.

'Fifteen, count them! Then I'll give him two more breaths.'

Once again his lips were against the man's mouth and he blew hard, took a deep breath and blew for a second time, then Onerva's hands began bobbing up and down again. Harjunpää felt for the man's pulse, and he thought he could sense something, but maybe it was only the result of Onerva's compressions. He recalled that you were only supposed to check for a pulse after the compressions. He breathed into him again and again, but still there was nothing, not the slightest pulse.

He remembered reading that resuscitation by amateurs very rarely succeeded in starting the heart again, that this required injections and all sorts of things, but that its purpose was to maintain a constant flow of oxygen until professional help arrived. They had no option but to carry on until the paramedics arrived, and they certainly couldn't leave him be or pronounce him dead, as there were no other obvious signs of death. In circumstances like this only a doctor can pronounce a person dead. Again he blew hard, he had to catch his breath, Onerva counted her compressions, and he could feel the stone floor pressing hard against his knees. It seemed to go on and on, minute after minute, everything lasting an eternity. Again he breathed in, again. Only then could he make out the faint sound of the siren switching off and soon afterwards the patter of soft shoes fast approaching.

The men were wearing white jackets, the same jackets that Harjunpää had seen at hundreds of different crime scenes; he even recognised one of the men - Ruija. He threw his bag to the floor and wrenched it open; his partner knelt over the man and felt around his neck.

'We've got a pulse!' he exclaimed almost in disbelief. 'You got it started again. It's an even, steady rhythm.'

'His eyes are moving too. They're opening.'

Harjunpää slowly withdrew from the group and wiped his mouth and tongue on the sleeve of his jumper, but it wasn't enough: he needed a toothbrush.

'What if we were mistaken?' Onerva panted, droplets of sweat sparkling on her forehead.

'We weren't... you felt it yourself.'

'Then he owes his life to us.'

The man was trying to sit up and the paramedics almost had to push him back down by force. He was frantically trying to say something, and only after a moment could they properly make it out: 'Whea ma teef?'

Harjunpää picked the false teeth from the ground and pressed them into the man's hand. He clenched them carefully and appeared to calm down considerably. Harjunpää instinctively wiped the palm of his hand on his trouser leg. From his inside pocket he produced his card and slipped it into the man's jacket. He swallowed. He felt as if he had tasted Death itself. He swiftly brought his hand up to his mouth and ran off towards the nearest of the decorative trees.

43. *Compact Disc*

'What SIM card?' his mum yawned. She was annoyed that he had come to the newsagent's. For some reason she didn't like him coming to her workplace at all. From the way she refused to look at him when she was speaking, Matti knew she was lying. 'If your father was stupid enough to leave it lying on the step, then you can be sure it's long gone.'

'It wasn't just lying there - it was in one of those packets.'

His mum didn't say anything and pretended to look for something on the shelf beneath the counter – but not for him. He didn't enjoy visiting her workplace either. The boys at school had described her as being the easiest of all the staff to pull one over on. One of them would ask her to look for a magazine they probably didn't even stock, while the others would fill their pockets with whatever they wanted, out of sight of the security camera. Thankfully they didn't know that she was his mother.

'Oh, the packet!' she said, trying to look surprised, as though she had just remembered something. That was how she had managed to trick and mislead the entire family, and now she was pulling the wool over Roo's eyes too; he did whatever she wanted. 'Yes, there was a packet in there... I thought it must have been a CD your father was returning.'

'You didn't throw it out, did you?'

'Of course not. It's on the shelf next to the video tapes. But don't touch them, they belong to Kari.'

'Thanks a lot,' said Matti, and now it was he who couldn't bring himself to look at her. He couldn't understand what she had meant by all this, she probably thought of it as simply another way to annoy him. He turned around and walked out.

'*A CD!*' he scoffed. '*She sells exactly the same packets in the newsagent's!*'

44. *The Teachings of Jabalpur*

'*Mortui non silent,*' he muttered to himself, fingering the card carefully, suspiciously, as if it were contaminated in some way. Once again he was twenty-five rungs underground, in his home at the heart of the rock. '*Eccu larum rosaece...*'

They had forcibly taken a scan or something of his heart. He was not quite certain, as he had not visited a doctor or been to a hospital for many years. But their scan had revealed nothing, so once he had begun playing the difficult patient – and he certainly knew how to do this when necessary – and showered them with horrific curses, they had all but thrown him out.

His heart had not really stopped: with the power of his mind he was able to slow his pulse so that his heart beat only once every ten or even fifteen seconds; and no one had the patience to check a lifeless artery for such a long time. He had learnt how to do this in India, in a town called Jabalpur, where he had spent almost five years back when he had first realised what a pack of lies the teachings of the church really were; but he had not converted to Hinduism, Buddhism or Islam. The only drawback was that he could only sustain this bodily state for four minutes at a time. His mentor in Jabalpur, Laximidas Tagore, could remain in this state for up to an hour. He was also able to dangle from a noose for a full two minutes, and could slide a knitting needle through his arm or palm without feeling the slightest pain, without shedding a single drop of blood.

It was strange being in a state of slowed heart activity; his body felt very heavy, but still he seemed to be floating, suspended in some form of liquid, and although he could not see a thing because his eyes were closed, in some miraculous way he was able to sense everything happening around him. Only once he had begun to discern a quiet rushing sound in his ears did he know that it was time to return his heartbeat to its normal rate again. He rubbed his forehead; a small bump had appeared. He had had to act at the beginning, pressing his hands against his chest and falling to the ground, but as soon as he was lying down he was able to control his heartbeat at will.

'Helsinki Police Department, Violent Crimes Division,' he read aloud from the card. 'Detective Superintendent Timo Harjunpää.'

This was the man that had startled him; he recognised him as the same man that had come to the underground station on the day of the sacrifice and to whom he had tried to preach. For a moment he had been sure that the man had recognised him too, for at first he did not remember that on that particular day Maammo had wished him to appear in the form of a woman.

'Timo Harjunpää,' he repeated. He did not like the name. He did not like the man either, for he had committed a gross profanity by touching the earth spirit's mouth –with his lips! This was simply not done and would not be tolerated, for the law of Maammo declared it an evil sin; and should anyone commit such a sin, he would not go unpunished. He wiped his mouth on the back of his hand, over and over again, for he felt as though something dirty had been left on his lips – after all, the man was an infidel and, as a policeman, he was a representative of the entire infidel society, much like a priest.

He sat there a moment longer, lost in thought, then stood up. Holding the card gently between his fingernails, he stepped over to the bedside table, placed it on the rough surface next to the storm lantern and knelt down. Stuck into the furthest plank of the chest were nine black-headed pins standing neatly in a row. Their colour was important; red, blue or white pins would not do. He picked one of them up and slowly stuck it through the card. There came an almost imperceptible pop as it pierced the card and struck the board beneath. He pricked it again, over and over, until the tiny holes formed a pentagon directly above the words 'Timo Harjunpää'; then, little by little, a large letter M gradually appeared within the pentagon, representing the word '*mortuus*' – body, death.

45. *Deep Underground*

Common sense had told Harjunpää that he probably hadn't caught anything serious, but as the day drew on he remembered the man's chapped lips all the more clearly, and realised that blood could well have been seeping out behind those loose flakes of dry skin. Finally he had decided to tell a little white lie: he claimed that the man had split his lip when he fell over, so that during the resuscitation he had come into contact with blood. He was therefore immediately sent to Aurora hospital for an HIV test and anti-hepatitis drugs.

He still wasn't sure how he would be able to tell Elisa.

As the day slowly faded into evening, the worst of the rush hour was over. Onerva, Piipponen and Harjunpää were on the upper underground level of the Central Railway Station, standing next to the compass mosaic on the floor. The letter N for North was directly beneath Harjunpää's feet.

'I think it would be best if we split up,' he said. 'Piip, you take the next west-bound train to Ruoholahti; Onerva and I can take the next two trains going east.'

'But won't it be a bit difficult to apprehend her if we're by ourselves?'

'Just shadow her to start with, and alert us by mobile. We'll only try to talk to her once we've all regrouped.'

'What about the stations in between?'

'Get off at every station and give it a thorough going over, wait for the next train and carry on. Have a look on the ground and in the bins for pamphlets or flyers of a religious nature. If so, she might be very close by.'

'And when the line splits?'

'You take the Mellunmäki branch, I'll go to Vuosaari; we'll do exactly the same on the way back too. Once we're done, we'll meet back here and decide whether it's worth doing another round.'

They looked at each other for a moment; they were all utterly expressionless, and the matter seemed to be clear. A camera dangled from Piipponen's wrist; at the very least they wanted to try and photograph her.

'Elderly female, grey hair down to her shoulders,' Harjunpää recapped. 'A beret pulled down to her ears, possibly some sort of long skirt. Sharp-chinned old crone.'

'More than likely preaching and handing out some sort of leaflets.'

'Let's get to it,' said Onerva decisively, and with that they turned and made their way past the ticket machines and on to the jolting, downward escalators. A light draught blew up towards them, carrying the slightest hint of dampness, of the underground; the odour growing stronger all the time, yet remaining virtually imperceptible.

Piipponen walked several metres ahead, a number of people stood between them, and above the clunking of the escalators he couldn't hear a thing. Harjunpää whispered to Onerva: 'I'll give him his due, he's pretty hard-working – works his arse off. I happened to see his timesheet and even yesterday he was there until about eleven.'

'Yeah, yeah' Onerva scoffed cynically, as though she were not amused in the slightest. 'So you've never worked with him before?'

'No. We've been on night-duty together a few times, but that's it.'

'Come on, Timo...'

'What's that supposed to mean?'

'It's not even worth telling you. For all I know it's probably just gossip.'

'You've started now.'

'Well... You know he lives in Kivihaka, only a few kilometres up the road. Word is he works late almost every night doing a spot of his own 'business'. Wills, some dodgy dealings, that sort of thing. That's his idea of overtime.'

'What the...?'

'Apparently he sometimes turns up in a sweaty tracksuit, like he's just come in from a jog, and paces around for half an hour with a pile of papers in his hands, making sure that everyone on night shift notices he's there.'

'You've got to be kidding…He's pretty convincing, though.'

'He even pretends to be angry if anyone suspects he's up to no good.'

They were approaching the underground platforms and the wail of a departing train could be heard: *phuii – phuii!* A moment later crowds of people began flooding on to the escalator opposite; men and women of all ages, and considering the time of day a great number of teenagers - children even.

'That was my train, it was going west,' Piiponen shouted back to them. 'I'll get the next one. I'll call you if anything happens.'

'Yeah, we'll be in touch. I'll meet you back at the compass.'

'Right!'

Harjunpää and Onerva turned left towards the eastbound platform. There were about thirty people waiting, among them a very drunk man, probably just back from a booze-cruise to Tallinn. He offered swigs from any of his numerous bottles to a young girl and boy sitting on one of the benches. Harjunpää let him be. They didn't have time to take care of every trouble-maker they saw; they had a job to take care of, though searching around the underground was rather hit or miss. And then he spotted her.

He recognised her immediately: her clothes, her posture, her slight limp – and for a moment something inside him froze. A chill spread across his skin. Had the impossible suddenly become real?

'Onerva…'

'Yes?'

'There she is. Over there on the far left. This time she's got a blue beret.'

'The skirt's the same. How shall we take this?'

'Let's stroll up closer like we're minding our own business. Then we'll ask her for her papers – there's still five minutes until the next train. Call Piiponen and tell him to get down here.'

'OK.'

They started moving closer to the old woman, slowly winding their way through the crowds of people. Her beret was pulled almost down to her ears and looked like a blue ball covering her head, and beneath it her silver hair flowed loosely. Around her waist was a black and very full-looking bumbag: that must have been where she kept her leaflets. They kept moving closer, the gap between them now less than forty metres. Then all of a sudden the old woman gave a start, turned around and stared right at them. In a flash she was on the move. She ran off towards the end of the platform, and as Harjunpää broke into a run behind her his mind was filled with a sense of victory: she's running into a dead end!

But to his surprise the woman stopped by the platform wall and began frantically rummaging through her bag. Only then did Harjunpää realise that at that point in the wall was a dark-brown, inconspicuous door. He vaguely recalled that the door led down into the shelter beneath the station, or else into one of the tunnels connecting the tracks, and he quickened his step, knocking people out of his way. 'Sorry!' he yelled.

The old woman glanced at him. There was something oddly familiar about her face, particularly her mouth, and from somewhere other than their encounter at Hakaniemi underground station. The woman clearly realised that she wouldn't have time to open the door, if that was what she was planning, the hefty lock gleamed in the light before her; she let go of her bag and set off running again. The hem of her skirt flapped behind her like the wings of a giant vampire, but she could do nothing about the fact that she was running into a dead end.

'Police! Stop!' shouted Harjunpää, the words echoed off the stone walls of the tunnel as though someone had repeated his command, but the old woman did not look back. It was then that she took him utterly by surprise: she hopped down off the platform and onto the tracks, as light and nimble as a deer. Her skirt momentarily fluttered up like a bell, and a moment later she was inside the rock-hewn tunnel. The darkness swallowed her, leaving only her white legs flashing behind her.

Harjunpää stopped running, but his shoes slid along the floor and he almost collided with the wall at the end of the platform. A white placard stood in front of him: NO ENTRY. TUNNEL. KAISANIEMI 597m. He could clearly make out the woman's steps crunching against the gravel as she ran. He knew full well that it was expressly forbidden to go on to the tracks - it could be life-threatening – but the woman running away might be guilty of two murders.

He hopped on to the tracks. The drop was well over a metre and he almost fell to his knees, but eventually he managed to regain his balance and began running into the darkness, all the time fumbling for the torch in his pocket. Behind him he could hear Onerva's frantic, almost furious cries. 'Timo! Come back you idiot!'

Harjunpää didn't pay any attention to her. The old woman wouldn't have run away unless she had a very good reason, not to mention risking her life by jumping on to the tracks. In addition to this, a gut reaction told Harjunpää he would catch her very soon, as there couldn't possibly be anywhere in the tunnel for her to hide. He would have to hurry, and he hoped that there wouldn't be a scuffle – there couldn't have been more than four minutes until the arrival of the next train from the west. His heart beat so strongly that he could feel it in his temples, and the back of his shirt was already drenched with sweat. Around him lingered the smell of stone, and of oil that had seeped from the trains over the years.

A gap appeared suddenly in the left-hand wall, enabling him to see the opposite track. Light shone in from the platform. Something must have warned him, perhaps a faint breeze from below, and he stopped in his tracks. He gasped for breath, took out his torch and switched it on. He had indeed stopped just in time: in front of him gaped a black hole in the ground, then another, a third. There was a whole series of gaps; at this point the track ran across a bridge of some sort. But what exactly lay beneath?

He aimed his torch into the first of the gaps: the light only just reached the bottom of the shaft, but it was enough for him to make out the tracks of an intersecting tunnel further down. He noticed a railing running down the right-hand edge of the gap and moved towards it. He had guessed correctly: it was a ladder attached to the side of the shaft, leading down to the tunnel below. From the light of the torch he guessed that it was between three and four metres to the bottom. At the base of the ladder lay something on the floor, and when he looked closely he realised it was a blue beret. The old woman had gone that way. But how many minutes did he have before the next train arrived?

He was careful not to go near the bright yellow metallic rail running upside down along the tracks; this supplied the trains with electricity - the voltage was enormous. He gripped the ladder firmly, turned to face the tracks and began lowering himself downwards. For some reason he counted the eight steps before he reached the bottom. The ground in the lower tunnel was covered in coarse gravel.

Harjunpää crouched down and picked up the beret. He knew that he ought to have been carrying a plastic bag in case of finding any potential forensic evidence, but on this occasion he didn't have one. Instead he carefully folded the beret –it might contain strands of hair, some of which could still be attached their roots, and these could then be used to determine the DNA of the beret's owner. He put the hat in his pocket.

Which direction now? At a loss, he stood there listening for a moment. A distant humming could be heard, like the sound of a large machine, as though the earth itself were drawing breath, and from the left he could hear something else. A scraping sound perhaps? The crunch of gravel beneath someone's feet? He decided to follow it. But before leaving he lifted the edge of his jacket, flicked open his revolver case and pulled out the gun inside; its rubber handle fitted his hand perfectly, and had a strangely calming effect on him.

A moment later and he was on the move again, sprinting forwards, the light from his torch caressing the ground and walls in front of him. Along the left at ground level ran a concrete gully containing a number of pipes and possibly a cable, while along the ceiling ran a set of even larger pipes which shone dimly in the torchlight. He recalled that this communal tunnel was used for almost everything: water and drainage, heating, electricity, telephone cables. It also occurred to him that he ought to be wearing a hard hat, as the rock faces hadn't been secured with concrete, but had instead been left just as they were after quarrying – a large rock could easily have fallen on any unlucky person passing through.

The tunnel veered round a corner and the distant light from the station disappeared entirely. Harjunpää was enveloped by the darkness, which was lit only by the weak beam of light from his torch. Something began to puzzle him. How had a beret that was pulled so tightly round her head simply fallen off? And how could a frail old thing like her have jumped down on to the tracks so easily, not to mention climbing down the ladder? His mouth felt dry and he wet his lips. Had he been lured into a trap? In such thick darkness the light from his torch made him a sitting duck. He held his hand to one side and covered the lamp, allowing only thin filaments of light to trickle between his fingers.

He pointed the light towards the ceiling. Fluorescent light strips dangled at regular intervals, but he couldn't see a switch anywhere. He focussed once again on the ground and something at the side of the tunnel suddenly caught his attention. Had the old woman dropped a scarf perhaps? Or was it something else? He listened carefully for a moment, but still could make out nothing but a distant humming, and the sound of his own rasping breath. He began slowly making his way towards the object; he stopped and crouched down – and at first couldn't quite understand what he saw.

In a neat row on the ground in front of him lay a collection of dead pigeons. There were probably a dozen or so altogether; some already shrivelled and decomposing, though a number of them looked fresh. Each one of them had had its throat slit, and when he turned one of them over he saw that its chest had been cut open too, exposing the bloody innards.

'Good God,' he stammered, and wondered how the pigeons had ended up so far underground. There was no way they could have flown down here, that much he realised at once; something or someone must have brought them here. It couldn't have been an animal? What animal could have gone outside to hunt them and then returned down here? And what about the cuts?

It had to be a person. But what sort of person? An wizard, involved in some evil form of witchcraft? The thought was a disquieting one, and Harjunpää had the inexplicable feeling that that same person was very close indeed, watching him – if not preparing to attack.

He spun around, but he must have been imagining it: there was no one behind him. Again he thought he heard something, this time from the opposite direction, and he turned back around – but still he saw nothing. He could have sworn he'd heard the gravel crunch beneath someone's cautious feet.

'Come out! Police!' he shouted. His voice echoed against the rock, stretching further and further into the depths of the tunnel before finally disappearing as though the rock had swallowed it. A fear grew within him, the terrifying thought that the rock would swallow him too. He sensed something dark and malevolent about the place, and wanted desperately to return to the surface.

He had spun around so much that he could no longer remember which direction he had come from. About ten metres behind him he could make out the opening of a subsidiary tunnel. Was that the right way?

'Calm down,' he told himself, but it didn't help. On top of everything else some sort of claustrophobic angst began to overwhelm him, though never before had he been affected by anything like it.

He could feel beads of sweat forming on his forehead and he wet his lips once again. And of course, the light in his torch began to falter; it glowed dimly, like the setting sun. Now he was in a hurry. Still he managed to concentrate: he had first noticed the pigeons on his right and now they were on his left, so all he had to do was carry on straight ahead.

He bent down and grabbed one of the dead birds with the same hand his torch was in – and only then did he notice that something had been sprayed on the rock in front of him. There was not very much of it, only a few droplets, forming small rivulets, and he realised that it must be blood.

'Ugh,' he spat, and broke into a run. He suddenly felt that the hunter had become the hunted, and that something was right on his heels. Just then a familiar buzz could be heard from above: the fluorescent lamps began to flicker, and a moment later they shone fully and Harjunpää was forced to shut his eyes. He could hear heavy steps approaching, perhaps the steps of several people, then he felt the powerful beams of two lamps shining directly at his face. Through his blinking he could see that the men were wearing the familiar helmets and reflective black jackets of the fire brigade.

'Put the gun down! Now!' shouted one of them. Another exclaimed: 'Harjunpää! What the hell's going on?'

Harjunpää recognised the voice. It was Eki Tattari from the fire station downtown.

46. *Headlines*

Although spring was well on its way, the mornings were still cold and bracing. The wind almost burned into the knuckles of cyclists, and because of this Harjunpää was wearing a pair of leather gloves. He was on his way to work in Pasila, peddling towards Masala station as fast as he could. He had left the house in a rush, unable to find his keys – he had later found them in his trouser pocket.

He sped past the kiosk at Masala Station and continued for about another twenty metres before he fully understood what he had just seen. He braked suddenly; the wheels screeched and the bicycle lurched forward. He jumped from the saddle, letting the bike fall to the ground, its mudguards rattling, and ran back to the kiosk.

'Christ Almighty,' he seethed; he had seen correctly after all. The headline of one of the tabloids read: COPPER BRINGS TUBE TO STANDSTILL. Another read: FIRE CREW SAVES POLICEMAN FROM PIGEONS. The first one came complete with a photograph of a fireman standing on the platform holding out his hand, and Harjunpää himself standing on the tracks looking bewildered by all the lights and fuss. He was carrying one of the dead pigeons, its wings dangling sorrowfully towards the ground.

'Christ Almighty,' he sighed once again, and he suddenly felt a wave of nausea wash over him. He recalled his possible infection too, how he hadn't dared kiss Elisa that night, and for a moment he had to lean against the wall of the kiosk, supporting himself with both hands. He vaguely remembered the flash of the cameras, but he had thought the photographer was just another fireman.

Onerva hadn't been sure that the next train would stop at all, leaving her unable to warn the driver – it could have been a service train rattling through the station without stopping – and so she had pulled the emergency communication cord on the platform, cutting off the flow of electricity to the trains throughout that whole sector of the network; and because one sector was down the entire network had had to be closed.

Outside the Central Railway Station a sea of blue emergency lights had been flashing in the dusk. There were two ambulances, a SWAT team, a fire engine and two squad cars. Central had reported the incident to the division responsible for the downtown area, but Harjunpää still didn't know whether charges would be brought against him. He wasn't particularly well acquainted with the laws on matters of this nature, but jumping on to the tracks might well come under 'causing rail traffic disturbance'.

From the sound of the engine and the screech of the tracks he realised that his train was just pulling out of the station – the next one wouldn't be along for at least another half hour – and for a moment he seriously considered returning home, going to bed and huddling under the covers. He was only too aware of what would be awaiting him at work.

'It's Tunnel-Boy Timo!'

'Since when is it our job to investigate animal deaths?'

'Screw that poor pigeon to death, did you?'

'Christ Almighty,' he sighed for a third time and trudged back to his bicycle. As if to cap it all off, the glass in the front lamp had shattered when the bike hit the ground.

47. *Surprise*

Mikko was pacing up and down along the edge of the platform at Hakaniemi underground station. He couldn't yet hear the screech of the tracks, or even the faint hum that always precedes it. According to the screen the next train would arrive in a minute's time. There were lots of different thoughts simultaneously spinning through his mind, overlapping each other. As one thought drifted into the background another would make its presence felt more powerfully. He thought of the strange sadness he had felt since Sanna had moved out. She and her friend had taken care of the entire move, and although he cherished his privacy and his peace and quiet, now it seemed that he had far too much.

His thoughts turned to Matti, and whether he would move in to replace Sanna. He wondered how the two of them would get on; since the divorce Matti had clearly felt estranged from his father. Perhaps it was because he had initially asked only Sanna to move in with him. For Matti the full onset of puberty was yet to come. He thought about the love between mother and child. This was generally considered the greatest and noblest of loves, almost sacred, but it wasn't always so perfect. For countless atrocities have been committed in the name of that love - poisoning the minds and souls of young people; abandoning them to drink and drugs; leaving them to wind up in mental institutions or to take their own lives.

The greatest of all loves is a child's love. It banishes all those demons, shuts out the beatings, the humiliation, the abuse. Children instinctively love their parents, because they need to believe that their parents are good people, so that when they are with them they can feel safe and loved. This love is so great that it can sometimes cost them their lives.

He thought of where he could hire a van to help Matti move. He didn't have a credit card and no firm would rent him a van without one. He wondered whether his old friend Kari Häyrinen would remember him. Though they had known each other since they were children, it must have been a year since they'd last seen one another, and even then it had only been by chance. After their meeting Kari had got into a dark-blue van. Did he still have his phone number? Then again, it would be a bit embarrassing to look up an old friend just because he needed his help. It would be no use asking people at the post office, that much he knew from experience. But how had Sanna sorted out her move?

He could just make out the distant rumble of the approaching train. Light reflected first off the wall where the tunnel gently curved round, then shone bright along the tracks. To Mikko it all seemed rather beautiful, like fire tearing along the tracks. The engine lamps came into view, growing larger all the while, then the first carriage appeared and the train began to slow. *Phiuu-phiuu...*

Mikko didn't quite know what happened. He felt a powerful shove from behind, almost like being tackled in a game of ice hockey; all of a sudden he was leaning forward, hanging over the emptiness in front of him, his arms thrashing wildly. His satchel went flying, his balance eventually gave way and he could feel himself falling. Two thoughts shot through his mind: *Is this the way it's all going to end? Don't fall!* A steely, metallic shriek pealed out as the driver desperately tried to slam on the emergency brakes.

48. *Set-Back*

There was quite a commotion in Mäki's office when Harjunpää finally arrived at the police station in Pasila. Piipponen was talking loudly, emphatically trying to get his point across: 'It would be insane not to look into this!'

'But there's well over two hundred kilometres worth of track in the network. Where would we get the man-power to investigate it thoroughly?'

'We'd ask for volunteers, the same way we get people together for door-to-door enquiries.'

'But a lot of the areas down there are shut off to the public,' said Onerva. 'Some of them belong to the army, some to the government. In any case, we'd need a team of guides from Geotechnics. As far as I could make out from that phone call they just can't spare the resources at the moment.'

Harjunpää realised that they were discussing the network of underground tunnels hidden beneath the city. It was also clear that Piipponen saw this as an opportunity to do as much overtime as he wanted. Harjunpää felt relieved. In the corridor he had bumped into the head of Violent Crimes, DCI Rantanen; he had been standing there holding both tabloids when he'd arrived.

'Timo,' Rantanen had said. 'Was it absolutely necessary to run into that tunnel?'

'Yes. The woman we were looking for ran in there.'

'Onerva has filled me in,' he'd replied, and there hadn't been the slightest trace of disapproval or amusement in his voice. Everyone who worked in the Crime Squad knew full well that at any moment you could be faced with some of the oddest situations. 'I'll be in touch with the downtown division. No need to worry about any repercussions.'

'Thanks.'

'And what's this thing about the keys?' Mäki asked, nodding towards Harjunpää. 'I see you've made the front page.'

'Looks like it.'

'Not to worry, only it's stirred up rumours of a serial killer again.'

'I'm sorry…'

'That's all right. So what about the keys?'

'It was seven years ago. One of the guards lost a set of keys, including the master key for the entire underground network. He thought he lost them in a scuffle with some troublemaker, and figured they'd been carted off to sea with the snow.'

'And they haven't noticed anything strange since?'

'No. That key gives access to well over a hundred doors, even some along the streets in the walls of certain houses. There's no way they could have changed all the locks and codes.'

'What about the alarm system?'

'It covers the platforms and pavements, but it's under renovation at the moment. Some of the doors haven't been used for years, the locks have rusted and not all of them work properly.'

'Have you been down there with a sniffer dog?' Harjunpää asked Piipponen, who had promised to take care of the matter first thing that morning.

'Yes,' he replied immediately, staring down at his hands. Red blotches glowed on his cheeks. 'But it didn't get the scent. It just wandered back and forth at the spot where you and the firemen were standing.'

'What about forensics?'

'They couldn't find anything, though there were a few decent hairs on that beret.'

'So it wasn't a complete waste of time after all,' said Harjunpää, and at that moment a thought flashed through his mind as clearly as if someone had whispered to him. 'I'll just throw my jacket in my office, I'll be right back...' he said.

He left the room but walked past his office door and continued further along the corridor. He pressed the door to Piipponen's office with the tips of his fingers, letting it glide silently open. The camera lay on the edge of the table. It was one of those new-fangled ones, light and easy to use; the kind that, apart from pointing it in the right direction, practically took care of the entire operation by itself. He turned the adjustor towards the green letter L at the sensor and looked at the tiny screen on the other edge. This indicated that there was no film in the camera. Immediately his eyes narrowed to mere slits across his face, though he realised that there might well be an innocent explanation for this.

He took his satchel and jacket into his office, and just as he was returning to Mäki's office Rummukainen from Central turned the corner in front of him, his belt quietly jangling. He was carrying a number of video cassettes and a notepad with a few lines of text in tight, pedantic handwriting.

'Good morning! How's our celebrity doing?'

'Give it a rest... Yourself?'

'I think I can shed some light on this shady case of yours.'

'The underground case?'

'Yes. My partner's sitting in the visitors' room with a Mikko Matias Moisio. Heard of him?'

'Isn't he a novelist?'

'That's the one. His novels very nearly came to an abrupt end this morning. Someone shoved him in front of a train at Hakaniemi.'

'And he survived?' asked Harjunpää, his voice coarse with disbelief.

'We're not exactly in the habit of bringing bodies in for interviews. He didn't fall, but managed to jump across the tracks and power cable and landed on the other side. There's just enough room there for a thin person between the train and the wall. He's pretty shaken up though.'

Harjunpää rubbed his neck, utterly dumbfounded. At least now one thing was certain. There was no doubt that what they were dealing with was two murders, plus a third attempted murder.

'What about the perpetrator?'

'Got away in all the commotion. But now we've got descriptions from five different witnesses and some fairly clear footage on these tapes.'

'The silver-haired old woman, right?'

'Not even close – a middle-aged man.'

'A man...?'

'Yes. The opposite of a woman.'

'And all this time we've been looking for a woman,' said Harjunpää. Now he was even more perplexed and began to wonder why things didn't quite add up.

'These things happen, there are always a few little set-backs along the way. 'I'll interview him right away. I'll go and tell the others.'

'Timo, the third name on the list is the one who can best describe the guy. We didn't bother sending forensics down there, as a thousand passengers had already trampled all over the place and we had to get the network back up and running. All the particulars are on page three, including all the measurements too. We photographed the scene and the film's in the lab.'

'Thanks a lot. This is definitely attempted manslaughter, if not attempted murder.'

Rummukainen walked off, his boots softly creaking, and indicated to his partner to follow him. Harjunpää hurried into Mäki's office and shouted from the door. 'We've got another underground case. This one managed to jump across the power cables and got away without a scratch. And guess what?'

'It's that same woman?'

'That's just it – it was a middle-aged man.'

'Great, that's all we need... don't tell me there are two of them on the loose?'

'Piipponen, go and watch these CCTV videos and print off any good images of the guy. Onerva, ring through this list of witnesses, ask them to go through the details again and arrange to bring them in for questioning. I'll go and talk to Moisio.'

'Not Mikko Matias Moisio?'

'The very same.'

'Great, now we'll have the media breathing down our necks again. Try and get him to agree not to go to the press.'

'I'll try.'

Mikko Matias Moisio was a slender man, he looked thoughtful and somewhat downhearted, and when they shook hands Harjunpää could feel he was quivering all over. It would have been wrong to call him shabby, he simply looked as if he didn't have much money; either that or he no longer knew how to take care of himself. Still, the most striking thing about him was his eyes: they were at once sharp and sympathetic.

'It must have been quite a shock. I'll give you the number for Victim Support. They can offer you professional help.'

'I'm sure I'll be OK... It just brought back a wave of bad memories.'

'Indeed,' muttered Harjunpää, allowing the silence to continue until the man sat down and glanced around.

'Perhaps you could tell me in your own words what happened back there?'

'There's not much to tell really. I was waiting for the ten to eight train and was standing at the edge of the platform, lost in thought. And when its lights came into view... Oh God... Then... then I just felt a violent shove at my hips. My bag fell to the ground and I spun my hands round trying to regain my balance. When I realised I was going to fall I tried to propel myself forwards and jumped over the tracks and on to the other side.'

'Did you see who did it?'

'No, I didn't even notice anyone hanging around near me. Those policemen said that you have a number of witnesses. But yesterday...'

'Yes?'

'This probably has nothing to do with it, and I may be mistaken... All day yesterday I had the distinct feeling someone was watching me and following me. Let me assure you I'm not exactly paranoid.'

Moisio's mobile started ringing in his pocket. Harjunpää had forgotten to ask him to turn it off; mobile phones going off during interviews were one of his pet hates. Moisio dug the phone out of his pocket, looked at the screen and clearly didn't recognise the number calling him.

'Moisio... Matti, is that you? So you did get it... I'll call you back soon,' he said quickly, but something inside him snapped and he burst into tears. His sobbing was heavy, painful, and Harjunpää realised straight away that Moisio was not crying merely because of what had happened that morning, but for years of ungrieved pain.

'I'll fetch those cards,' said Harjunpää. He stood up and walked out of the room, went to the toilet, picked up a handful of paper towels and filled a paper cup with water.

The cards for Victim Support were in his desk drawer.

49. *Light*

No meeting had officially been scheduled, but everyone had slowly made their way into Harjunpää's office once he had finished interviewing Moisio and had seen him out of the building. Each of them read the text in turn and gave a sigh of disappointment.

'He really didn't see a thing. The guy came at him from behind. He didn't see anyone staring at him before-hand either.'

'What's going on with this case? Someone's really taking the piss.'

'I just can't believe there are two psychos on the loose shoving people in front of underground trains.'

'Unless they're both members of some weirdo cult,' suggested Piipponen.

Harjunpää knew Onerva well enough to see that she had something important to say, but one of the others always managed to butt in first.

'And what's with the dead pigeons in the tunnel? You don't think these are some kind of devil worshippers?'

'They tend to be younger, and the clothing doesn't suggest any involvement with the occult. Perhaps we should look into it nonetheless.'

'Koskinen called from the security company. Almost all the guards know the old woman. But apparently she's never been any trouble, they've never had to remove her or check her ID. They call her the Easter Witch.'

'Still we should get in touch with the guards and give them the photofits of both suspects.'

'Listen!' Onerva finally managed to get a word in. 'Rummukainen said that one of the witnesses got a good look at our man, and she did. But before I say anything else… Timo, could you write down any distinguishing features of the man we resuscitated?'

'Why?'

'Just do it. You'll see what I mean soon enough.'

'All right,' Harjunpää conceded, knowing Onerva wouldn't ask something like that without good reason. He grabbed a sheet of paper from the printer and picked up a pencil, but he had to think hard for a moment before he could remember the details properly. The situation had been so nerve-wracking that he had only been able to concentrate on what was most important: reviving the man. Nonetheless, the policeman's eye in him had been at work all the time and he very quickly jotted down a list of bullet points.

'About 180cm tall, thin, bony,' he began to read aloud. 'Grey checked cap, the grandad type. Brownish overcoat, straight dark-grey trousers. A pair of worn trainers that didn't match the rest of his clothes... I think they were brown.'

'Anything else?'

'Let me see... False teeth, but of course a witness couldn't possibly know that. Ah yes, big, thick-rimmed glasses. Hang on a minute, Moisio said he had noticed one person on the platform because he reminded him of President Kekkonen, and it was because of the huge glasses!'

'You see?'

'It's quite a coincidence... I know he behaved oddly, but would he do something like this?'

'Hold on,' Mäki interrupted. 'Could you let the rest of us in on this, please?'

'Of course,' said Onerva, the joy of being in the right dancing across her smiling eyes. 'This description perfectly matches the one our witness gave Rummukainen.'

'I'll be damned. You took down his details, I assume.'

'There was such a commotion that it completely slipped our minds. But he was admitted to hospital later on.'

'Somebody get hold of the paramedics to see where they took him.'

'And he's more than likely still there.'

The change in atmosphere in the office was almost tangible. Someone restlessly changed positions, someone else eagerly rubbed his hands together, and faint smiles lit up their faces.

'But how does this explain the old biddy?'

'Let's take care of the guy first. We can cross that bridge later.'

'What if it's some kind of tranny?' exclaimed Piipponen. 'Do you remember that film where a transvestite killed women so he could make a dress out of their skin?'

'*The Silence of the Lambs*,' said Onerva matter-of-factly. 'But that's rubbish. There's nothing in transvestites' behavioural patterns to indicate such violence. For most people it's something secret and shameful. People used to think of homosexuality like that too.'

For a moment the room was silent. Harjunpää slowly stood up and gestured towards Onerva.

'His hair... What was it like?' he asked.

'You were closer to his head than I was.'

'It was tied up in a bun under his cap, a ponytail tied into a knot. And it was grey!'

'And when it's loose would it reach down as far as the old woman's?'

'I'm certain of it. And once I took out his false teeth... When I think about it, the woman running about at Hakaniemi had the same sort of sharp chin.'

'My god, anyone would think we're a bunch of secret agents,' said Piipponen, deadly serious. At times he could be quite the comedian. Once – as a joke – he had made such a good case for a new and completely useless motor boat for the arson department that the Chief of Police had eventually given the go-ahead. He was also in the habit of putting small popping devices under toilet seats so that when anyone sat down it would make a small bang. Now he seemed so sincere that everyone burst into much needed laughter.

Only Harjunpää's laughter was short-lived, and his expression suddenly turned serious with disbelief. As if in slow motion he took a pair of tongs from the box of pens, stepped around his desk and on towards the metallic coat rack by the door.

'What now?'

Harjunpää didn't respond, but perhaps he hadn't heard the question. His pulse was racing as he stared at the row of police jackets hanging on the rail. A moment ago he had remembered the last time he'd worn one. He undid the zip of one of the breast pockets and opened it carefully, as if he were approaching a bird's nest and expected something to fly out at him at any moment. Then he slowly inserted the tongs into the pocket.

'Look,' he said, turning to face the others. Between the tongs he held a roughly folded piece of paper. 'I took this from the old woman at Hakaniemi so I could get rid of her. There was so much else to think about that I'd forgotten all about it...'

'So the old mare gave you a piece of paper. Now what?'

'There must be at least two sets of fingerprints on this. One will be mine and...'

'The other the woman's!'

'Exactly.'

'Christ, Timo!'

Harjunpää placed the paper on the desk, carefully trying not to make any new prints that might obscure the old ones, and prised it open using the tongs and the end of a pen.

'The Truth is Nigh,' the paper declared. 'Prepare yourself: renounce greed and sin! *Ea lesum cum sabateum! Pica pica setilius omni vibera berus! Custorae carboratum idiopatis!*'

'What kind of language is that?'

'Is it Esperanto?'

'Looks more like Latin to me.'

'*Pica pica,*' Harjunpää read aloud. 'I was quite a bird-spotter as a lad. And if I'm not mistaken this *Pica pica* is the Latin name for magpie.'

'What the bloody hell has a magpie got to do with this?'

'This must have been written by quite a lunatic.'

'I must have learnt something in biology classes,' said Onerva. '*Vibera berus* means adder.'

'Adder?'

'Yes. And that's exactly what we're up against.'

50. *Amends*

'*Vascea cantrum esfobi,*' he repeated, over and over, for he could not understand why the attempted sacrifice that morning had failed. As though his chest were being crushed between two enormous sheets of ice, he had a strong sense that Maammo was displeased with him, that she would rescind her love for him and cast her wrath upon his shoulders. And perish he who befell such a fate. He would be lucky to survive without killing himself, or without at least having to spend time in a mental institution – he of all people should know.

Deep underground he pulled the tarpaulin across the door of his little nook, popped his head outside into the pallid light seeping down from above, and listened. The silence was foreboding. Not a single one of the Orange Apostles had whistled him a sign, a message from Maammo. At the sacrificial moment he had not even heard the screech of the tracks, the sound he cherished so dearly.

He stepped out on to the grille and walked across the platform, stopping at the wide open door of the chamber opposite. From his pocket he removed a small lamp, offering only a speck of light, and stepped inside the room. Although the room appeared empty apart from a few pieces of piping and steel railings, this was not entirely true, for the floor and the corners of the room were filled with all sorts of clutter - rubbish, cardboard, pieces of wood - which the earth spirit had been collecting. He formed them into a small pile in the doorway, barely the size of two fists clenched together, for although he was almost certain there would be no one wandering on top of The Brocken, there was always the possibility that one of those graffiti boys might be loitering up there, and he did not want the smoke to attract their attention.

He crouched down in front of his miniature bonfire, dug a box of matches from his pocket and lit the fire. The flames were sparse and low, barely five centimetres tall, but it was enough. From his jacket pocket he produced one of the pins that had been standing in a row at the edge of his bedside table, closed his eyes and prayed nine times: '*Ea lesum cum sabateum, Mamollae non vihcum!*'

After the ninth prayer he began pricking the knuckles and fingers of his left hand, not quickly, but infinitely slowly, causing himself the greatest possible pain. This time he did not take refuge in his special powers but allowed the pain to engulf him, and let the blood flow. He opened his eyes: how he bled! The back of his hand was like mincemeat, covered in small pinpricks, each of them starting to swell, and bleeding profusely. He curled his fingers loosely into a fist, leaving only his first finger drooping downwards, then he watched as the blood ran down it, trickling into the flames in a chain of droplets. The smell was familiar - he had been forced to make amends for his unworthiness before - and it was such a distinct smell that it could not be described, let alone compared to any other.

He crouched there for almost ten minutes, until not a single piece of cardboard remained glowing amongst the embers. Only then did he stand up. He kicked the pile of ashes three times with each foot and stepped out on to the grille where he carefully wiped the soles of his shoes. This done, he pulled the tarpaulin aside and stepped into his home and the reddish glow of the storm lantern. He strode up to the edge of his bed against the far wall, knelt down, raised his hands into a praying position and stared at the poster depicting a far away galaxy - perhaps a Big Bang billions of light-years away.

'*Sublimator surmontilos, picea exelsa cum narilarum,*' he prayed in a whisper, repeating the words over and over as devoutly and with as much concentration as he could muster. But no, nothing happened. Still Maammo would not deign to grace him with her gaze, would not pardon him. Was this because, in addition to ruining the sacrifice, other people had now seen him and what had happened? Did Maammo think this even worse because now the infidels, the police, were on his tail? If he were caught it would jeopardise the task with which Maammo had entrusted him.

'*Sublimator surmontile!*' he cried out imploringly, but still his chest felt gripped between two great floes of ice. He humbly lowered his hands, rested them against his knees and thought hard. He did not need to think for very long, for he knew precisely what lay ahead. He would have to face his fear of mortality – and defy death itself. Of all acts of devotion to Maammo this was the greatest, and now that he was no longer in her favour he had no chance of becoming a part of her, of spending eternity blessed by her love. Instead he would die like the infidels; he would rot away and worms would feast on his remains.

A sound almost like a whimper passed through his lips, or perhaps he just breathed too quickly. Only twice before had Maammo been so displeased with his incompetence that he had been forced to make amends by facing the possibility of death. Both times he had stood on the central train line's tracks, at night, waiting for the intercity train to appear from the north, and had only jumped out of the way at the very last moment. These had been extraordinary experiences: the approaching train thundering closer and closer, the ear-splitting sound of the horn, the trembling of the ground, the engine and the headlamps growing larger at a phenomenal speed. The last time he had done this it had been so close that the train had torn off his jacket sleeve as it sped past. Nonetheless, after this act of contrition Maammo had been very merciful to him indeed.

'*Ea lesum cum sabateum,*' he finally intoned. The zeal and pleading had disappeared from his voice, and now he sounded like someone standing in front of a firing squad, ready to accept his fate. For he already knew what he would do to atone this time. He stood up and tied a rag around his hand, so that his clothes would not become soiled with blood. He then took from behind the piles of books a black rucksack, the kind that can be seen on the backs of dozens of people every day. It was clearly very heavy, and his arms trembled under the strain of lifting it. He undid the drawstring around the bag; inside there were nine small, closed cardboard boxes with a space in the middle for a tenth. He lifted the lid of one of the boxes and peered inside, though of course he knew all too well what lay inside: rusty screws, nails, bolts, all manner of sharp, lascerating objects he had found on his night-time excursions along the rail tracks.

He straightened his back, walked over to his bedside table and lifted its lid to one side. Inside was the alarm clock he had stolen, and next to it the tenth box from the rucksack. The clock's blue and yellow cables wound their way into their home, inside the box where the sticks of dynamite were. They were not like the ones seen in cartoons or films, they were more like sausages; their surfaces oily and sticky to the touch. When he had pressed the cables – which were tucked inside metal caps, no larger than his little finger - into the sticks of dynamite it felt as though he were pressing something into a block of marzipan: the substance was resistant at first, but eventually gave way.

With blood still seeping through the bandage on his left hand he picked up the box, took the clock in his right hand, and moved towards the rucksack. He slid the box into the space between the others, placing the clock on top; then he sat down in a lotus position and shuffled his buttocks against the floor. Finally he took the rucksack and placed it between his legs, like a mother protecting her child. Fine beads of sweat appeared in a row on his upper lip, and his mouth was extremely dry, as though he had not drunk anything for a week.

He picked up the clock and stared at its glassless face. The connecting wire was still rigged up to the minute hand, set five minutes away from the screw jutting through the clock face at number twelve. He turned the clock around; the battery door was open and the battery had been left only halfway in so that it did not provide a current. He hesitated for a brief moment, then wet his lips decisively; he had tried this with his headlamp many times before and it had never switched on when he had pushed the battery inside; it would only detonate once the wire came into contact with the screw.

What if this time he had made a mistake? Perhaps the rucksack would explode at once. Was this precisely the kind of fear Maammo wished him to face and overcome? Should he go one step further and attach the battery, and then wait until there was only a minute left before disarming it?

'*Ea lesum cum sabateum*,' he said, his voice quivering, for Maammo had answered him immediately, and only the latter method would warrant forgiveness. And with that he took a deep breath, held it in, clamped his eyes shut and slipped the battery into place with a 'click'. Straight away he could hear the clock's soft ticking, but nothing more.

Once again he turned the clock so he could see its face. Just as he had thought: the second hand was ticking away, as was the minute hand, though its movement was steadier and almost imperceptible. Four minutes. It suddenly seemed like an eternity.

All he could think was: what if? What if the boxes of nails ripped him to pieces, what if the little nook he called home collapsed upon him and his body were never discovered? In all the seven years he had lived there not a single caretaker had been down there, not a soul. But would it matter? Perhaps this – the ultimate sacrifice – was what was required to set in motion a series of events leading to the New Big Bang.

'*Ea lesum cum sabateum*,' he repeated once again, but now his voice was hoarse. His shirt was so damp that it stuck to his skin, and he would have given almost anything for a gulp of water. But he did not dare reach his hand towards the bottle of water, for he had to be vigilant, ready to grab hold of the minute hand.

At that moment Maammo gave another command: he must let the clock tick until there were only thirty seconds left before the explosion! His cheeks began to tremble and he almost dropped the clock. Now each second felt as long as the four minutes that had just passed, and he began to count: 'Six. Five. Four. Three. Two…'

51. *Leaps*

Harjunpää turned the steering wheel sharply to the left and revved the transporter into Leanportti. Once he had passed the row of hedges he took another left, then swung round to the right, and pulled the car up on the pavement a few metres from the imposing gates leading into the central police station. Hidden from view, a radar device or an electric eye of some sort examined the transporter, received a confirmation signal in reply and accepted that this was indeed a police vehicle. The gates gave a shudder and slid slowly open.

He drove inside and reversed the car into one of the parking spaces allocated to Violent Crimes. He was in a strange mood, like a partially clouded sky. On the one hand he was content and even slightly excited that the Criminal Police had agreed to treat the issue of the fingerprints as a matter of great importance, and to prioritise it over other tasks in the queue. After all, there was a very good reason for this: as impossible as it seemed in a country like Finland, they were on the tail of some kind of serial killer, and it was only a matter of time before the next unsuspecting victim would be pushed in front of an underground train.

But what excited him even more was that he had been able to watch the leaflet being treated with ninhydrin; and more to the point, to see the wonderful clear prints it had yielded. They appeared on so many different parts of the paper that they couldn't possibly all belong to him.

Still, he couldn't quite figure out what was bothering him. He didn't consider himself old – nor was he – but somewhere in the back of his mind he sensed that a train bound for an unknown destination had already departed, and that he had been left standing on the platform. He had felt this most strongly while his fingerprints were being taken for comparison with the leaflet. For years now the staff in Pasila had done all of the lab-work, and this meant that those investigating a case had only to send the appropriate requisition form to the right people. Even now, no one had asked him to dirty his own fingers with ink; all he had done was place his fingers and hand on a glass plate resembling a small photocopier. Then a computer linked to the device had photographed it, and almost immediately afterwards the printer had spat out a sheet of paper displaying his fingerprints.

The wonders hadn't stopped there either. His prints were then fed into a computer programme called AFIS which then compared them to every set of prints on the national register, as well as to any unidentified prints found at crime scenes. The same was then to be done to the other set of prints found on the leaflet: they would be photographed, scanned, and if the old woman had had any previous trouble with the police the machine would match the prints and provide them with a name in an instant.

Harjunpaa was overwhelmed by even the most basic technological advances. His computer, for example – as soon as he'd acquainted himself with the hidden wonders of its programmes they were replaced by new and ostensibly better ones, and so the cycle of clumsily teaching himself to use the new software could start again. No IT training was ever organised; in fact they were lucky if someone took the time to introduce the new system at all.

Harjunpää was too agitated to sit in the cafeteria and strode right up to Onerva's office. She and Piipponen were examining a set of images laid out across the table. They were both radiating a gleeful excitement about something, and Harjunpää realised it meant they had come up with a new lead.

'There were some fantastic prints on that leaflet,' he announced. 'Santalahti promised to photograph them today even though they'll show up better in a few days' time. If we're lucky we'll have a name by the end of the day.'

'Seriously?' asked Piipponen.

'Yep.'

'That's great. Come and look at these,' said Onerva.

Harjunpää stepped closer to the table; he had been right. Strewn across the table were several dozen sheets of A4 paper, each with a print-out of a face. But they weren't photographs: forensics had created them on the computer, building up the features one bit at a time according to the witnesses' instructions. This allowed them to change the nose or the lips until the face matched the description.

Harjunpää glanced over the images and stopped almost immediately at a picture of the sharp-chinned old woman. Perhaps this was because before leaving the house he had drawn a rough pencil sketch of her features. As he looked at the wrinkled face built up of small individual elements, the same woman he had met in Hakaniemi stared back at him.

'That's the one,' he whispered, cautiously, as if he were afraid that by speaking out loud he might break the spell. He allowed his gaze to drift along the row of faces. The second image from the left: this was an almost exact likeness to the man he and Onerva had resuscitated in the Sanomatalo.

'How did you do that?'

'It was Piipponen actually. That woman was reconstructed according to your sketch, but as for the old guy in the glasses... I called our star witness again, the one that gave us the best description. She agreed to leave work and come in. That image is based on her description. I managed to interview her too.'

'And guess what?' quizzed Piipponen.

'Well?'

'Those photofits have been distributed all over the place, and all the duty sergeants have printed them off and posted them in police stations around the city together with our brief.'

'He, they...whatever; they'd be well advised not to show their face for a while.'

'It won't be long before every officer in the city recognises them.'

'We've taken quite a few steps forward today.'

'More like leaps, I'd say.'

They stared at each other for a moment. Only now did they dare to smile, broadly and unashamedly, as though they had just made a full recovery from a debilitating illness. The magic was broken as Harjunpää's work phone began to ring.

'Crime Squad, Harjunpää,' he answered, then listened for a few seconds, reached into his pocket for a pen, flicked over one of the photofits and began scribbling something down. 'Could you repeat the social security number again? Thanks. Send a formal statement when you get a moment. Once again – thank you.'

He ended the call and slipped his mobile back into his pocket.

'You'll never guess…'

'Well?'

'Turns out our old biddy is a man after all.'

'Who is it?'

'One Markus Luukas Paavali Heino. Master of theology, teacher of religious studies.'

52. *Playboy*

Piipponen was by no means a bad person. He was in fact a far better person than most of his colleagues realised; he was actively involved with a number of aid organisations, charities and societies. Part of the reason for this was that he enjoyed being in the thick of different projects and working with large sums of money, while at the same time he took great satisfaction from acting as MC at important functions and events.

Aside from this he was quite a schemer and a plotter; what's more, he knew it, too. If he had ever been asked to fill out a self-assessment form, he would probably have put a tick in the box marked 'Scoundrel'. Less charitable colleagues may well have ticked the box marked 'Cheat'.

Of course there was an understandable reason for all of this. Piipponen was the fifth son of a caretaker; life had been hard and of all the children in the family he had suffered the most. He had always been left to settle for his brothers' hand-me-downs: worn-out pairs of shoes; darned, threadbare clothes; an old bike that had already been well-used by four young rascals before him. Hobbies had only been allowed for the two eldest brothers; in any squabbling and quarrelling between them all Piipponen had always fared the worst.

Nonetheless, Little Piipponen – or Lilliput as his elder brothers had called him – had found his own method of survival: he had started running small scams. Little by little he had become quite the playboy, though gambling had never been one of his pursuits. For him, daily life was one big game, a game in which the smartest always came up trumps, while the stupidest were left cowering with their tails between their legs. Now this had almost become a lifestyle in itself, and he always felt put out if on any particular day there was nothing even remotely exciting going on. As a result, he would often take a squad car and drive around sorting out his own business.

He had more than enough matters to attend to. Spending his childhood and teenage years in poverty had made him eager to succeed, and very thrifty with money. He had all manner of little business projects: taking care of wills and estates; buying, selling and supplying almost anything; helping people move house. Those who knew him well were sure that his little enterprises weren't always entirely legitimate.

Still he tried hard – mostly on police time – and he had been rewarded with ample material comfort. He always drove the newest American car on the market; his cars were so new he almost never had to take them in to be serviced. Being the runt of the litter hadn't turned him into a loser in the slightest; on the contrary, he had grown into an ambitious, successful man.

It was just after six p.m., but Piipponen was still sitting at his computer terminal in Pasila police station, absent-mindedly chewing the end of his thumbnail. He was astonished; everyone else was astonished too. For the last twelve years "Apostle Heino" - as they had named their suspect because of his first names - had managed to live in such a way that there was not a single mention of him in any of the national registers. Throughout that time he had had no fixed abode, so it would have been understandable if at some point he had been picked up for a minor offence of some description. The last time he had been registered was for shoplifting. But since then, for twelve years he might as well have been dead.

And although the others had already decided to call it a day – Harjunpää had taken his youngest daughter riding, and Onerva had gone to a concert she had booked months ago – Piipponen had stayed, going over everything again and again, but now even he had to admit that he was at a loss. It didn't really matter; he was being paid the highest rate of overtime and he had come up with a few good ideas for the following day.

First they had to establish the man's last known place of work and contact the employer, as no living relatives could be found. They would have to check whether the man received a pension and which cash machines he used regularly. They would also have to contact social services, as it was highly possible that he received some form of benefits from them too, or even that he picked up his pension from their office.

Piipponen yawned, rubbed his neck and glanced at his watch. He was marginally disappointed, as it would have been a sweet moment the following morning to throw a pile of print-outs nonchalantly on the table and scoff: 'So there was no information to be found on him then?' He still had some hope for the evening: they had managed to recruit four volunteers from Violent Crimes to work overtime, and at that moment they were all searching the underground network.

The telephone warbled. It only rang once, which meant that this was an internal call.

'Piipponen.'

'Evening. It's Alho from downstairs.'

'Evening. How's it going?'

'The computer here says you've got a unit looking for a Heino. A Markus Luukas Paavali Heino?'

'That's right,' Piipponen replied. He anxiously shifted position, suddenly filled with renewed hope. 'Don't say you've taken him in…'

'That's exactly what I'm saying. We've got him in cell number two.'

'Who picked him up?'

'A unit from Central. Underground security first noticed him travelling back and forth from one station to the next, then they recognised him from your photofit.'

'Well I'll be damned…'

'Are you coming down to pick him up now or do you want us to bring him upstairs?'

'You bet I'm going to pick him up. Do us a favour and process him for me, will you?'

'No problems.'

'Thanks. I'm on my way.'

Piipponen hurled the receiver back into place. Something inside him froze and he took a deep breath. He could feel his temples tingling, and the sudden tension made his stomach churn – this was his big opportunity. He could almost see the others' expressions as they arrived at work the following morning to see him calmly placing the interview transcripts on the table saying:'Here are three confessions, by the way.Two for murder and one for attempted murder.'

'Jesus Christ!' he exclaimed, and then he was off.The excitement of a game in full swing fizzed inside him so strongly that he felt the palms of his hands begin to itch.

'Good evening. I'm Detective Sergeant Piipponen'. He introduced himself at the door of the cell and extended his hand, but the sullen man inside made no move to touch it. 'And you are Markus Luukas Paavali Heino?'

'In a way.'

'In a way? And what does that mean?'

'I was once. Now I am merely the earth spirit.'

'Of course,' Piipponen uttered after a moment's silence, and now he felt certain that the man was a lunatic. This gave him even more hope because, although people like this were often difficult to question, they were sometimes keen to confess everything during the initial interview; they were proud to take responsibility for their acts. However, Piipponen knew he'd have to be careful with the details, as head-cases like this often confessed to anything and would take the blame for other people's crimes just to get some attention.

'OK, follow me. When we get upstairs I'll explain your position and your rights. Is there a lawyer you would like to have present?You do have the right to one.'

'No, I do not need one,' the man hissed. 'My defence comes from another world.'

'I see, that's right,' said Piipponen; although he never tried any of his tricks in an interview situation, it was always easier to get the suspect talking when there were only two people in the room.

They stopped to wait for the lift and Piipponen examined the man out of the corner of his eye. He matched both his picture on the criminal register and his photofit almost perfectly, though now he looked slightly older and haggard. He was surprisingly calm; he wasn't shaking, twitching or moving restlessly; he wasn't even looking anxiously around himself; he stood perfectly still, his eyes fixed on the wall. Piipponen thought quickly what tactics to employ in the interview.

'Listen,' he said once the lift started moving. 'Have a look up at the ceiling.'

They both raised their eyes. On the ceiling there was a square pane of glass and behind that a camera staring at them.

'They're everywhere nowadays. It's impossible to move around the city without being picked up on three or four different cameras.'

The man remained silent, and Piipponen thought this was a good sign. He allowed the lift to go up another few floors before adding: 'And there are even more of them around all the underground stations and inside the trains – hundreds.'

Still the man remained silent. He merely stared past Piipponen far into the distance. Only his throat moved as though he were swallowing very slowly. When the lift came to a standstill Piipponen continued. 'You see, the thing is, I've got a feeling there are several tapes with you on them.'

They left the cells and walked across into the Violent Crimes building and Piipponen strode off along the endless labyrinth of corridors.

'Follow the leader,' he turned and gestured to Heino. 'I can honestly tell you there are two ways we can sort this out...'

Again he let the silence settle for full effect; all he could hear was the creak of his new shoes.

'There's an easy way and a difficult way. The easy way is you help us to establish exactly what happened. You tell us the truth. The difficult way is if you don't want to cooperate. But even then you'll eventually be forced to tell us the truth. All it takes is time and strong muscles in your backside. And I can assure you I've got plenty of both.'

He stopped in front of the open door leading into his office and directed the man inside with a polite movement of the hand – nothing less for the man of the moment. But just then he was struck by an icy chill, as if a set of small hooks had sunk into his neck, and goosebumps appeared on his skin. There was no one behind him. He was standing in the corridor alone.

'How the hell...' he growled, then something snapped and his cheeks began to burn. He had made a stupid, amateurish mistake: he had walked in front, turning his back on the suspect. He also realised that he could thank his lucky stars that a suspected double murderer hadn't gone straight for his jugular.

He dashed towards the nearest door, but it was locked – the man couldn't have gone in there. He began rattling the handle of the next door, and the next. His heart was pounding so much that his heart rate must have been well over a hundred. A thought occurred to him and he sped towards the end of the corridor: the man must have slipped out of the door in the stairwell; it could be opened from the inside without a key, and as for the main outer door, nobody could get in without a key card, but they could certainly get out!

His shoes squeaked on the floor as he came to a stop by the thick glass door. He had been right: the door was still ajar, resting on the latch, and this meant that the man must have closed it slowly and with enough cold-blooded, steely reserve to make sure that the mechanism didn't click shut. He hurriedly leant on the door and shoved it open, then stopped for a moment and listened carefully: the stairwell was so large that you couldn't take a step without it echoing up to the fifth floor. But he couldn't hear a thing; no steps, no rustling of clothes, no panting.

Piipponen stumbled forwards and began running down the stairs as quickly as if he had wheels on his feet. The blue railing creaked beneath his hand and he could feel his palms burning. Once he reached the landing between the second and third floors he was overcome by the nauseating facts: the man was gone. In a daze he tried to catch his breath and looked around.

However, he only stood still for a few seconds. He quickly shrugged off his jacket, tied the rough sleeve around his neck and began yanking it back and forth like a sponge. His skin instantly started to burn, and as he continued rubbing it turned a bright red colour. Blood had risen to the surface, he could feel it. He then slipped his jacket back on, tore his shirt open – a button flew on to the stairs and he picked it up. He knew precisely where it should be found: in the corridor on the floor next to his office door. Finally he took his mobile phone out of its case, and without a moment's hesitation slammed it at the corner of his eye with full force. It broke on impact: the phone's battery fell out and a crack appeared on its screen, while a warm stream of blood trickled from the corner of his eye. Before long it reached halfway down his chin.

'Help!' he shouted, his voice booming through the stairwell. 'I've been attacked! The suspect's escaped! Immediate assistance required!'

53. *Holy War*

'*Belaboris botulium diaboli vascenata,*' he said to dispel the uncertainty from his mind. This was more than uncertainty, for a moment it had been pure fear; denying it was pointless. He had not experienced such a thing for years, as Maammo had always given him strength. But now for some reason Maammo was testing him. In some respects she was still on his side – the events of the previous night had been an indication of that. As an opponent Maammo had chosen such a stupid infidel that he had managed to slip away easily. He had not liked the man in the slightest: he stank of greed and pride, of money stashed in an old sock.

The backpack was very heavy, he could feel it pulling at his back. Would the boy have the strength to carry it?

The worst of it was that now they had begun their religious persecution, for that and nothing else was what the previous evening had been about. They could not accept that he worshipped Maammo, the only true deity, and that his faith demanded that he carry out necessary sacrifices. It would have been that same bigotry had he broken into their churches, kicked over the font and trampled their consecrated wafers into the ground.

In fact, this was not merely religious persecution, this was a holy war – and they had declared it. They had declared it by making it impossible for him to visit his sacred shrines: the Railway Station, the underground stations and the trains themselves - the holy Orange Apostles. After that policeman had told him that there were cameras everywhere he had checked – and it was true. And not only at the stations, but almost everywhere, on the streets, outside every shop and government office. This meant that at any given moment he was on camera for all the nosy heathens to see. For this reason he was now pacing around the streets behind the Railway Station and wandering through Kaisaniemi Park. Although he had taken precautions to avoid being followed, he was still in the form of a man. After all, on their cameras they had already seen him in the form of a woman. This time, however, he was wearing a long raincoat and a cap with an extended brim. When he lowered his head the brim all but covered his face from view; in addition to this, he had left his hair half open so that it flowed down his back and was only tied at the end with a rubber band.

Another reason he had been unable to assume the form of a woman was that the boy had to be able to recognise him. That was, of course, if he turned up. It was late in the afternoon and school would certainly have finished for the day. Throughout the day – and the previous night for that matter – he had been sending the boy powerful messages to come and meet him, for now that war had been declared it was time to carry out the final strike - especially now that the future of the New Big Bang might be in danger, and would be fatefully delayed if they managed to catch him. As an extra precaution he had left his glasses at home; they were very distinctive and he could see well enough without them.

Still, all these factors – the war situation, continuously having to watch his back, living in an unnatural way – considerably weakened his concentration and perhaps even his powers, and he was not at all sure whether his messages had found their way inside the boy's head. In addition to all this, his left hand ached constantly, distracting him and making it difficult for him to scale the ladder down into his home. He had been unable to stop the bleeding and had resorted to putting a leather glove over his hand. Now that the blood had dried the glove was stuck to his hand so tightly that he had not dared to take it off.

His hand had also been a hindrance in making his final preparations and in putting the bomb together. It had impaired him so much that he had had to start again many times and adjust the various settings, but there it finally was in the rucksack on his back. The clock was not yet ticking, but it would start the moment he pressed the battery into place, and after that only an hour would be left until the final BOOM! He could only imagine how the nails and bolts and pieces of metal would be cast in a great cloud in all directions, and how they would tear the infidels to pieces; their blood, their flesh and their splintered bones whirling in a wild, red storm.

He had already decided upon the place of the sacrifice. It was appropriate in many ways, a temple of material greed, awash with people, and what's more its structure was open, a grand hall, allowing the force of the blast to move freely upwards, right up to the top floor. There was even a glass ceiling and he was certain that it would collapse, shattering into millions of razor-sharp shards that would shower down upon the heads of the infidels who had been spared from the initial blast.

'*Ea lesum!*' he uttered, for something told him that the boy might be on his way after all. He did not know how he knew this; perhaps it was the pigeon that hopped out of his way on the path through the park, its head jutting back and forth. His mind was made up: he would start the clock. Let it be a test: it would force the boy to come to him. And if the boy did not come, he would once again demonstrate his bravery and his devotion to Maammo by stopping the clock only half a minute before detonation.

He stopped by a park bench, removed the bag from his back, placed it on the bench beside him and, somewhat hindered by his hand, began untying the cords. And although those stalking him thought that by fortifying the underground with cameras they could prevent him from reaching Maammo's sacred temples and his home, they were mistaken. In the centre of town he could make his way underground at five different points, through unmarked, almost invisible grey doors in the foundations of buildings; although in fact he had only managed to deactivate the alarms on two of them, using aluminium foil so that they appeared to be shut even as he slipped in and out of them. The only true hindrance was that he now had to walk much farther. He finally managed to open the rucksack and picked up the clock. He had replaced the glass at the front so that the hands would not accidentally snag on anything inside. He placed his thumb upon the battery and pressed. First came a click, then the regular tick as the clock was set in motion.

'*Cum sabateum!*' he murmured, like a blessing. 'Come my boy, come to me!'

54. *Pizza Outing*

'I'm only now beginning to realise quite how terrible it would have been,' said Matti, and now he meant it, for at first he hadn't fully understood the seriousness of the matter. 'I would have been stuck with Mum and Roo, and they would probably have sent me to a foster home.'

'How's he doing?' Leena asked, but avoided his gaze. She was behaving oddly, as if she were nervous or felt guilty about something. They were sitting on the underground train rattling its way towards the centre of town, and this time they had even bought tickets – Matti had insisted.

'He's OK, I suppose. He knocked his knee quite badly.'

'I meant how's he dealing with it?'

'He's good at hiding things, but he didn't seem in shock or anything.'

'Terrible that someone would do something like that,' said Leena, staring ahead strangely as though she couldn't see a thing.

'It was only last week someone got themselves killed at Hakaniemi.'

'What made you decide to go and see him now?' she asked, quickly changing the subject. 'The priest, I mean?'

'It's just a strange feeling, I feel like I need to see him. I suppose I ought to thank him for healing me. Somehow… I thought he might be able to take care of Dad.'

'I'm sorry… Maybe he isn't a priest after all. And I don't know whether he's all that good either.'

'What do you mean?'

'Just a hunch,' she said and turned to look out of the window. She started chewing the nail on her little finger, and for a long moment neither of them said a word.

'Haven't you figured out the whole SIM-card thing yet?' Leena asked finally, though she still didn't seem like her old self.

'What about it? She said she thought it was a CD.'

'Oh come on, Matti, don't be so gullible. She sells the exact same cards at work. She knew what it was all right. She was probably going to sell it off at half-price to some customer, and pocket the money herself.'

'Really,' Matti replied slowly. At first he was ashamed that his mother could be so conniving. Gradually he began to feel happier than ever that his father hadn't been killed in the underground accident.

At the same moment he realised how painful it was waiting to move in with his father, and how he wished it would happen soon – that same day even. Only then did he remember the terrible fact that there had never been any discussion of him moving whatsoever. He had made it all up, and he had lied to Leena so much that for some reason he too was now beginning to believe it was all true. He let out a long, deep sigh and wondered whether to own up to everything once and for all.

'Leena, listen,' he said and took her hand, but his lips suddenly began to tremble and he couldn't bring himself to tell her.

'What?'

'Just that I'm really glad Dad didn't die.'

'Who wouldn't be? But will you promise me something? When we meet him – the priest.'

'What about it?'

'If you could make yourself scarce for a minute; I've got something personal I need to give him.'

'What?'

'I can't tell you. There's just something I want to ask him.'

'OK.'

They fell silent again, each focussing on their own secrets. The train pulled into Hakaniemi. It was rush hour and people were flooding out into the shopping centres, heading back to their homes.

'You realise…?' said Leena. They were still holding each other by the hand, but now Matti no longer found it embarrassing. 'We haven't checked any of the other stations in case he's there.'

'Of course not, because he'll be at the Railway Station.'

'How do you know?'

'I can feel it. Or he might be somewhere outside the station.'

'Does it feel like he's calling you? You know, like by some weird telepathy or in some spiritual way?'

'Well, now that you ask… It's just, I haven't been able to stop thinking about him all day.'

'That's it, that's exactly what happened to me.'

'Really?'

'Yes. OK, let's do a test – just for fun. Shut your eyes and concentrate really hard. Now guess exactly where we're going to find him.'

Matti closed his eyes. He couldn't feel anything out of the ordinary; nothing happened that might have meant someone was sending him thoughts. On the spur of the moment, just to please Leena, he said: 'He's outside on the square by the Railway Station, down there where the buses leave.'

'Are you sure? You didn't just make that up?'

'No, not at all.'

'Well, good. It's just that I've never seen him anywhere other than the Railway Station or in the underground.'

'We'll soon see, we've just gone past Kaisaniemi.'

They ascended the slowly jolting escalator at the Railway Station in perfect silence, a silence held tight by something almost magical. They didn't dare look at one another, though as if by accident their fingers gently touched each other on the black moving handrail. They both looked around, and Matti expected to see the priest at any moment. The decision to meet the priest seemed suddenly wrong, as though if he were caught a terrible punishment would ensue.

'Leena,' he whispered as they arrived at the level with the compass. 'I'm not sure I want to see him after all.'

'You're not?' said Leena, stopping in her tracks. They were standing in people's way, right in the middle of the crowds coming up from the train, passengers barging into them on all sides, forcing them to move upwards with the mass.

'I don't know either,' she whispered finally. 'I've got a bad feeling about this, like an omen…'

'Maybe we should just go back?'

Leena bit her lip for a moment; they could already here the station announcements echoing through the vast hall.

'No,' she said after a moment's thought. 'Let's go and see if he's there; if you guessed right. Then we can just go home, we don't need to go and talk to him.'

'OK, but we will leave, won't we? I can feel something in my stomach…'

They walked through the underground hall, weaving their way in between the groups of people, loitering first beside the numerous kiosks, then the toilets. The main door was only some twenty metres away, and a gust of wind caught them as people walked in and out. They stepped outside and stood beneath the massive stone pillars, staring out across the street and down to where the buses departed. There were dozens of people, hundreds maybe, making it impossible to distinguish anyone in the crowd.

'I was wrong. He's not here. Let's go.'

'Wait a minute. Do you see that man down by the taxi rank?'

'Good afternoon, children,' came a voice from behind them, and they both recognised it instantly, though it wasn't as tense as normal – it was almost gentle. They spun around: the priest was standing behind them. This time he looked somehow different; instead of his normal jacket he was wearing a raincoat that reached almost down to his knees, and a baseball cap pulled so far down that it hid his face almost entirely.

'Where are your glasses?' asked Leena; it came out rather stupidly, but the priest didn't seem to mind.

'At the optician's,' he replied with a smile, then his voice turned suddenly sharper. 'Did I invite you too, my girl?'

'No… but… Matti called me and asked me to come along.'

'Is that so, Matti?'

'Yes.'

'Do you have something to tell me?'

'Yes, thanks a lot. The stone worked great.'

'Why, think nothing of it. As a matter of fact, I have something to tell you too. I don't see why I shouldn't tell both of you, seeing as things have turned out this way.'

When the priest looked Matti in the eyes, so closely, he was overcome by a strange sense of helplessness, as though he had just been sick. He also felt that he could no longer leave, even if he'd wanted to, but that now he had to obey the priest. He glanced at Leena, and she too seemed a little confused. In an incredible way, it felt as though they were the only people in the world, as though the sea of people around them had suddenly disappeared.

'Do you children like pizza?'

'Yes.'

'Yes… Especially ones with garlic.'

'I see,' said the priest, removing his hand from the pocket of his raincoat. In his fingers was a crumpled bank note; judging by the colour it must have been at least a hundred euros. 'I shall buy you any pizza you want. And then I will join you later. First I must take care of another appointment.'

'Well…'

'I insist,' he said and handed the note to Matti; sure enough, it was a hundred euros. 'You know the Forum shopping centre?'

'Yes, we know where it is.'

'Down in the basement there are many different kinds of restaurants. Choose your pizzas, then go and sit at the table nearest to the small pool and the stone pillars.'

'I've eaten there before.'

'Well, that's nice. But I do expect a favour in return. In fact, it is no real favour. It is more a test of your maturity.'

The priest slipped his hands beneath the straps on his shoulders and removed a large rucksack from his back. It was a perfectly normal rucksack; black, the kind almost everyone took to school. Matti could see that it was rather heavy.

'Matti, put this on your back. And although it may be heavy, do not once take it off. It contains something very precious to me. It is also a symbol of life's burden. If you can bear the weight of this rucksack, you shall be able to carry on fearless for the rest of your life.'

'It is very heavy,' said Matti, shrugging the rucksack on to his shoulders.

'As for you, my girl, you must support Matti the way a wife supports her husband. And if you succeed in this, you will succeed in everything you do for the rest of your life. Do you understand?'

'Yes…'

'You must wait for me there until I arrive, then we will have ice cream for dessert. And remember: you must not open the rucksack. For if you do you will tarnish and sully that which life shall bring you.'

'We won't open it.'

'No. And I won't take it off.'

'And when I return, each of you shall receive something else as a reward…'

'More of those vibes?'

'Yes. Sublime, incredible vibes.'

The priest performed a series of strange hand signals in front of them while muttering something almost inaudibly. It was as if he were blessing them, and in a terrifying way it all resembled a funeral. Matti could already feel the straps of the rucksack chafing against his shoulder blades, but decided that he would be able to cope. Leena groped for his hand and her fingers were sweaty with excitement. He allowed her to take his hand; the moment was strangely solemn.

'*Ea lesum cum sabateum! Mamolae sub extriensa!*' the priest said finally, waving his hand in a circle above their heads. 'Now – go!'

He hastened them towards the grand doors of the station and they understood that they should go immediately. As they were about to walk through the door Matti glanced over his shoulder. The priest was not following them, he trusted them. And just as the doors swung shut behind them he thought he could see the priest turning and walking down the stone steps, heading diagonally across the square towards Kaivokatu.

It was the busiest time of day: people coming and going in every direction, more and more people appearing from nowhere. It was difficult to see the crowd as made up of individual people; it was swarming and pulsating like a giant organism. For some inexplicable reason it occurred to Matti that if someone were to go mad and start running amok with a machine gun, the station would be a scene of mass slaughter.

They not so much walked as dodged and wound their way through the station hall and down into the underground shopping level, and still neither of them said a word. They even avoided looking at one another, though they were still walking hand in hand. Matti's mind was strangely numbed, as though he had been sedated. This in itself meant that he didn't particularly want to speak. They wandered around the upper level of the underground station – they could barely make out the compass beneath the crowds of people – then they headed towards the tunnel running under Mannerheimintie, leading to the basement level of the Forum shopping centre.

'What do you think all this means?' Leena whispered, clearly puzzled and perhaps even slightly afraid. 'Something about this freaks me out…'

'I don't get it either. Maybe this is one of his religion's holy rituals.'

'Yeah maybe… I don't understand… When he looks at me it's as if he can control me by some magic.'

'Me too. It makes me feel… Like if he told me to jump off a cliff, I'd do it.'

'Do you think he can hypnotise us?'

'I don't think it happens that quickly. Don't you have to stare at a swinging watch or something? And I read somewhere that you have to want it to work too.'

'What do you think is in the bag? Should I have a peek?'

'No, I don't want to know. Let's just do this the way we agreed. Still, it's really heavy though…'

They were far enough along the tunnel that the traffic and trams along Mannerheimintie must have been thundering directly above their heads, though they couldn't hear a sound. All at once the air changed, making them hungry instantly; the smell of food wafted out of the numerous restaurants in the lower level of the Forum.

'Let's go over there,' said Leena nodding to the right. 'My Mum and I have been there a few times, they have really good toppings.'

'I've been there too, but I've never eaten there.'

'Have the Della Casa, it's got black olives and loads of onion.'

'I'm not too keen on olives. I want one with prawns.'

'Then you should have the Cam…Camberetti - and a large Coke?'

'Yeah.'

'Look, those people by the fountain are just about to leave. Give me the money, I'll order and you can save the table.'

'OK. I'm not really used to being in a real restaurant.'

'Garlic on the pizza?'

'Yes please, lots.'

Barely ten minutes had passed before the waitress laid the plates in front of them. They were enormous, like the steering wheel of a bus. Matti's pizza was piled high with prawns and the rich smell of garlic filled his nostrils, whetting his appetite. He had propped the rucksack against the back of the chair, making it almost comfortable to sit down. Dozens of people chattered around them, knives and forks clinked, and beside them water rippled softly in the pool. Two thick blue pillars rose up towards the ceiling. The pillars united several floors higher; undoubtedly a work of art of some kind, situated right at the heart of the shopping centre.

'They're here already?' Matti asked.

'Yes!' said Leena, and Matti followed her example, spreading a napkin across his lap. Then he picked up his knife and fork and started slicing up his pizza. The crust was so crisp that he didn't have to saw at it like pizzas from the supermarket; a gentle cut was enough. The first mouthful was a glorious experience. Matti closed his eyes and let one prawn after another melt in his mouth.

To his amazement he realised that, despite being so nervous a moment ago, for the first time in a very long while he felt happy. He had a friend, Leena; he had his own mobile phone with prepaid talk-time; and then there was the priest who, with all his strange little quirks, had saved him from his tormentors. Then there was Dad. When he thought about all this he had a strong and warm feeling, a certainty that his father would take him in - all he had to do was ask.

'This is amazing…'

'I know. Maybe he's a nice guy after all,' replied Matti.

That's when the music started. It was the same kind of beeping as a mobile phone, but far louder. People started looking around, wondering why no one answered so that the noise would stop.

'What's that?'

'Old Macdonald had a farm…'

'I know that,' said Matti. 'But where is it coming from?'

'Somebody's got their phone turned up really loud.'

'No,' said Matti, bewildered. He placed his knife and fork back on his plate. 'Leena, I think it's coming from this rucksack...'

Leena's mouth stopped chewing. She stared at him in disbelief.

'You're right,' she whispered after a moment. All the while 'Old Macdonald had a farm' played on and on in the background; the sound seemed to grow louder the longer it rang. 'It might be an alarm clock. I stayed over with a friend one night and her clock sounded just like that.'

'Do you... Do you think we should have a look inside?'

'But what if it really is some kind of obedience test?'

'How about if I don't take it off my back, so at least we don't break that rule. Then you can have a quick look inside.'

'OK.'

Leena stood up, the legs of her stool scraping across the floor. Some of the people sitting around them realised that they were the ones causing all the noise and looked at them angrily, as if to say *'Give it a rest!'* Leena was already standing behind him and Matti could hear the bag rustling and feel it moving on his back. 'Old Macdonald had a farm' played on and on – until there came a click and the music stopped all at once. Now there was only the sound of Leena rummaging in the rucksack. Then she closed the zip, walked back round the table and sat down.

'I was right,' she said. 'It's the same little white clock my friend has.'

'What else was in there?'

'Well,' she said, lowering her eyes. 'Nothing valuable, just boxes full of rusty bolts and stuff.'

'No wonder it's so heavy.'

'The box in the middle had some kind of blocks in it, like sausages. Then there were a load of cables going from the clock into the blocks.'

'I don't get it,' said Matti. He gave a shrug and picked up his soda, but the glass hadn't even reached his lips before his expression changed into one of bewilderment.

'Hang on.'

'What?' asked Leena, her mouth full of pizza.

'Have you read in the papers...' he stammered, his hands shaking so much that Coke spilled over the rim and he had to place his glass back on the table. 'Could it be a bomb?'

'A bomb? What on earth makes you think that?'

'It was in the papers. The kind they blow up in England and Israel...'

'What?'

'Oh God,' said Matti breathlessly, as his face and lips began to tremble.

'Matti,' Leena whispered and placed her hand on his. 'I'm scared...

Let's leave the bag and get out of here, just to be on the safe side.'

For a long moment Matti was silent.

'We can't,' he stuttered finally.

'Well what then? Should we call the fire brigade?'

'What time is it?'

'The clock wasn't right. It was ten to twelve.'

'What if it goes off at twelve?'

'I know...'

They stared at one another with fear in their eyes, and only after many long seconds of silence Matti finally said: 'But what if we're wrong? Things like that don't happen in Finland...'

'Really?' said Leena, as though she too wanted to believe it, then added stiffly: 'But what about... Don't you remember what happened in Myyrmanni? And the car bomb downtown?'

'Yes,' said Matti, carefully standing up. 'Let's go. We'll leave it on the street. It can't do as much damage if it's outside.'

'I'm not so sure it was a bomb after all.'

'We can throw it down a sewer...'

'OK,' Leena finally agreed, and they began to make their way towards the escalators leading up to the ground floor. Matti was suddenly filled with an urge to ditch the rucksack there and then and run away, but it was as though Leena had sensed this and she grabbed his hand, holding him tightly.

There were still crowds of people and the escalators were so packed that it was impossible to walk up past the queue. All they could do was stand and wait, wait and suffer as the escalators edged slowly upwards. Matti wondered what would happen if it really was a bomb and if it exploded right now. At least a hundred people would have been blown into oblivion; Leena amongst them, and him too. Would he have time to register anything? Pain? Or would it be as though someone had simply switched off the lights?

They arrived at the main door and wove their way outside among the thick throng of people. Matti could no longer control his fear; he had already slipped his hands beneath the straps on his shoulders and broke into a run, but he only managed to take a few steps before Leena grabbed him by the sleeve.

'Don't leave me!'

'I won't,' he panted. His upper lip was moist with sweat and a few drops started to trickle down his neck.

Then he saw the priest, and Leena clearly saw him too – as impossible as it seemed in such a crowd. He was standing on the other side of the street staring up at the shopping centre. Then he noticed them, there was no mistaking it. For a moment he didn't move, then he turned sharply and took a few quick steps towards the corner. He stopped still and raised his hand as if he were looking at his watch. Immediately he started waving at them, gesturing as if to say 'Come quickly!' And although the distance between them was great, Matti could feel his electric gaze sizzling and boring into him.

The traffic lights would not change. Matti didn't dare cross. Cars sped past like sharks or piranhas, their tyres thundering along the road, and the lights continued to shine red at the waiting pedestrians; they shone so insistently that he began to feel as if the little man were never going to change, but had been painted permanently red.

'Dear God,' Leena mumbled, but Matti couldn't manage even that. Only an indistinct sound passed his lips. Perhaps it was a whimper.

55. *Tinkerbell*

'Why won't it change?' The words pounded through Leena's mind, almost as fast as her heartbeat. There wasn't room in her thoughts for much besides the priest whom, despite the crowds of people, she could see as clearly as if she had been looking through a telescope, and a desperate hope that it wasn't a bomb after all, that nothing bad was going to happen, that there would be something good that she could look forward to in the future, something she could live for.

And in a flash it became clear to her what that thing was, so clear in fact that she no longer had to think about it, and she clung even tighter to Matti's hand. She turned and looked at him; the expression on his face was that of a scared child – he was crying, without making a sound, tears simply running one after the other down his cheeks. And there amidst the chaos and the danger he suddenly asked: 'Do you like me?'

'Ye–yes.'

'Are we going out?'

'Yes.'

The crowd split around them and began flooding across the street, shoving them backwards in the process. The cursed little red man had disappeared and had now been replaced by a sprightly green one. Leena managed to urge her legs into action and dragged Matti behind her. They were soon in the middle of the street, on the tram tracks, only one platform and another lane of traffic separating them from the pavement opposite. It wasn't a very long journey, it just seemed long – all the more so because the distance was being measured by the little alarm clock in the rucksack on Matti's back. It didn't tick as such, it whispered: *'tih, tih…'* And although he didn't want to, he couldn't help thinking how many times it still had to say *'tih'* before it was too late.

Finally they arrived at the other side of the street and stepped on to the pavement. The priest ran towards them at an incredible speed; he didn't say a word, but spun Matti around by the shoulders and began almost tearing open the top of the rucksack. He was hampered by the glove on his left hand, and something at the side of his mouth was quivering so intensely that, amidst all the commotion, it resembled a fish tugging at a worm on the end of a hook.

'Sabre delicatus helveticum!' he growled, almost like a wild animal. It had to be a curse of some kind. Eventually he managed to undo the top of the rucksack and open the strings, ripped the neck open, shoved his hands inside and began fiddling with something. He clearly succeeded in what he was doing, took a deep breath, removed his hands from the rucksack and let it fall to the ground. His posture seemed to collapse, he slumped and whispered: *'Cum sabateum…'*

'What?' asked Leena. Speaking was something of a relief, as for the last few minutes her tongue had seemed paralysed. 'What exactly is going on?'

'Pons asini…'

'Enough of that gobbledygook. I think it's time you explained exactly what's going on. You have the nerve to ask us to carry this machine of yours… It started ringing.'

'Vox Mamolae.'

'Well?' Leena pressed him. She couldn't understand where she had suddenly found such courage. But the priest didn't even look at her. He tore the rucksack from Matti's back, slung it on his arm, left it there dangling and looked around a number of times, as if he were waiting for someone – or rather afraid that someone might appear.

'I asked you to explain what this is all about!'

'It is nothing. It was merely a test that you two wretched children have failed miserably. Now – go to hell! I never want to see you again!' the priest snarled. His voice was now as rough as a lump of steel wool. Then he simply turned and ran off as quickly as before, and before they knew it he had turned the corner into Kaivokatu.

'What should we do?' asked Leena, but Matti was still so disorientated that he seemed not to hear her. 'Let's go after him and cause a scene until he tells us what's going on.'

She grabbed Matti by the hand and started running, and together they wound their way in between all the people walking along the street. The priest had to be running very fast. He had already passed the Seurahuone building and was running flat out, his shoulders hunched, towards the steps leading down to the upper level of the underground station. All they could make out were his shoulders and his baseball cap, and from beneath the cap crept a few strands of loose silver hair.

'Faster Matti!'

'I can't. My legs feel like they're numb…'

'You've got to! I want some answers from that freak!'

She strained even harder, all but dragging Matti like a weight behind her. Soon they had reached the steps and began nimbly making their way downwards. She had guessed correctly. The priest had turned left, and there was only one place he could be heading: towards the compass mosaic and the underground.

'Come on, we can't lose him. He could blow the whole place up…'

They struggled their way through the crowds down to the compass level, and just before they reached the ticket machines Leena realised that she ought to go on by herself after all, if only because of what she had originally planned to speak to the priest about, and now more than ever before she didn't want Matti to overhear. She stopped, grabbed Matti by the shoulders and tried to catch her breath. Looking past him she could see that the priest was almost there. It looked as if he were afraid of something; he looked almost shy as he peered around, pulled up the collar of his raincoat and drew the cap even further down on his head.

'I'll go by myself,' she gasped, turning to look Matti in the eyes.

'No... what if he does something to you?'

'With all these people around? He wouldn't dare. I'll start screaming and say that he was trying to touch me up. The security guards or the police will arrest him.'

'Still...'

'I'm going after him!' she snapped. She shook Matti by the shoulders – they were running out of time. She couldn't let the priest get on a train without her. 'Remember what you promised me. You said you'd make yourself scarce so I could talk to him in private.'

'OK... I'll wait here. But promise me that you'll come back.'

'Of course I'll come back,' she said, and with that she was on her way. She didn't care that she didn't have a ticket.

The priest had already arrived on the platform and turned left once again – he was waiting for a train heading east, unless he knew of a secret door or some other way of escaping unnoticed. Leena had also made it on to the platform. She pushed her way between two men and almost tripped over a pram, but managed to regain her balance in time. The priest was some twenty metres away from her. He was standing behind the mass of people on the platform, waiting for the train like everyone else. Leena inched her way forward, further and further, until only a few boys stood between them.

She walked around them and stopped right beside the priest. Only now that she had stopped running and her breathing had finally returned to normal did she realise how painfully the feeling of anger and disappointment stung inside her. She grabbed hold of the priest's sleeve and pulled sharply. He turned, but now his expression was utterly calm, as if nothing had happened, as if they were old friends who had accidentally bumped into one another.

'Oh, it is you, my girl,' he said, raising his eyebrows in mock surprise.

'Yes, it's me. And now you're going to explain a few things.'

'Lower your voice. Do not shout.'

'I asked you to do something to Matti's Dad so that they wouldn't move away...'

'Yes?'

'And you... You tried to kill him. You pushed him in front of a train. And now today you tried to blow me and Matti to smithereens – and hundreds of other people too. What's going on? Are you some satanic priest or what?'

'I do not have the faintest idea what you are raving about.'

'Raving? Do you know what'll happen if I start screaming that you groped me?'

'And that, little wretch, is something you will not do,' the priest growled, raising his right hand in a trembling fist in front of his face. Leena somehow sensed that he had no intention of hitting her. He then spread his fingers as far apart as he could. 'Look at me!' he commanded her.

Though she didn't want to look at him, in some strange way she felt that she had no choice. Her anger had disappeared, and she suddenly felt as timid as she always had in the presence of the priest. He stared at her through his outstretched fingers, unflinchingly, not even blinking, and she felt the full power of his gaze; like the pull of water through a drain, it sucked out her own will and left her with nothing.

'What are you?' he asked quietly, though he clearly did not expect her to answer and continued almost straight away. 'You are a fat, ugly slob that nobody could ever truly love... Answer me: what are you?'

'A f-fat, ugly... Slob that nobody could ever truly love,' she whispered. She could feel the tears welling in her eyes, for it was true – she was exactly as the priest said; Matti must have been mistaken. She could have burst into tears, but managed to stifle her sobs to a mere whimper.

'But what would you like to be? What could you become?' wheezed the priest, and he bent down so close to her that she could smell his breath. 'You would like to be beautiful and slender. You would like to float in the sky in a bell skirt with nylon tights on your legs. You would like to be Tinkerbell. Tell me: am I right?'

'Ye-yes.'

'And you have already experienced it once. Your life could be like this forever... But you have gravely offended both me and Maammo. First you must make amends. Would you like to do so?'

'Yes,' she whispered softly. Once again the priest had her in his power, and all the people around them seemed to have disappeared. She could no longer hear the crowd's faint murmur; she and the priest were all that existed. Or rather, all that existed was the priest.

'Then you shall accept the holy kiss of Maammo.'

'Wh-what?'

'Maammo's hallowed kiss. Can you see the yellow rail on the other side of the tracks?'

'Yes, but… There are people standing in the way.'

'Go over to it. Kneel before it and place your hand inside – the underside is open.'

Leena was breathing heavily. It was as though she were drunk, but she could still clearly remember how incredibly beautiful it had felt to be thin and slender, pretty stockings on her legs, floating between the rooftops with nothing in the world to fear; it was then that she realised she truly was Tinkerbell.

'But… It says DANGER…'

'Of course, that is because of the tracks. A train might come along, but you can see from the screen up there how many minutes are left before the next train is due, so that you will have enough time to walk across.'

'What… What is the holy kiss of Maammo like?'

'It lies inside the railing, just to the left of that sign. It is a round stone, and when you bring that stone back to the platform you will notice that it is filled with silver grooves. And whenever you clasp it in your hand, then you can be Tinkerbell again.'

A train pulled into the station and people began to cram inside. Almost immediately the signal to close the doors rang out and the motors revved up again: *Phuii-phuii…* More commuters instantly flooded on to the platform; it was as if Leena saw them through a veil of mist. The only thing she saw clearly was the yellow rail running along the ground on the other side of the tracks.

'Now!' commanded the priest. 'Go and receive the holy kiss of Maammo and you will be saved!'

'I will,' Leena heard herself say; perhaps someone else said it in her voice, but in any case she started moving, walking steadily towards the edge of the platform. She didn't hesitate for a moment, but jumped straight down on to the tracks. The gravel crunched beneath her feet, and somewhere far off she could make out the concerned, terrified cries of the people on the platform, but she didn't pay them any attention. She thought only of her poem:

Her face in the mirror –
how pained the sight;

how keen the girl there feels your spite.
Lips pursed in a smile, tight and long,
breasts large and strange and long.

56. *Suicide*

Harjunpää was driving, Piipponen was sitting in the passenger seat and Onerva was in the back. They were on their way back from a frustrating day's reconnaissance, and the silence in the car was like a sheer wall of steel that none of them could break. As if each of them were sulking inside their own steel bubble.

'Can we please knock off the silent treatment?' Piipponen tried to sound pointed and irritated but his words did not have the desired effect. His voice sounded as though his cheeks were full of cotton wool, softening his every word. Around his neck was a thick foam support clipped shut at the back; its rim was so high that he couldn't move his mouth properly. He had a large bandage on his forehead, and he had taken such a whack that the underside of his eye had turned progressively bluer throughout the course of the day. Despite this, he had flatly refused any suggestion of taking sick leave.

'As if I'd let him escape on purpose,' he mumbled with considerable difficulty. 'It could have happened to anyone. All I did was turn my back for a second to find the key and put it in the lock and he was at my throat like a tiger...'

'No one doubts you,' said Harjunpää flatly. He always found it difficult giving people negative feedback, let alone directly criticising or blaming someone. Even now he had to clear his throat for a moment before finally stammering: 'I'm just pissed off at how you handled things in the first place. What a cock-up! We should have pooled everything we had on him and had a meeting about how to proceed. In any case, I'm in charge of these two cases so I'm the one that should have questioned him.'

'Here we go, so our Timo's ambitious after all! You want to play the hero and be the one to get a confession out of him. That's just great... I wasn't even planning on questioning him. I just wanted to straighten things out with him so that come the morning he'd be like putty in your hands.'

'Give it a rest,' Harjunpää snapped and stared angrily at the traffic jam in front of them. Suddenly Onerva, who had been listening carefully, leaned forward between the front seats and pointed at the police radio.

'Quiet, you two, and turn that thing up. There's been another suicide somewhere.'

'... take care of it, and back-up's on its way. Grönlund's still in charge.'

A number of patrols acknowledged the call, but no one commented on the nature of the incident.

Harjunpää grabbed the microphone from the dashboard.

'This is Harjunpää from Violent Crimes. Where is it?'

'The eastbound line at the Railway metro station.'

'Jesus,' Onerva gasped.

'And you're sure the victim jumped in front of the train? Were there any witnesses?'

'Over twenty. A couple of security guards turned up and took down contact details and what have you. This one wasn't hit by a train; just jumped on to the tracks and stuck her hand into the power rail at the back...and there's enough electricity flowing through that thing to fuel a nuclear plant.'

'And people actually saw her walking? Was she by herself?'

'Yes, she seemed to do it by herself. Surely it'll be on the CCTV cameras. The body's so badly burnt that only the breasts indicate it was a woman. She died instantly. Are you going to take this one?'

'Not in that case, give it to the guys on evening shift,' said Harjunpää and then replaced the microphone in its holder. For a moment there was something almost like relief in the air, but the silence was every bit as impenetrable as it had been before.

57. Guilty

'*Apartus ecolea mobilata,*' he panted and snarled, for he was in a very tight spot indeed - clinging desperately to the steel rungs of the ladder leading up from within the rock, barely a metre beneath the grille and the door to his home. But his stamina had simply run out. Perhaps this was not so much a matter of stamina as a culmination of events. First he had run through the network of tunnels all the way from the Railway Station to Pasila, and his ascent up the ladder had been hindered by his confounded raincoat which had repeatedly become stuck beneath his knees and shoes. On top of this he was still carrying the rucksack, which now felt so heavy that it may as well have been packed with paving stones. But by far the worst part was his left hand; it stung and ached as though the glove were full of small red-hot shards of steel. His grip would not hold.

'*Nessum tasea tacitus*,' he puffed and decided to try again, for he had no alternative other than to plummet back down the shaft, battering himself to death, and the thought did not appeal to him. He took a deep breath, gritted his teeth and quickly attempted to haul himself upwards using his feet and his good hand – and it worked! He collapsed on to the grille and lay there for a moment, a rushing sound in his ears and bright sparks dancing in front of his eyes. His clothes were soaked in sweat; he only realised this now that he was lying still and could feel the eternal, gentle draught wafting up from the depths.

For almost ten minutes he lay there perfectly still. Only then did he attempt to clamber to his knees, then to his feet, finally stumbling over towards the tarpaulin hanging across the doorway. He could not for the life of him understand why Maammo had decided to treat him so cruelly. It was as though she had abandoned him, condemning him to failure in all his endeavours. He managed to pull the tarpaulin to one side, slipped the rucksack from his shoulders and gently laid it on the floor next to the pile of books. His fingers trembling, he lit the storm lantern and collapsed outstretched on his bed.

A single thought spun through his mind: why should Maammo treat him, the highest of earth spirits, so wrongly? Had Maammo forsaken him forever? An eternal union existed between them, though Maammo could of course rescind the union, but only should he sully himself with greed and lechery, or if something beyond his control should pollute him – and he could not imagine what such a thing might be.

Eventually he rose slowly to his knees, clenched his right hand into a fist and made the first sign of prayer – with his left hand he could do nothing. Then, as loudly as he could muster, he cried out: '*Maammo! Mamolae, lama sabaktani?*'

His cry boomed from wall to wall, slipping past the tarpaulin and out into the shaft; it resounded in a faint echo up to the top of The Brocken, and travelled downward into the underground darkness from which he had risen. He listened carefully, to the world outside and to himself, but there was no reply. His chin slumped against his chest in bitter disappointment.

Since when had Maammo's displeasure plagued him? From the time he had adopted the boy? No, for nothing in the adoption went against the laws of Maammo; he had carried out everything exactly as he should. From the time he had adopted Mikko Matias, the boy's father? No, for that too had been conducted in accordance with the law, and after all he was allowed five adoptions. When had his disgrace begun?

'*Cetera desunt,*' he whispered after many minutes of silence, for a thought was beginning to form in his mind, a revelation. Everything was not quite as it should be - the end was yet to come. He thought of the Five Wise Ones. He had asked for their guidance, they had given it to him, and he had followed their instructions, so this could not be the source of the problem.

But still his thoughts remained with the Five Wise Ones, and after a moment everything became clear to him - in a flash! He ought to have realised straight away – it was the infidel, the policeman who had thought he was reviving him! It was he who had polluted him! He had polluted him by touching his mouth to the sacred mouth of the earth spirit, which had been blessed to utter prayers to Maammo. The policeman was guilty!

'*Mortuus et diapoli,*' he croaked, rose to his knees, and from the box beside his bed picked up the card the policeman had left. Placing a curse on the card with needles had clearly not been enough; this would require something far more powerful. Perhaps revenge would cleanse him and allow Maammo to grace him once again.

He untied a small bag hanging from his belt, opened it and allowed its contents to spill out on to the bed. The bag contained dozens of pebbles, the majority of which held the captive souls of people who had wronged or offended him. However, some of the pebbles were still vacant. One at a time he fingered the available pebbles, but did not yet empower any of them. His spirit, his senses and instincts were tired, and were not as acute as normal. He tried again and finally selected the third pebble. Yes. This felt like the right one; he could fit the policeman's soul inside, perhaps it was already inside. It nonetheless contained something which strongly resembled it. Around the stone he made the holy marks of Maammo, then the mark that would finally seal the infidel's soul within the pebble forever.

He stood up, taking the pierced card and the soul-pebble with him, pulled the tarpaulin aside so that he could slip out on to the grille and into the opposite room, which he often used as a redemption chamber. He switched on his headlamp once again and it shed a faint pool of light on the stone floor. In the middle of this he laid first the card, the text facing the ground and the underworld, then on top of that the pebble. He then rummaged in the left-hand corner of the chamber and quickly found what he was looking for: a jagged stone that fitted his hand perfectly.

After feeling the stone for a moment, he knelt down and began pounding the card and pebble. He hit them hard, again and again, his hand moving like a piston. There came a loud crack as the pebble broke apart, but he carried on battering them, spitting out a deluge of venomous curses between blows. Eventually the pebble was nothing but dust, the card was reduced to a few pulpy lumps of paper.

Only then did he finally stop. He stood up, caught his breath and kicked the dust and tiny pieces of paper out of the chamber. There they disappeared through the slats of the grille. Immediately he felt better. He felt energised, as though he had once again been allowed to suckle at Maammo's breast, and he quickly made the holy mark of Maammo in thanks.

His thoughts returned to the bomb. What in damnation had gone wrong? Why had it started ringing in the middle of the operation? Had blood perhaps dripped from his hand and dried on the clock-face causing the alarm to go off? Or had he, either accidentally or out of sheer carelessness, moved the switch as he had replaced the clock in the rucksack? He had to find out at all costs.

He quickly returned home, turned up the storm lantern and allowed his headlamp to remain switched on. He then picked up the rucksack and placed it next to the pebbles on his bed, opened it, took out the clock and laid it on the mattress. He glanced at the middle box where the cables disappeared into the sticks of dynamite, reached out his hand and grabbed the…

58. *Sleeper*

Mikko had taken off his slippers so that the smack of their rubber soles against his heels wouldn't wake Matti, though it now occurred to him that this wasn't necessary – the road works on Neljäs Linja meant that every passing car caused the cobbles to rattle considerably. In addition to that it seemed that the previous night there had been far more call-outs at the nearby fire station than usual.

Still, most importantly Matti was now sound asleep. He seemed peaceful, and he was no longer frantically twisting and turning as he had done just before one of his fits. Mikko rested his hand on the edge of the screen and looked at his sleeping son. Now that he had calmed down he looked almost the way he did as a little boy; he was even sleeping in the same way, almost a foetal position. His hair spilled across his ear and on to his cheek, forming the same wisp that had once been there - it seemed like millions of years ago.

They weren't really 'fits'. They were nightmares during which Matti lay wriggling and crying, still asleep. Mikko could tell this from the fact that his son's face had been limp and expressionless, and he had been unable to rouse him. Matti had simply curled up on the floor, sobbing so inconsolably that it was almost frightening, and crying out the name Leena.

When Matti had appeared at his door earlier that evening – accompanied by a police patrol unit, for which Mikko was very grateful indeed – the boy had been hysterical and had barely managed to explain that his friend, or possibly even his girlfriend, Leena, had for some inexplicable reason crossed the underground tracks and had received a fatal electric shock. Matti had recognized her from her trainers, but the rest of her clothes had been burnt beyond recognition. On top of this, he had slipped past the guards and lifted the sheet laid out across the body, and he had barely been able to recognise her face. That alone would have been more than most adults could stomach.

Mikko tiptoed silently through to the kitchen and took a cautious swig from an open bottle of beer. He didn't want to get too drunk, so that he could be of some support should Matti wake up again, but he desperately needed something to calm him down. What Matti had told him had reminded him that he too had been shoved on to the tracks. He remembered the oily smell of the air; the lamps on the front of the engine growing larger and larger; the horrified look on the face of the woman driving the train. And all this had exhumed the terrible fear he had experienced as a child every time his father had tried to kill himself. But here he was despite it all. A single thought spun through his mind: had he been saved because Matti needed a father, a home? Was this the will of God?

On his desk stood a lamp. Its light shone through the rice paper shade and fell softly on his son's face. He was fast asleep, even his eyelids had stopped twitching. And although this recent change in his life had once again come as a complete surprise, everything seemed finally to be falling into place. The following day he would accompany Matti to a therapy session. The police had left a calling card which he'd stuck in his jacket pocket. He would spend at least the next week with Matti, helping him adjust to his new life and surroundings. If everything worked out, he'd be able to spend the rest of the spring term in his old school in Kulosaari, then they could decide what do after that. Come autumn they might no longer live in Kallio.

But what should he do about his workroom in Kontula? Surely Cecilia would be obliged to pay him some sort of child support. And what would life be like once he returned to the post office?

Despite everything he somehow felt lost, helpless. He walked into the kitchen, picked up the beer bottle and crept into the dark hallway. He opened the toilet door, switched on the lights, put down the toilet seat and sat down. For a long while he stared at the floor tiles between his bare feet and eventually he managed to block the outside world from his thoughts. His mind was filled with a profound silence.

'Kikka?' he called, his lips barely moving. He sat and waited. Nothing happened. He called again, over and over, his final cry was almost panicked. 'Kikka!'

It had stopped working. It couldn't be because Matti was sleeping in the other room, it had worked dozens of times with Sanna sleeping there.

'Kikka,' he whispered a final time, but already it sounded dispirited and plaintive, for somehow in his heart of hearts he knew that his time with Kikka was gone. He could no longer imagine her as a living being – his very own golden-haired, beloved miniature woman.

He remained there, dejected, full of sadness, staring at the toilet door. It needed to be washed and painted, he had been meaning to do it for a long time, but hadn't found the energy. Now as he stared at the spot next to the handle where the paint had worn away, an even deeper silence reached out to him, as if someone had wrapped their arm around him. A moment later and the paintless spot no longer seemed like a smudge reproaching him for his inefficiency. It was now a strong spruce branch, standing firm against the gentle morning breeze. He began to see more: the sky brightening more and more in the north-east, the spruce grove appearing all the darker against the light. He saw red rays of sunlight shining against a turf-roofed cottage built in a clearing where hay and crops had grown. In the first rays of sunlight they looked almost fragile; like distant whistling willows.

And from within the cottage came the sounds of sleep; there rested the happy family he had lost years ago.

59. *Name*

Jaana could only register a few things at once. First it had been the wail of sirens, their cries screeching high and low, then different cries at a faster tempo, like a dog barking. But now that too had stopped, and more distinctly than before she could feel the movement around her: she was being wheeled on a stretcher along a hospital corridor; fluorescent lamps and their mesh covers dazzled her eyes. It seemed like of an illusion; it felt almost as though she were moving upwards, shooting far up into the sky.

The next thing was the pain. There it was again, gripping her from the neck downwards; this time so strongly that it felt like a new experience altogether, a state of being in which she was entirely removed from what was going on around her. She no longer understood that she was being rushed into a birthing room, and she no longer had the strength to be afraid, not even for the baby that was almost two months premature. Somehow instinctively she reached out for help, her fingers grabbing at the empty space next to the stretcher. She was searching for Tero's hand, though she knew that she would never be able to hold it again.

'... Completely green,' someone said. In the distance she heard the words: 'Tell them to get an incubator ready!'

'It's coming... It's blue...'

'... Umbilical cord round the neck... Oxygen!'

'... No heartbeat...'

Then amidst the commotion came a faint cry, like a kitten when someone stands on its tail, and immediately someone wearing a paper mask over her mouth leant across Jaana and all but shouted: 'Mrs. Kokkonen! Jaana! You've just had a little girl. What shall we call her?'

'Is it a... an emergency baptism? Is she going to die?'

'Not at all. It's a healthy baby girl. Any idea what you're going to call her?'

And although before his death she and Tero had come up with a number of different options, for a girl or a boy, suddenly she couldn't remember a single one of them. For some reason she simply said: 'Sinikka.'

'Sinikka?'

'Yes. Sinikka.'

More weak cries could be heard. A new being had been born and was about to embark on the long journey called Life.

Who could know what it held in store for her.

60. *Catching Up*

Elisa was sitting cross-legged on a wooden kitchen chair, her upper body bare, her elbows leaning on the back of the chair. Harjunpää was standing behind her; he squeezed more of the pungent, herbal gel on to the palm of his hands, spread it across her back and continued massaging from the left shoulder blade where he had left off. The girls were all out somewhere.

'Is it getting any better?'

'Maybe a bit.'

'No wonder you've got a headache all the time, you've got enormous knots in the muscles here. You really should see a physiotherapist.'

'It'll be so difficult once I go back to work,' she said and quickly changed the subject. 'What exactly caused that explosion in Pasila?'

'We still don't know, but around the Exhibition Centre and the Hartwall Arena there was a distinct smell of explosives.'

'But they haven't located the site of the explosion?'

'No. We've been through the whole of central Pasila, we even brought in some helicopters. If a group of kids blew something up on a spot of bare land it wouldn't necessarily leave any trace at all.'

Harjunpää continued the massage in silence; by now the gel had been absorbed, making it much easier. His hands moved almost by themselves, finding one awkward knot after another.

'You're worried about something,' said Elisa, more a statement than a question. 'This is not your normal kind of silence.'

'Do I have a normal way of being silent?'

'You know very well what I mean,' she said softly.

Harjunpää muttered quietly in agreement, but the silence continued for a long while. In the living room the wall clock ticked, but Harjunpää was so lost in thought that he didn't count quite how many times.

'I don't know… Is this some kind of envy or what?' he said finally. 'I've never before felt like I wished for something that belonged to someone else but…'

'Maybe it's a feeling of injustice?'

'Maybe. I haven't told you yet: Piipponen got promoted to the DI position left open by Old Lörtsy.'

'Piipponen? How on earth did that happen?'

'Especially since Central had already decided not to fill vacant positions due to cut-backs... Apparently he was the most hardworking of us all, does the most overtime. And he apparently displayed exceptional bravery and initiative fighting off that guy's attack and organising the search for him.'

'But there's still no sign of him?'

'No. The boys will spend the next few weeks looking for him on the underground but after that they'll have to call it a day.'

Elisa didn't reply but laid her fingers on her husband's hand as it rested on her shoulder.

Harjunpää continued massaging. Beneath his hands Elisa felt warm and familiar. He felt a certain pleasure at being able to provide some form of help to someone else. But all of a sudden he felt something change. It was as though she had tensed herself suddenly or tried to stand up, and then her body went limp and she fell back sharply into his arms. He tottered several steps backwards and eased her on to the floor.

'Elisa!' he shouted, tapping her on the cheeks. 'Elisa, wake up!'

He felt her neck, remained there motionless for a split second, then leapt up and dashed towards the telephone in the living room. His imagination was running wild, and he could do nothing to stop it: he felt as if a curse had been had been hanging over him these past few weeks, a curse that had plagued him at work – and now that same curse was about to take Elisa from him! The journey seemed endless, he ran and ran, and everything around him started to spin, to warp, making it difficult for him to stay on his feet.

61. *Elisa*

Elisa was standing on the top of a white wall, her gaze fixed in front of her like a tightrope walker. But she was not afraid of falling; she felt warm and at peace.

When she looked to her right all she could see was a flood of light, opaque and soft as though it were shining through frosted glass, and at the centre of the light she could make out what seemed to be a number of different figures, but she was not sure whether they were people or trees. Nonetheless it was something immensely beautiful and good, powerfully drawing her closer.

And when she looked to her left – she saw what looked like the wall in their kitchen, though it was much higher, and she could see herself lying on the floor, and Timo running in from the living room, kneeling down beside her and fretting over something. She turned again to look towards the light. There was no one beckoning to her, no one to block her path, and at this she realised that the choice was entirely up to her: she could step to whichever side of the wall she chose.

She waited for a moment longer, but still no one appeared from the light to greet her. Meanwhile Timo kept repeating her name: 'Elisa! Elisa!' And at that she turned back towards the kitchen and prepared to take her first step.

62. *Timo Juhani*

'Elisa!' Harjunpää called out between gasps of breath, as he frantically patted his wife's cheeks. Again he felt her throat. A pulse! Was he mistaken? He thought he could feel the artery faintly beating beneath his fingers. Again he thought he felt it, but then came a long pause, longer than time itself, and the wail of approaching sirens, the sound that he so longed to hear, just would not come.

'Elisa!' he called out again, and all of a sudden he could hear through the open door the sound of the girls returning home. He could hear giggling and it sounded like one of them was hopping on one leg; then he heard the echoing sound of a stone being kicked through the tiled hallway. He stood up; he knew that he must go to his daughters, prepare them for what they were about to witness. He took a step towards the hallway but was struck by a stinging fear - almost a certainty - that if he left Elisa now he would lose her for good, and at this he fell to his knees, laid his head beside his wife's head and sobbed. And he felt so profoundly small, and so alone - never before had he felt so small, and so terribly alone.